ZACHARY JEFFRIES

Oracle of Fate

Angels of New York State Book Three

Dedication
For Charlie, a great editor, an authentic teacher, and a personal hero of mine

ANGELS OF NEW YORK STATE

ORACLE
OF FATE
ZACHARY JEFFRIES

Author's Note

Dear Reader,

Please don't keep this book a secret! Feel free to let your friends, family, loved ones, and strangers know what you're reading. Post about it on social media. Spread the word to your bookish friends! Each of books is an investment of hundreds of hours and thousands of dollars. Every moment you can spare helping this book find the right readers is appreciated more than you know.

Sincerely,

-Z

Reader, Be Aware

This book includes:

Anxiety

Death, including death of immediate family

Sickness of a pet

Mental Illness

Occult

Mentions of substance abuse

Kidnapping

Physical violence

Chapter 1

Bazrael

"Is Aurora Marie Seitsinger home? She summoned me from heaven to murder a deity." Bazrael matched the polite smile of the put-together middle-aged woman, making sure to maintain eye contact. Humans loved eye contact.

"Excuse me?"

"I know her from the school we are both forced to attend." There was an odd deliciousness to dishonesty, a tartness that felt wrong yet delighted his nervous system.

"That's not what you just said."

"You're right, I'm lying!" A new bolt of adrenaline left a wide smile on Bazrael's face. It was not returned. The woman's polite expression melted as she closed the door.

That was fine. Bazrael hadn't wanted to use the front entrance in the first place.

The house was grand, proud, and impeccably white. Something about its properness begged to be ruined with unsightly clamoring. A tree stretching up to the second-floor window beckoned him. A twisting journey from trunk to branches showed him a well-laid path, both challenging and innately beautiful. Organic. Chaotic.

So much of Earth stood as a playground custom-made for humans, as if Bazrael had found a wardrobe tailored to his precise dimensions. Sure, he'd already experienced this world, viewed it as a guardian angel, but this was living. Touch and taste. Comfort and strain.

His strong hands of long, tawny fingers gripped the tree as his extended legs walked up. His tall, athletic body worked in perfect cooperation despite all of its moving parts. He was grateful he didn't have to think too hard about breathing or tell his heart to pump. While he had all the memories and experiences of his old ward, eighteen-year-old Miguel, the operation of a human body had its own learning curve, like the piloting of a giant robotic form from the cartoons Miguel would watch.

Inching out on a branch that thinned as it tapered and reached for the bedroom window, Bazrael could see a room of yellow filled with picture frames—the walls, the tables, even the floor, all tiled with photos. And even without having seen her, he felt her, just as he had felt her while approaching the house; the female human who summoned him was here, the air viscous with her presence.

The window was locked, but his arms were strong, and with a pop of some hardware, Bazrael entered the room easily.

He was met with a gust of his summoner's energy, a cool, sweet breeze electric with supernatural power that magnetically pulled him toward her. The air in the room smelled of cocoa butter. The figure under the blankets snored softly. Aurora Marie Seitsinger. Somehow, breaking open the window hadn't awakened her. Neither did her mother flinging open the bedroom door.

"The hell you doing in here?!" The pitch of her voice skyrocketed as she rushed at Bazrael. Without missing a stride, she laid hands on his torso, continuing forward.

Bazrael was surprised. Since being on Earth, he'd been struck with impact several times—fist, open hand, foot, even a baseball or two. Much of a male youth's existence was blunt force.

But this woman simply power walked into him, through him, using the momentum of her gait in one linear swoop to knock Bazrael off balance and back out the window through which he'd climbed.

The luxuries of climbing into a window included choice of footing and pace. Going at a comfortable speed and finding purchase with each foot and handhold on the way up. Such luxuries were unavailable to him on the way down. Despite the valiant efforts of his reaching fingers, Bazrael couldn't slow his descent and hit the ground with a thud and a cracking sound.

His vision flashed red, and a sharp tangy taste filled his mouth. His lungs stopped working, and he gaped like a fish, attempting to inflate them with breath. What an incredible sensation.

Eventually, air came into his body, and with it, pain, simultaneously needle sharp and omnipresent. It was an overachieving injury affecting everywhere all at once, so large he couldn't place it.

Fantastic.

Bazrael laughed in the glory of such agony, specific in its generality. What a feeling, to be so alive with a nervous system under such assault and alarm. An experience so novel was delicious and hilarious, though. As he shuddered with laughter, his ribs and back spasmed. But also the back of his head. And the part of his tongue his teeth had bitten into.

But he'd seen her, *felt* her. Not the middle-aged human adult who'd shoved him through the window. Aurora Marie Seitsinger.

"Hello there. Hello, supernatural creature," a husky voice said in a sing-song tone, like syrup poured over rocks. The source of the voice, a petite and curvy figure with a face somewhere between smirking and angry, stood over Bazrael's injured body, obviously self-satisfied and confident. She was dripping with the metaphysical residue of Aurora Marie Seitsinger, as though they recently shared proximity. Maybe also an emotional closeness. Plus, waves of some supernatural energy flowed off the human in cool blue tendrils.

"I couldn't help but notice that you fell out of a second-story window and laughed about it. So I have to ask...what exactly are you? And what do you want with my girlfriend?"

Mark

"But if he doesn't bring the apocalypse to Earth,"—Mark downed the rest of the second cup of coffee—"Anthony dies from complications caused by the stomach problem."

"He ain't going to cause the apocalypse!" Beth insisted. When she got mad, her already-broad shoulders flexed, making her seem pretty jacked and threatening.

"I don't know if he causes it. I just see him as one of the four horses to...you know...usher in the apocalypse."

She slumped back in a pout, brow wrinkled, shoulders

relaxing somewhat. "So then, what if we don't do the stomach treatment at all?"

"Okay, let me see." Mark let out an enormous sigh. "Could you grab me a water? Tap's fine."

While she rifled through the Cecilia family's kitchen cabinets, Mark closed his eyes and began.

Ever since a near-death experience, the visions came more easily. He could control them, pushing forward in time and warping the possible futures in his mind by adding different hypotheticals, adding forks in the road to see how things would work out differently. But since the visions were a dream-state, a surrender of his present mind to his subconscious, they were now accompanied by the terrors.

Anything too closely resembling drowning, car accidents, or fire would stir up his trauma, and he'd be flooded with the all-too-familiar panic on the cliff's edge of death.

As much as he loved Beth's horse, Anthony, peering into the animal's future, looking into his oncoming death, could easily trigger Mark Cecilia's fight or flight. And he wasn't the fighter he used to be.

He breathed deeply and allowed the vision to come to him. Anthony was a chestnut brown horse with some white spots on his nose and around one hoof, dark brown and black hair from his mane and tail. The animal was strong, solid like a car. Bulk and power reminding Mark of the body of a pro football player. Mark could feel his skin as the horse's, covered in coarse hair, able to shiver and shake specific spots to keep the flies away. A powerful sense of smell that led him toward fresh grass and away from mildewed straw. But the suffering...

Clenching and searing heat coursed through his stomach. An infection. Or was it cancer? Mark couldn't diagnose the animal, but when he stepped into the animal's future, he felt it. Just like he felt the lightness, the warmth, the flow of love when he looked up at Beth. This was Beth in the future, and she looked terrible. Eyes filled with tears and bags underneath, reddened by crying without sleeping. Worry. Stress. Grief. But to Anthony, she was so beautiful.

The horse loved Beth more than anything, in a way beyond how a pet loves its owner. They were best friends. And it weighed on Anthony that his health could cause such agony in her. He sucked it up, not allowing himself to wince or cry at the stomach pain. He walked with her, keeping it together, moving at his normal pace even as his belly burned. Keeping upbeat. Pretending to be happy. He nudged her with his face, nuzzling into her straw-colored hair. She smelled of the usual chemicals that humans did, but also flowers, clothing, and tears. How could he ease her pain?

Summoning the energy, he pushed her away then kicked and frolicked off. An invitation to run and play, like they did when they were both so much younger. With high knees, he pranced away, kicking hoofs up, beckoning her.

'Come play.'

Throbbing pulsed through him with each step, and his snuffling, joyful taunts turned into tormented whinnies. Tears filled her eyes as she rushed to him, but he trotted away playfully. 'Chase me,' he thought. 'One last time.'

"Anthony!" she cried. "Stop, you're hurt."

No. He couldn't hurt when she was around.

Mustering strength, he bucked, hopping around like a hyper foal. Each jolt tore through his body, like his muscles were ripping him apart. But if he could just hop higher, get her to chase after him one more time, she'd stop being sad. She'd forget that he was a dying friend dragging her down.

He leapt away and kicked into the air, but his body betrayed him.

He couldn't bring his legs back down fast enough to catch himself. Impact with the ground knocked the breath out of him. Something within him cracked. Burning. He couldn't breathe. He wriggled to get back to standing, but every motion injured him further. His body begged him to stop, to stay still. Forever.

He was afraid. What would happen if he stopped? What would it be like to stay still forever? What would Beth do without him? Her warm hands wrapped around his neck, her body hugging him close, and she shushed him.

He stopped trying to get back up, barely able to breathe. He smelled her hair, her clothes, her tears. She cried and cried as their bodies shuddered together.

Goodbye, Beth.

Mark jumped to his feet, gulping air. He kicked the coffee table with his bad leg, sending hot needles up his bones and digging into his ankle joint. Tears and snot streamed down his face as he wiped them with his shirt as if he could wipe away the visions, the aftertaste of grief and fear.

Once he caught his breath and dried his cheeks, he saw it again, Beth from his vision, but there in the Cecilia living room, breathing heavy, red-eyed, crying. He almost smelled her clothes for a second.

She knew.

Tears stung and threatened Mark again, and all he could do was press his lips hard to keep it together, shaking his head in an apologetic no.

He was safe from the vision now, no longer feeling the hand of Death on him, no longer poisoned with the emotions of a dying animal. But that didn't make him safe.

In his mind, his human mind, he was trapped in that car trunk again, panicking as the world closed in on him. He was drowning in water and choking on smoke. He was helplessly bound and simultaneously banging against his restraints. He was no longer dying as Anthony. He was again dying as Mark.

Strong hands gripped his shoulders and ripped him back to reality. He snapped back to his living room, standing in the clutches of Beth shaking him by the shoulders.

"I'm fine," Mark said, shrugging out of her grip. He was anything but fine, but he couldn't tell her that. Beth was there for his help. He was the only one she could turn to as the most important thing in her life slipped away. He couldn't be a burden as well. He refused to be. "I don't know if Anthony's getting any better without the treatment."

"You just freaked out, Frosty," Beth said gently, using his nickname to cushion the seriousness of the room. "You were gasping. It was like you were drowning."

"I said I'm fine."

Beth obviously wanted more out of him, but she would not get it. Pity welling up in her eyes alongside the tears, she sank into his couch, holding his gaze.

"Look, the visions are getting a little wild. I'll try looking again later when I can focus better." It was a lie, but no one besides Mark knew how his foresight worked. And not even Mark knew exactly how.

Slider sauntered into her lap purring, and she gave the cat some love. Maybe she had some kind of beast magic, maybe she could talk to animals. Her connection to Anthony had to have been supernatural, though Mark could never place it. Maybe it was all animals. Maybe that made Beth more powerful than Mark ever gave her credit for.

But she wasn't powerful now. She was suffering. And Mark couldn't help her.

Beth

Everyone in her life was in pain. Anthony was quickly dying from cancer, racked with pain from colic. Mom was lonely in a new city without her favorite daughters around. And Mark had been an absolute mess since he stopped drinking and Lord knew what else he put in his body.

How much of all this was Beth's fault? If not for her, Anthony wouldn't be suffering like this. Without a surprise youngest kid, Mom could have followed her daughters off to some college town. And Beth knew asking for Mark to look into her future was putting him through more pain.

Maybe she was just being selfish by holding onto all them, holding them back.

"Will you be at group tonight?" she asked, giving the cat some deep scratches behind the ear.

"I don't know; I've got a game." Mark limped over to grab the glass of water.

Beth almost laughed at his answer, considering how pitiful he looked. "You can't play like this."

Mark at least had his hard plastic brace on, even though he didn't use the crutches she'd loaned him.

"I'm not going to play. I'm going to support the team."

A team. Something as foreign to Beth as speaking Greek or reading hieroglyphics. She'd admitted as much to Mark, just about her only friend in this town. So maybe he was taking a shot at her. Or maybe Mark was just lashing out in self-defense. He did that. Like an injured animal, hurting everyone around out of a panic for survival.

She didn't want him to hurt anymore. Maybe someday she could even be the cure for Mark. More than a friend. She thought about it, walking over to his wide frame, falling into his brawny arms, kissing away his pain.

"My mom's new boyfriend's gonna be here any second," Mark said without looking her in the eyes. "You should probably take off."

The pain was still there. On his face. In his injured leg. The house was brimming with it. And as she left, Beth took some pain with her for the road.

Bazrael

"I am seeking the one who summoned me." There was no need for Bazrael to keep his purpose a secret; few humans believed in direct purpose, anyway.

"Oh, great. What did that little witch manifest now?"

Since Bazrael could smell the aura of 'that little witch' on *this* little witch, he had to assume she was being endearing and not derisive. It was so confusing being an American teenager. There were so many instances of using language that meant the opposite of the concept being expressed. But it wasn't sarcasm or lying. The more someone liked someone or something, the more proper it was to speak badly of them.

But Bazrael couldn't go around explaining the intricacies of his own ties to Aurora Marie Seitsinger. He knew from watching over Miguel in Cuba that when someone claimed the divine, if a woman were to tell others she'd seen or spoken with an angel, either it was assumed she was mentally ill, or worse, she gained a following that studied and scrutinized her every gesture. America seemed much less pious and demonstrated poor treatment of the mentally disabled, so Bazrael could only reveal so much about his mission on Earth. And he definitely had to keep his angelic origins a secret.

"That is none of your business." Bazrael loved that phrase. He'd heard it a lot while asking questions to understand the social customs around him. And it was exciting that he now had business of his own. "That is between me and her."

He stood, his limbs electrified with singing nerves, which may have been from broken bones. He folded his arms and mirrored her posture, cocking a hip to the side and smirking. A valiant attempt at gaining control over the conversation, though he was unsure if he achieved it, especially with the blood dribbling from his lip.

She studied him closely, her smirk sliding into a scowl.

"Listen, pal, I've been summoned as well. Pro tempore security for this house and the witch residing within. Any gentleman callers, especially those attempting to climb up the second floor into her bedroom, are indeed my business."

There—she'd called Aurora Marie Seitsinger a witch again. It wasn't some term of endearment but a label, a classification. An inaccurate one at that; she was much more powerful than some Earthly witch.

"You must be mistaken. As far as I know, no witches live here. I imagine, based on those markings on your arm and the one peeking up from your neck, that you should have a little more first-hand experience with witchcraft, or at the very least, diablerie."

For a fraction of a moment, her eyes went wide, eyebrow arched, her posturing sneer dropped. But only temporarily. She recovered quickly, and her angry mask returned. Delightful! Bazrael managed to score a point in a game of wits, a sport in which, so far, he had a losing record.

"Cute." She seethed, face pursed, eyes squinting. Her lips, eyebrows, somehow even her nose, all tightened up in united defense. "Seems you have a better handle on the situation than I credited you. It's a mistake I don't plan on making again." She rolled up long sleeves to reveal even more tattoos and brands, runes from different cultures. Fascinating. He could read her like a book if he had the time. Her body was a story of man's attempt to supersede gods. And she wasn't just playing the games of immortals, she was throwing the entire rulebook at them.

Her focus narrowed, shifting to her hands. Her fingers flexed, contorting, making odd shapes Bazrael had never seen before. It looked like it hurt. Bazrael made a mental note to attempt them later.

She whispered to herself, barely audible, though not English. Was it Aramaic? A word in Sanskrit...something Phoenician...a mishmash he only caught crumbs of: "losing hours," "banishment from this place," "I command you." Energy built around him like humidity. The air grew syrupy and alive. A static charge rose from the ground to the top of his head as his arm hairs stood on end. Wisps of her hair floated up. The well-kept yard was filled with witchcraft, danger, and deliciously interesting possibilities.

Her hands froze in mid-contortion. Her eyes closed. And when she spoke once more, her voice didn't just come from her mouth but vibrated from her entire body through the air, through Bazrael. Through the universe. Whatever word she said, it was the spark to an explosion.

Her eyes opened wide, her pupils faded to white.

Impact.

A concussive blast collided with Bazrael's torso, knocking

him backward.

Chapter 2

Mark

"Are you supposed to have girls over when you're home alone?"

Curling dumbbells on the couch, Mark was doing his best to ignore his mom's new boyfriend, but the guy pulled the weight away.

Mark shrugged. "No laws against it."

"Well, has your mother said it's okay?"

Mark got up to get his water again. Chugging water and coffee was all he could do to stop the shakes from not chugging alcohol. Maybe it would be just easier to sweat and itch it out, but he knew that the more he stressed, the more the visions would come. "She didn't bring it up in the two hours I saw her last week."

"That's 'cause she's busy providing a roof over your head and food on the table!"

The boyfriend, who actually used to coach Mark's middle school team, blocked his path to storm off to his room.

The shriek of Anthony's neighing tore through his mind.

Coach Boyfriend went on, "From now on, if you want to have people over, you have to pass it through her."

A vision of an earthquake shaking Lockport spread across Mark's thoughts.

"You still have to mow the lawn!" The demands kept coming.

Mark could see the Earth crack open.

"Have you done the laundry yet?"

The room was spinning. Mark mumbled a reply, desperate to stay in the moment, in the now. "The yard is mud," he answered. "My game's at two."

"You're in an air cast; the team is fine without you."

No. Mark wasn't going to lose baseball now, too. "It's the two best teams in the state. Scouts could be there."

"And they'll be impressed with how you sit on a bench?"

Through the fire and the rupturing ground, Mark could hear screaming—the final pleas for help from people dying.

"Mow and clean your room now, and you'll get there in time."

Mark was sweating, feverish, yet his skin chilled. "You can't boss me around."

"The hell I can't! We both see your mother working her hands to the bone to provide for you. And you just coast by: drinking, smoking, skipping school, failing most your classes."

Mark didn't know if he was going to vomit or faint. He gnashed his teeth, gripped the kitchen counter, and growled, "I got high Cs."

"That won't get you a good job or into a good school."

"Who cares?" Mark lashed out. "Baseball can take care of me! You know that."

The only thing worse than envisioning a world full of dying screams was the silence afterward. It meant there was no one left to call out for help. A darkened world empty of life.

Coach Boyfriend kept on with his lecture, the words fading in and out. "What I know is that every player is one injury away from never lifting a bat again. That ankle doesn't heal properly, you're done. Bad break on your collarbone, you're done. Catch an inside fastball to the eye, screw your vision, you're done. Then what? You'll just be a burden on your mother 'til you die?"

Mark pounded the rest of the water and wiped the sweat off his face. He was out of breath and shaky all over. But the vision had ended.

"I know you love her," Coach boyfriend's tone softened as he kept on. "You just got to show it by helping out. Clean your room. Mow the lawn. Laundry. And catch up on those dishes."

Mark was tired of the lectures. He spat back, "Why don't *you*?"

"Because I got a home of my own, and I keep it clean. Right now, it's the nicest place your mom gets to stay! Lawn. Room. Laundry. Dishes. And where you at on your summer reading?"

Mark limped back over to the couch and his dumbbells. "I don't know."

Coach Boyfriend rested a foot on the weight, blocking Mark from picking it up. "Well, crack a book and find out. Might as well get something accomplished while you're riding the pine."

"I'm not gonna read a book during a baseball game! Are you crazy?"

"No, I ain't. But I know a guy who is. Best hitter on my high school team. Had scouts and everything. Was gonna go to college on it or maybe the minors. Got a DUI and killed an old couple. Guilt drove him crazy. No more baseball, no more sleeping at night. Died homeless two years ago."

Mark glared knives, saying through his teeth, "I don't drink anymore."

"Oh, really? Then what's this?" Coach Boyfriend reached behind the couch and pulled out a half-empty fifth. Mark had forgotten it was there. "Vodka? Your mom doesn't drink it, so I guess I'll just pour it out."

"Fine." Enough was enough. Mark hobbled back to his room. If he made sounds like he was cleaning, maybe the guy would shut up.

"Fine! Don't tell me you don't drink anymore when I found empties in the bathroom garbage yesterday."

"Those are old."

"Then take out the trash more often!"

Mark slammed his door.

Beth

As she drove the hand-me-down Toyota to the end of Mark's street, headed for the barn to see Anthony's veterinarian, an old white van pulled up to block her. The name of a church was stenciled on the doors in curled and flaking blue paint. Next to that and on the front trunk was a newly stenciled logo in black: a circle with a cross within it, split down and hinged open vertically. Crosses and idols hung from the rearview and filled the dashboard. A smiling white man in his late twenties or thirties wearing aviators and a wide grin even faker than his clean, preppy look stepped out.

"Hello, little lamb!"

Beth just squinted against the morning light and stared back, pulling the keys from the ignition and adjusting them in her hand in case they needed to become weapons quick.

No way this was Mark's mom's new boyfriend.

"Did you see the prophet? Did he speak with you?"

The words, friendly but thick with reverence and gospel, tightened Beth's body all over.

"Just visiting a friend."

"Is your friend the young man who talks to the Lord about His just and righteous plans?"

Whatever this guy wanted, Beth was not about to rat out Mark, even if someone knew about his ability to see the future.

"No, sir. Just a guy who does dumb stuff and tore his leg up."

"The Lord works in mysterious ways. More than once, He picked 'just a guy' to carry His glorious message."

Everything about this man, from the ease with which he spoke to strangers to how his crisp, clean clothes clashed with his beat-up church van, pushed Beth into unease.

"Well..." Beth struggled to keep her tone friendly. "My friend's about to get whooped if his step-daddy catches me here, so I'm gonna take off. Reckon you might want to follow suit."

Maybe stretching the truth about Ma Cecilia's marital status was fine if it kept this guy out of her family's hair.

"Understood. When a pretty lady talks, I always listen."

Creep.

"But I obey Him first and foremost." The man pointed a reverential finger at the sky. "Have a blessed day," he said it as a threat behind a brightened white smile and climbed back into the creaky van before puttering off in a stream of stinking exhaust.

Beth was happy to stand up for Mark and be a good friend,

but what kind of trouble was hunting him down?

She kept a sharp eye on her mirrors for the church van as she drove to meet the vet at her barn.

Bazrael

Bazrael flew back from the enchanted blast, not flying as he had as an angel through the air, but falling, at first backward and then through dimensions. His body flailed as it ripped through realm after realm until he landed on hard dirt. The ground smacked him on the back, knocking the breath out of him yet again.

His hands fumbled over his body, reassuring that he could still move and his human vessel had not become mangled or liquified. He was indeed still alive, still in this human form, and somehow feeling much better than he had after toppling from Aurora Marie Seitsinger's window.

His eyes opened and took in the world around him. He was at the baseball fields, dressed in his uniform, complete with his gear bag containing his bat, glove, and hat. His team was warming up. The star Sol was past its zenith. Hours had passed. Along with levels of space and time, he'd also traveled across town.

It was afternoon now—time for his game. But how could he focus on baseball when he'd just encountered something he never imagined in all of his time as an angel or a human? He'd just seen witchcraft powerful enough to banish him, a wholly unholy power. Helpless fear was a novel sensation but not enjoyable. It was viscous. Icky.

He could not return to the Seitsinger house; he felt himself warded away from even the thought of it. There would have to be another means to fulfill his purpose. But this was destiny, and it could not be rushed. If that guard witch prevented him from approaching Aurora Marie Seitsinger at home, he would discover another way.

Clean, green waves of patience calmed him, settled into his bones until all frustration had released. There. Now he could enjoy the human experience while he still had the time. While the human experience still existed.

He would pass the afternoon playing baseball and fulfill his purpose of bringing the end of time later.

Mark

After a lifetime of playing baseball, being relegated to the dugout because of an injury made Mark realize how boring the game was to watch. He was so used to the unseasonable cold of this past month's freak weather that he was uncomfortably hot and sticky, even though it was only in the high 70s. But then, the boot on his ankle and girdle strapped on to hold his ribs only added to his heat and discomfort. Even though he wasn't playing, he insisted on wearing his full uniform, which must not have helped either. He also made sure his coach included him on the roster, maybe in case a scout showed up, maybe to nurse his injured ego.

Constantly itching his boot and medical tape, the pace of the game, this one in particular, was unbearable.

Chances were he wouldn't be back to full health before this early summer league finished and crowned a champion, but sitting at home wasn't an option. Besides, their team was pretty good, and there was always the chance a college scout was watching. Not that he'd impress anyone in his current state, but if he were absent, that could look bad and hurt his chances.

Mark had always played baseball, from catch in the backyard before Dad left to pickup games with older kids. And now he was supposed to just sit and watch as his team was in tight competition to determine which team made it to the championship series.

With each of his teammate's at-bats, his hands flexed the grip of an imaginary bat. His shoulders and back tensed in time with every would-be swing. And of course, his mind wandered through the future, seeing possible outcomes for each pitch, hit, and on-base runner.

Another out. The game was winding down, and things weren't looking good for his team. They were two runs down with two out and one runner on base in the ninth inning.

Mark had to get to the championship. There'd be scouts from local colleges, maybe even out-of-state schools. And the elusive wish that a minor league scout could show. Watching without being able to help was torture, no matter how many times his mom, Coach Boyfriend, or his teammates tried telling him that losing wasn't the end of the world.

The true end of the world came to Mark whenever he lost focus, if he let boredom of the dragging game let his mind wander. Then he saw the baseball fields differently, now under relentless rain in the dark, lighting outlining floating figures in the sky, and a sharpened sword suddenly flying straight for his own eyes. Then his coach clapped to rally the players, and Mark was brought back to reality.

They had to find a way to win this game. He was certain a

couple coaches from colleges around the state would be at the final games. The redheaded batter in the box was no power hitter; neither was his teammate up next. But of course, nobody hit better than Mark. This uselessness was driving him mad.

The next pitch flew in tight, nicked the redheaded batter's chin, sending him flying back. The redhead's bat flew from his hand, sailing right into the upcoming batter on deck, striking him in the hand. What a fluke. The next batter crumpled to his knees, screaming in agony, cradling his hand. The hitter took his base. It was a near-impossible series of events. Someone would have to step in and hit, or they'd forfeit the game. Coach tapped Mark to step up and bat.

The flash was over as fast as it started. A vision. A possible future opening itself up in Mark's mind. Not reality. Mark chuckled to himself. Maybe it was just a daydream, wishful thinking. A series of events like that would be impossible.

And then it happened. High pitch inside clipped the batter. The bat whipped back and crushed the other player's hand. Everyone in the dugout stood. Coaches rushed to check on the player to see if he was okay.

But Mark already knew—the hand was broken. There'd only be a short window for the coaches to figure it out as the umpire demanded the next batter.

Mark stood and asked the player next to him, "Give me your left cleat?"

"What?"

Mark was already grabbing a batting helmet and unstrapping his oversized boot.

"I need your left cleat."

The coaches were helping the injured player off the field.

"I've got to bat, or we forfeit," Mark told his teammate

matter-of-factly.

Mark grabbed a bat and used it to kneel, asking again, more urgently, "I need your left cleat."

He removed the boot, a cool rush of relief to his foot where his skin screamed to be scratched, the ankle joint longed to be stretched. No time for that.

"Cleat. Now."

"Coach," the umpire called out, "we gotta have your next batter, or it's gonna be a forfeit."

"We're a little short today. Can we rotate in our starter?"

It was against the rules to bring a pitcher already pulled from the game, and Coach knew that. But he probably hated losing his chance at the championship, too.

"Can't do it," the umpire said. "Are we calling this game?"

"I got it, Coach!" Mark yelled, shaking an outreached hand out to his teammate, impatiently demanding his shoe. The teammate rushed to untie it.

"Cecilia, forget it. You're injured."

"Come on, Coach, I ain't injured, just bruised a bit."

"Can't let you on that field; your mom would chew me out."

"She won't know." Mark shrugged in an attempt to downplay how much he wanted this. How much the team needed this.

"Coach," the umpire said, growing weary, "we need a batter in the box, or it's a forfeit."

Mark grabbed his teammate's shoe—a few sizes too big, but that's what Mark needed. He lifted his wrapped-up foot and fed it into the opening of the shoe. Spasms ran up and down his ankle, foot, and calf. He buried his face in his knee to cover up any reaction.

"Yeah, we got our batter right here," Coach said.

Mark didn't even bother tying it, just pushed the laces into the shoe. He stood by pushing up on the bat like a cane, clamping his jaw shut to keep from groaning. Hiding any limp as best he could, he sauntered to the batter's box slowly, gripping the bat and taking light practice swings.

And of course the other team called timeout.

Good. They knew about him then. Mark was always happy to know his reputation preceded him. Now in the batter's box, he knew no pain. No visions of the apocalypse distracted him. He was dialed in. He was more alive here than anywhere else on Earth. And he was more than willing to save the day.

Bazrael

Bazrael had never seen baseball players in such a state. When the All-Star, thought to be out with injury, took up a bat, the panicked simultaneous gasp from the team formed a gust of wind. Their sweat was sour with fear.

The young man was thick with muscle, his arms tight and flexed, wound ready to strike. His torso was stiff, yet his grip on the bat and the swing of his hips were loose, carefree. His eyes were focused, steady and still as a tree trunk, but his smile was bright and airy. He was filled with contradiction. And purpose. Singular, direct purpose that Bazrael hadn't yet observed in humans. Suddenly, Bazrael's guts turned to jelly, but not in the same ferocious fear that his team was experiencing.

With the All-Star's clear limp, surely he couldn't pose the threat Bazrael's team feared. Bazrael was an excellent ball player, learning from Miguel's lifelong obsession in Cuba. But on this elite American team, Bazrael didn't get to play too often.

If needed in the clutch, he could muster up enough focus to help out his team, batting or substituting on the field as needed. Coaches and players alike didn't enjoy depending on Bazrael for the duration of an entire game, but he made himself useful in short durations. The coaches deemed him as distracted, not invested in winning. So he rode the bench.

And now, everyone was shaking in their cleats. On the field, Bazrael's teammates were getting heated, huddled at the pitcher's mound.

Coach let out a deep sigh. "I guess I'll go out and talk him down. Maybe we can pick off a runner."

It was a longshot and wishful thinking. This loss would eliminate them from a championship in a summer league dedicated to getting players' attention. Attention for scholarships, attention for minor leagues, attention from dads who missed out on their own glory days. The team needed a miracle, a burst of baseball excellence, a window of focused athleticism. This was exactly the kind of instance in which the coaches *did* trust Bazrael. So he spoke up.

"Let me pitch to him."

Coach let out a chuckle and raised an eyebrow as if there were some joke Bazrael should have understood.

"I can do it, Coach. I don't have the strongest arm, but I'm the only one who's not scared of this guy." Bazrael knew it was a good point and was satisfied to see it land. The snickering smile on Coach's face relaxed into thoughtfulness. He nodded to himself, slow at first, then more vigorously, as if persuading himself with an interior conversation.

"All right, Munoz," he said to Bazrael, "Get up there, throw some practice pitches. Now don't get gassed, but give it all your heat warming up. Make them think you do this every day."

Maybe Bazrael could pretend enough to fool the All-Star, but Bazrael wasn't the best liar. He could pitch, that much was true, but he had no 'heat' as they called it, no strength of arm to make someone miss on a fastball. Hopefully, he'd be accurate enough.

So he trotted out to the mound with Coach. The dumb-founded starting pitcher handed the ball to Bazrael, who took his position at the mound. The coach and the rest of the team left him there, where the loneliness of baseball became exaggerated. Here, the game was a duel, just the pitcher and the batter. The rest of the team were just onlookers. The catcher transformed into a glorified coach, in some ways involved but relegated to advice, not action. The umpire seemed several kilometers away, a judge to declare the winner of each offensive attempt.

With all of his strength available, Bazrael levered his long body into warm-up pitches, just as Coach said. He should've been happy with those pitches, his aim on target, but instead, he felt naked under the gaze of the All-Star, an unsettling focus, a smoky glare.

Thankfully, the catcher's hand signals broke Bazrael from his trance. The catcher wanted a fastball outside, a perfect pitch for the situation. If the All-Star truly did have an injury, he would not be able to chase an outside pitch. But of course, he would be expecting something outside and might adjust. And if he was indeed healthy enough to play, maybe he was faking his injury entirely. Sure, he had a lopsided walk up to the plate, but that could be acting. He could just be resting for the championship.

He shook his head to the catcher, rejecting the suggestion of the outside fastball. The next proposed pitch was high and inside, but Bazrael couldn't be sure that had the control to throw it without hitting the batter. The next suggestion, low and down the middle: no. High and outside: no. The catcher was getting frustrated and signaled with an angry hand, 'Fine, you pick something.'

But what to pick? The runner behind Bazrael inched away from the base. The All-Star loosened his grip on the bat, bobbing it behind his head somehow threateningly. The catcher squatted deeper.

What to throw? Bazrael felt his leg pull up, beginning his pitching mechanics. His mind raced. Inside? Outside? His body fluidly went to work and leveraged his leg forward, tightening his torso, dragging an arm behind. He was already pitching and hadn't decided yet. His leg lurched forward, finding purchase in the ground. His arm was launching the ball without knowing the pitch.

Suddenly, the All-Star's eyes lit up, growing wide and wild. His brows and nostrils flared together in seeming confusion. What was he thinking?

Bazrael didn't even know what pitch he threw. The ball left his hand. It sailed in a tight arc, a slow throw, an easy lob, a pitch that could get crushed into a home run with a little effort.

It landed with a pop in the catcher's mitt.

"Strike!"

The All-Star, face still contorted in confusion, didn't step back from the batter's box, staying upright in aghast disbelief, not disguising his surprise. It was a terrible pitch, an easy hit, a big opportunity the All-Star hadn't taken. The catcher tossed the ball back, practically with the same ease as the first pitch, then gave the signal for Bazrael to choose the next pitch.

The befuddlement on the All-Star's face scrunched into

anger and intent. Even from this distance, Bazrael could see the All-star squeezing and twisting his grip on the bat. He was angry, whether at the pitching or himself for missing. Good.

Affecting another human warmed Bazrael all over and sent a thrum through his extremities. This was power, socially accepted consensual control. And it was scrumptious.

The All-Star held an angry stare, drinking Bazrael in from cleat up to his hat. Pretending to be unbothered under the batter's scrutiny took more exertion than the actual pitch had. And it wasn't the All-Star's prowess, his inherent threat as a hitter. It wasn't even the weight of the situation. It was those deep brown eyes.

Behind, the baserunner took an even larger head start, an effort at distraction. Little did he know that Bazrael was distracted enough in the eyes of the batter, determined, angry, chilling. But something about the discomfort was savory. Bazrael wished he could look into those eyes forever. But he and the batter had business to conduct.

He began his wind-up. This time, ideas of possible pitches came to him in a flurry. He pictured a dot-by-dot outline of the strike zone and dozens of possible pitches landing. Variations of outcomes, an entire game of chess in an instant. And again, before he even made a decision, the ball flowed out past his fingers. It spiraled down, spinning while sinking. The All-Star unleashed the bat, chopping air.

The catcher had to throw his mitt forward to the ground just to keep the ball from skipping away.

"Strike two!"

The catcher was smiling by now, jaunty and loose with a throw back to the mound. Bazrael's teammates and coaches called out, clapping, sending encouragement. His blood sang.

The All-Star took a step back far enough to place one foot out of the batter's box. He talked to himself, whispering nothing, giving a few practice swings, never peeling the black-brown eyes off Bazrael.

Was this what pitching always was like? It was so intimate. And so embarrassing. The two of them were experiencing a connection, a fluid exploration of each other in the middle of a game in front of everyone.

Now that Bazrael finally had this opportunity of greatness, this distillation of the beauty of the game that is baseball, he was experiencing something else entirely. He was getting bogged down in goopy, sticky, utterly teenage boy feelings.

Bazrael had to defeat this unnerving humanness overtaking him. He needed to best the All-Star in their duel, to embarrass him publicly. How dare the All-Star make Bazrael so self-conscious with his calm, confident air? How dare he enter into this sporting duel with no fear?

As he stepped back into the box, the batter smiled. Bazrael melted.

And out of the self-satisfied smirk came a bark: "Throw a curveball."

For a moment, Bazrael just enjoyed the sound of the All-Star's voice. Steady and deep. Then the words hit him. The umpire warned the batter, who didn't acknowledge but set his lips into a grimace, his jaw flexed.

The silent dance of wills between the pitcher and batter had escalated. The All-Star had dared to break the silence. Was that a challenge? Was he expecting a curveball now? Or would he know that Bazrael wouldn't throw the requested pitch?

If for no other reason than to impress his rival, Bazrael was determined not to lose. No curveball. This time, Bazrael decided before his wind-up. Another fastball, this one a little farther outside. He set his feet, checked the base runners, and put his entire body into this one pitch.

The All-Star smiled.

The base runners sprinted.

The ball sailed for home plate, as if on a string, right toward the catcher's mitt.

Chapter 3

Beth

She brushed out his mane as she'd been doing a lot lately. There were no tangles, but it was soothing, seemingly to both of them. If he were still a show horse, she wouldn't do this. But he wasn't. He was a dying friend.

Horses don't live forever. But they should live a hell of a lot longer than eight years.

Anthony wasn't technically a real horse, despite his accurate biology.

"Saw Mark today." Beth kept a light, conversational tone. "Says hello."

The horse let out a grumbling whinny and nudged at her.

"Stop that; we're just friends."

Another whinny.

"Mark don't think of me like that. Got enough issues without dealing with some dumb girl and her crush."

The next whinny was screeching high.

"Whatever. Probably has whole classrooms full of girls who would throw themselves at him. But he don't seem like he's got a lot of friends. Maybe teammates, but not real friends, you know? So maybe I could be that for him. And maybe that's more special than another high school girl that would sleep with him."

Anthony didn't answer this time, and Beth hoped he understood. She couldn't tell how much he understood and how much she just spoke to herself and created the other side of a conversation in her mind.

"I've got to go to group, but I'll check in when I get back.

It was nice that Anthony listened. She kissed him on his velvety nose, walked him back to his stall, and headed to her car.

The second she turned off the barn lights, she heard the whine of the horse, high-pitched and pained. It pained her, too, squeezing yet another tear out of her from what was obviously an endless supply.

She couldn't put up with more. She couldn't see him get worse. When she got home later, she'd have to do something about it. Something she wouldn't be able to share with anyone, not even Anthony.

Mark

The bat connected with the ball. The loud crack was deafening, the jolt of impact shocking Mark's arms. He knew it was a home run before he swung. He'd seen it. He saw the pitch before it came. He saw himself round the bases, pretending it didn't hurt his foot. He saw himself after the game, giving excuses not to celebrate with the team.

He'd done it, gotten the team to the championship. Gotten

himself in front of scouts. This meant scholarships, maybe a chance at a farm league offer. A future.

But looking across the field as he trotted along, he didn't see the sun shining on the still-muddy crushed brick. He didn't see the celebrations or the frustrations.

He saw red. *The baseball field cracked and tilted. His ex-girlfriend Aurora screamed into the rain. His hands wrapped around the handle of a sword, and he raised it above the pitcher's head before bringing it down with all his might.*

Hands slapped his back, returning him to now. Teammates shook him by the shoulders, knocking off his hat and tousling his hair. He'd done it. They'd won. But he wasn't floating on air, basking in glory. He was shaking the visions from his mind, begging himself to focus on the present. He was on the baseball fields. It was daytime, and he'd just won the game. There was no rain. No sword. No red.

And on the pitcher's mound, ignored by teammates who were slinking off the field, the pitcher stood tall, staring at Mark. A twinkle in his eye. A sly grin. What did this guy know that Mark didn't? How could he not be devastated by this loss, holding his chiseled chin high?

And why on Earth was Mark foreseeing himself striking down this tall, pretty boy with a sword?

Bazrael

Pizza was a normal celebration of victory in American baseball. Bazrael had had his share of the traditional American dish after winning games, and he was correct in thinking this was where he would find the rival team.

The walk wasn't too far as Bazrael held the All-Star's discarded 'boot.' It was an L-shaped splint, hard plastic encased in fabric, with dangling velcro straps. A token of the batter. Bazrael's best chance at interacting with him off the baseball field. Would Bazrael even recognize the batter out of uniform? Surely, he would. The All-Star's eyes had bored into Bazrael's, had pierced him like a needle. Bazrael could identify those eyes, that smile, that careless saunter. Then Bazrael could ask how: How had the All-Star command such control over him? What magic did the All-Star wield, less overt than the witch's but just as powerful as Aurora Marie Seitsinger's ability to guide Bazrael's actions?

It had to be some secretive power the All-Star held. That was how he'd affected Bazrael like he did, mushing up his thoughts, liquefying his resolve, entrancing him with an intimacy across the distance of a baseball field. Bazrael had to know how the All-Star did it.

Unfortunately, by the time Bazrael had reached the pizzeria, the All-Star was nowhere to be seen. He'd resolved to wait and see if the All-Star was just in the bathroom when the rest of the victorious team recognized him.

"Hey, you're that pitcher!"

"What are you doing here?"

"Is that Cecilia's ankle brace?"

"You stole Cecilia's ankle brace!"

Cecilia? Could that be the batter's name? Bazrael recognized it as traditionally feminine. But the All-Star wasn't traditional. It was a beautiful name for someone who played the game beautifully.

"You here for trouble?"

"Can't win on the field, so you're looking to beat up on an

injured guy after?"

Most of the team was standing now, the larger athletes approaching Bazrael.

"Hey!" an adult behind the bar barked. "Don't start any trouble in here!"

"I just wanted to return this." Bazrael held up the ankle brace. "But if the owner isn't here, I'll just keep looking."

Bazrael left the pizzeria, uncertain of where to look next. The night was tepid and slightly humid, adding a fuzz of fog around all of the light sources. Bazrael loved humidity. He thought of Cuba and Miguel, though he would never have a chance to see them again.

The pizzeria door opened behind him.

"We'll take that boot."

"We'll give it back to Cecilia."

"Leave it with us, and you can get out of here."

There was an edge of danger to their voices, not a confident threat, but a quiver behind it, a secret hope that this tough posturing would be taken seriously. These young men didn't want to fight.

Bazrael deeply and completely wanted to fight. He was made for it, designed for it. But humans were so fragile. These bodies of muscle and bone, skin and sinew, were made for repair, not trauma. And most humans lacked the single-mindedness required for battle. They were too easily distracted, unwilling to weigh the fate of one arm against their opponent's, one life against another.

So it would be unfair for Bazrael to attack them. But as Cecilia's four biggest teammates surrounded Bazrael in the yellow circle of light beneath the glowing parking lot street lamp, they must not have been thinking of the fairness of an attack.

Fine. Even if Bazrael wouldn't attack them, perhaps thwarting an assault would sate his bloodlust. One doesn't prepare oneself to assert violence without preparation to experience it.

Within Bazrael, something stirred, an idea to ignore the fragility of humans and to sharpen the weapon of his purpose. The bloodlust had grown every time Bazrael learned a fighting skill or studied a battle of the heavens. This feeling, this instinct, was something else entirely, a creature inside Bazrael's mind so intent on conflict, it argued against any restraint.

Let me out.

No.

"Where you going with that boot?"

The player was closer than Bazrael had realized. He was surrounded now, under the needling attention of all the players. The prickly focus of many eyes, the barbs of juvenile mouths. The heavy weight of teen boys encircling him.

"I'll return it." Bazrael struggled to know who to direct the claim to as each player edged toward him.

"You'll give it to us or get beat."

But this ankle brace was Bazrael's only link to this Cecilia, his only chance to see the All-Star again. If time on Earth was as short as Bazrael knew it to be and Bazrael's purpose as isolating as he expected, it would be nice to see Cecilia again. No, not nice. It was imperative. And besides, these guys couldn't injure Bazrael.

This would be his first actual fight.

Let me out.

Was this his purpose calling out to him, demanding to be unleashed?

"I will not fight," Bazrael said, both to the teens confronting him and this bestial urge within him.

"Then get beat." The player closest, chest puffed out with his arm reared back, threw the first punch, maybe it was an elbow, right into the center of Bazrael's back. An elbow—such an odd choice to begin an ambush.

Then the next attacker took a skipping crow-hop and unleashed a wide haymaker. It landed perfectly on Bazrael's jaw. The boy yelped, cradling his fist. Bazrael remained standing tall, amused by how strong the punch was. And accurately placed. Well done.

The rest of the group descended. Fists and elbows and kicks. Quite exciting. They were great working together as a winning baseball team, but as a violent mob, these guys were top-tier.

It was almost sad that they were wasting such an exciting group effort on an undefeatable target. But they were scrappy, not giving up, losing steam, losing accuracy. They yelped with pain, shaking out hurt hands and feet. One guy even started crying. But they were slow to give up. Admirable.

"Be careful," Bazrael warned sincerely. "You still have a championship game."

Thankfully, their attack ended as they heaved curses through out-of-breath gasping.

Fighting really does fatigue. Plus, these guys just finished a full game.

Bazrael couldn't fault their conditioning and didn't want to mock the effort. So, he silently stalked off into the night, still holding the ankle brace, unsure how to find Cecilia.

Mark

Group nights were the worst part of Mark's life, hands down. He'd much rather have ten heart-to-hearts with his mom's new boyfriend, a hundred batting lessons with sickly kids who hated baseball, a million nights of the sweats as his body ached for alcohol. None of it compared to sitting in the back of some empty church dining hall in a circle of folding chairs, sharing feelings and updating other weirdos on his progress toward becoming a well-adjusted, normal sober person.

And maybe he was subconsciously rebelling against it, but he was always late...which inevitably made it worse.

Wincing, Mark squeezed the handle of the door, swinging it open slowly, closing it carefully behind him, drawing as little attention to himself as possible. But the moment the door shut completely and he released the handle, Mark wheeled around on the grungy linoleum floor under the harsh overhead lighting to see everyone in group silently turned to him.

He limped in, taking forever to cross the dusty room that smelled of Pinesol, mothballs, and vague Italian food (maybe just oregano?) to sit at the empty chair someone was nice enough to leave out for him.

"Where's your cast, Mark?" MaKayla Colfax asked with admonishment in her tone.

"It's not a cast; it's a boot," he corrected the goody-two-shoes who practically ran group with all her therapy experience and know-how. Though Colfax was supposed to be just another member there to share.

And then Mark tried to remember where his boot actually was. Coach had given him a ride from Tony's pizza; maybe it was still in his car. Coach was the only one on the team who knew Mark was in group therapy, and Mark was grateful it was kept a secret.

"And aren't you supposed to be wearing it?" the goody-two-shoes asked.

"Is there something about the boot," the therapist, whom Mark knew all too well, asked, "that makes you feel like less than your former self, Mark? Does it represent a change from who you were when you were abusing alcohol and drugs? Or perhaps it reminds you of your rehabilitation?"

Mark stared the therapist down. "Are you doing this because I pushed you out of bed?"

She puffed up, sitting up even straighter as the yes in the room settled on her. "I'm doing this because not abiding by your doctor's prescribed recovery plan is a form of self-sabotage."

"I just forgot it. My foot itched, I changed shoes, and left it, that's all." That much might have been true; his ankle itched like hell. Maybe Mark left the boot at the field. "Sorry I interrupted. Who's up?"

"MaKayla was sharing."

Of course she was.

The little goody two-shoes changed her tone, like she was in the middle of a valedictorian speech. "I've rewritten my amends and shared them at my mother's gravesite. Cain was very nice, listening to some amends. He just sat there and let me read them, then he shared with me, and I appreciate that. I'd hoped he'd come tonight, but he's still not feeling well—"

"Please," the therapist, whom Mark liked to think of as Dr. Slider, interrupted, "don't feel responsible for anyone else. You're here for you. Let's focus on that."

"Right. I still have amends written for others, who I hoped to actually see tonight, but...we don't have to talk about that. It's my responsibility to share my amends, and I'll be working on that. Thanks to you as well, Mark."

Mark had already been the victim of MaKayla Colfax's amends. In fact, he received her amends plus several amendments. It was just as overblown and studious as he'd imagined. He was surprised it didn't come with a PowerPoint, a trifold posterboard, or a diorama.

"I guess it's just hard because as I sharpen my…abilities," she spoke carefully.

Group was about sharing feelings, but not too many details about powers. MaKayla Colfax was a Fate. She could see the connections between people, their auras, maybe even their futures. And she could cut any of them short. Her boyfriend, Cain Morrigan, was a Reaper. The perfect couple. Mark wasn't positive what that meant, what powers or responsibilities Morrigan had, but the guy was always okay with Mark. Being a supernatural being of death just made him more badass.

Colfax continued with a guarded tone, "I'm starting to see more about Cain and I and what our future is leading toward. And I know I'm not alone in seeing what's coming."

Eyes darted to Mark. Great. Way to keep abilities a secret, guys.

"And to be completely honest," Colfax said, "I'm terrified about the future. And I feel like I can't talk to my boyfriend about it because he's been so preoccupied for days."

Mark had been injured for days, so he somewhat understood. But if goody goody Colfax admitted her perfect little life was less than flawless, something big must have been up with Morrigan.

Dr. Slider thankfully ended Colfax's sharing, "Thank you so much, MaKayla. It can be difficult when our normal outlets for thoughts and emotions aren't available. And I know you've been dealing with a lot. I'd consider reaching out to your father, who's always been pretty understanding, right?"

Colfax nodded. She was tearing up now, the girl sitting next to her consoling with a hand on the shoulder. The girls seemed to thrive on crying and touching. It all just made Mark want to run out of there screaming.

"So maybe find things to share with your dad, and maybe pick up your journaling again, or find ways to express yourself through collage again? Also, I'm going to challenge you for your next group share to not prepare anything."

That shocked Colfax, her eyes widening with fear. Poor thing; she couldn't imagine anything worse than not being allowed to do homework. She and Mark were all kinds of different.

"Thank you again, MaKayla," said Dr. Slider before looking around the room as if trying to pick someone from a huge crowd. "Who'd like to go next?"

People looked around a bit, all eyes tracking to Mark. How late *was* he? Had everyone else already gone?

"Don't really feel like sharing." Beth's voice was raspy from distress. She'd been crying too, most likely over Anthony. Mark felt the instinct to reach out and comfort with a gentle hand, but she was on the other side of the circle.

Someone else did share, a girl Mark didn't know. She was stressed out about picking a college, and Mark couldn't help but laugh to himself. He wished picking a school were the biggest stress in his life. Must be nice not to constantly worry about seeing your friends burn alive while magical horses bring about the end of the world.

"Mark, what did you have to say?" Dr. Slider asked in an even tone.

People were staring. College girl looked pissed. Had he

laughed out loud?

"I'm good." Mark shrugged and forced a smile. "Just won a baseball game today. Hit the game-winning home run. We made the championship."

"Mark, you played baseball with your leg tore up?" Beth's hoarse voice was thick with judgment and disappointment.

Mark shrank into the uncomfortable metal chair. "All I did was hit once; they didn't even make me round the bases," he lied.

"Mark." Dr. Slider tilted her head curiously. "Do you ever worry that you tie your value as a person to your ability to play baseball?"

"Are you kidding me?" Mark scoffed. "I *love* that my value is tied to baseball. I see everyone else walking through life, confused about their worth, anxious that they aren't loved enough or if they're making the right choices. I know I'm making the right choices. My team is in the championship. I'm All-State. I can hit clean up on any team. I'm good."

"And what happens when baseball is over?"

Mark smiled. "That's the beauty—there's always next season."

"But what if there's not?" Colfax asked like a jabbing accusation.

Mark held her eye contact and leaned forward. "There's not a future I see when I don't go down swinging, and I'm good with that."

"Mark," Dr. Slider asked, "have you ever tried to define yourself outside of baseball?"

"What, like a dictionary?"

"Like a person," Dr. Slider pressed.

"I'm the guy who sees things coming," he threw right back

at her.

"And is that a good thing?"

"To know what's about to go down? Of course."

"Why?"

"Why what?"

"Why is it good to know what's about to go down?"

The room had grown still, watching this game of cat-and-mouse. Mark tried to play off his answer lightly, like he didn't care. "So you can be prepared."

"To do what?"

"What's necessary."

"That sounds cryptic. Do you believe your ability to see things coming inevitably leads you to cause harm to others?"

"I thought we weren't here to talk about abilities." Mark chuckled, seeing if it would catch on. It didn't. Tough crowd. All eyes were intent on him, waiting for him to open up, accusing him of being unable to. Prying, poking, goading Mark. He tried to explain, "Harm happens. All the time. Humans do harm. They kill and do violence and break hearts." Mark's voice cracked, and that infuriated him. He must have been thinking of his mother. Or Aurora, his ex.

"So you feel the need to do harm to others before others can harm you?"

"I don't *harm* anyone." Mark stood. He wasn't going to be accused of anything without defending himself. "I don't know what this third degree is."

"I've found, Mark, that you don't share much without prompting."

"Maybe that's because I see what's coming. And I think everyone here, no matter their 'abilities,' sees it too. Bad stuff. Bad stuff is coming. Big time harm. And no amount of sharing is going to help fight it. We've got to be tough. Trust our instincts. And be willing to go down swinging."

"Thank you for sharing, Mark."

Mark sat. "Yeah, well, don't expect any extra treats tonight."

"Do please refrain from inappropriate comments. I think that's a good way to end. Everyone, please take the time to do some affirmations before you go to bed. And as always, I'm available to text if anyone needs to. Goodnight."

People began shuffling out, and Mark, still riled up from his share, started collapsing chairs to do something with all this extra energy. Of course, Beth wouldn't let him, taking chairs from his hands and placing them on the racks. And of course, Colfax cornered Dr. Slider afterwards and talked her ear off. Then, after all the goodbyes, they left. Dr. Slider waved as the other cars drove off and locked the church, hid the key, and morphed back into Mark's gray cat.

The walk home from the church was short, and Mark enjoyed the silence. Slider padded along beside him, nearly invisible in the dark save for her reflective eyes.

After a full day of pushing his ankle to its limits, the soreness pinched and squeezed his bones with every step.

Maybe Coach Boyfriend was right. He had to take it easy to heal. This early summer league would end with the upcoming championship, followed by another tournament league, and Mark wanted to be healthy for that one. He had to show out for the stats, his last summer league before he'd be on a college team, or even better, a minor league team.

Unless the world ended.

Pushing the final days of Earth out of his mind was pretty tough. He couldn't think about life two weeks from now without seeing Anthony's hoof meeting grass, fire sprouting up from cracks in the ground. The fire would rage and consume the planet, destroying everything it its way.

The battle. The final battle. Good vs Evil. God vs Devil. One on one, and for an arena, they chose Lockport, New York.

When he saw it, the battle stretched into infinite possibilities — giants dueling with oversized swords, an angel wrestling a demon, an eagle and a snake. Numerous matchups filled his mind, too many to name, too fleeting to focus on.

It was a fight so intense, it would break the Earth beneath their feet. But the most surprising part wasn't the force of the battle; it was the fighters. They didn't want to fight. They had to, were forced to.

And a crowd gathered to watch helplessly. Mark would be there, along with Beth. His ex, her new girlfriend, and even that goody-two-shoes Colfax, all together to scream and plead for the fighters to stop. But they wouldn't. And everything would die.

Mark napped out of it, seated on the side of the road, sweating and crying with Slider in his lap sniffing him and peering into his eyes.

"I'm fine," he said, pushing the cat away and struggling to his feet. More steps flooded his leg with more misery through muscle and soft tissue to bone.

He directed his vision to see how the foot would look all healed, but he couldn't conjure up that future; all he saw was the end of everything.

Chapter 4

Beth

The spade bit into the dirt around the rose bushes. There was no way for Beth to dig up the demon without wrecking the plants. That's why she'd buried it here when they moved in. To deter her from doing this very thing.

Not even Anthony knew this secret, knew that she still held onto it, that she kept it hidden.

The thorns stabbed through her gloves into her hands as she pulled it up. She had no idea what she'd tell her mother in the morning about the mess in the garden. Maybe she wouldn't have to say anything. Not that Mom wouldn't notice, but that she'd chalk it up to grief over a dying pet and let her daughter be.

Roots tore and popped as Beth wrenched the plant out of the ground, gripping it again and again as she pulled and jerked. Once the plant gave way, Beth went back to digging until she hit something hard. The tinny sound of metal on metal.

She removed the gardening gloves to reveal her red-streaked fingers and dug around the old metal box, wrenching it out of the ground from the caked dirt.

She sat, breathless, on the mulch, covered in dirt, with an old candied pecan tin in her lap. It probably would've been smart to take this somewhere quiet or hidden, but if she was unearthing it at all, she knew she wasn't being smart.

Such a normal-looking box, dirty, scratched, and dented. But holding such evil.

She ran her thumbnail under the lip of the lid and pried it open.

Within sat the coiled snake of a necklace, glinting in the moonlight. She threw it over her head. "Elizabeth," the demon's voice slithered along the air into her ear. She didn't dare conjure him completely from his amulet prison. But as long as she wore it, she could see and hear him.

The sight of the demon Puka sickened Beth, and she'd never been able to convene with him without losing her lunch. His skin was slick fur and constantly undulating with movement beneath the surface. His horns always pointed directly at her in threat. His animal eyes unsettling on an otherwise abundantly attractive human face. Tall, hairy donkey ears reached to the sky and twitched and moved with his expressions. He was a nightmare. And he knew saying her name disgusted her.

"Can you save Anthony?" she whispered in shame. She swore she'd never speak to the demon again, that she would allow him to rot in stagnation, that his memory would one day die with her.

Somehow, sitting around collecting dust had strengthened the imp.

"I did," he said, his voice cloying with an Irish lilt. "I saved the poor toy from the fate of all playthings of children."

"Can you stop him from dying from the colic?"

"Of course, Elizabeth."

He taunted her, calling her by the wrong name. She was filled with a nauseating hope and hated it, knowing a barb was coming.

"The horse will live to break the realm, to destroy the world. And from all the deaths, I shall be free again."

"Is that the only way? Can I command you to stop it?"

"Elizabeth, you commanded me to start it."

She froze. Of course, this was the trick. This was the sticky end to the deal Beth had waited for. When she had made her agreement with the demon, she knew he couldn't be trusted, that something about the deal would turn on her. She just thought it was going to happen back when she made the deal. Not nearly a decade later.

But here it was. She'd gone into a contract with a demon for Anthony's life, but he'd agreed so he'd eventually be free. And he didn't mind that everyone on Earth had to die to get his way.

"Is your desire to save the horse?" The demon's slick voice vibrated low. "There is another path to thread the needle in a windstorm."

"No," Beth said, quickly ripping the necklace off and closing the amulet back into the box. Not another deal. Not again. Not something worse to come back and bite her in the ass in another decade.

Even trapped within, the demon's laughing escaped, echoing in the night as Beth replanted the rose bush. This time, she did not bother with the gloves, getting dirt under her nails and thorns in her skin.

She was stuck. Anthony mattered more to her than anything in the world...but that didn't mean he mattered more than the world.

Bazrael

Without the advantage of flight, traveling was slow. Bazrael considered stealing a car to get around- or better yet, a go cart, sliding along the paved maze of roadways these humans trap themselves within. Perhaps one day. Until then, it was walking using the sun, the stars, and the geographical constant of the canal as his guide.

It was nighttime before Bazrael made it back to the abandoned neighborhood. Just outside of town, devoid of trees or any plantlife higher than overgrown grass, stood a street of dead homes like an elephant graveyard. Corpses of houses, some skeletal, abandoned mid-construction, others nothing more than concrete slabs geometrically breaking up the brush, all gathered along a road behind Bazrael's home. It was an example house to convince humans to live there, a peek into a future of what life would supposedly have been like. But it had been years since this neighborhood was abandoned, and someone decided it made more sense to leave it in various states of unfinished rather than sell or repurpose.

So he'd been living in this zombie home. Bazrael wasn't used to electricity, and in his co-opted youth in Cuba, days of blackouts were common. The comforts of furnishings made up for it.

Bazrael hadn't been the first person to squat here, and thankfully, the residents before were not only neat but well-off. They'd cached riches of possessions, then left, a theme for the area. Bazrael managed to pawn or sell some possessions as consignment. Jewelry and fine women's clothes stuffed the master bedroom closet, even a couple antique trinkets somehow hundreds of years old.

Bazrael often wondered who these nomads were, leaving a life of expensive belongings, even abandoning a toothbrush. They'd had a cat, who theoretically left with them. Bazrael remembered the cats of his false youth, wild neighborhood roamers who fought fiercely over territory. Like humans, in retrospect.

So in this shell of a house, Bazrael ended his day as he usually did, with sustenance and practice. He chewed beef jerky and readied his weapon. There was an End of Days to prepare, after all.

The touch of a familiar book was a favorite sensation of his, a soft, comforting reminder of a known friend. Bazrael's bible didn't house the same attachment many humans had. This bible was a collection of angelic capabilities and responsibilities as recorded by humans. This was a guidebook that had governed Bazrael's training to become an apocalyptic weapon.

The book listed each angel's realm, as well as tasks and feats throughout history. More than that, it was a war plan, the personnel strategy for the final battle. But plans changed over millennia, and the long-held theory of infinite angels crossing weapons with infinite demons was now obsolete.

But these weren't the reasons that Bazrael opened this ancient bible every night. Secretly, this book was much more than any information contained within. It was a sheath for a weapon. The pages were a scabbard for a sword. So Bazrael cracked the book, reached within, and withdrew his blade.

He practiced. The similarities between baseball practice and apocalyptic practice would most likely disturb most humans. Taking swings at recreational balls, quickening reflexes, and strengthening muscles could be put to many uses, and not all of them were wholesome.

Most of the money from selling the old clothes and baubles Bazrael converted into tennis balls. They were practically free when he bought them used in bulk, but the new ones, a happy yellow-green, came from a can that smelled of bright spring and poisonous chemicals, an overall pleasing mix somehow. So he destroyed dozens of new tennis balls nightly.

But tonight was different. There was an eagerness in his muscles, his purpose pressing down on him. Time was running short. He felt it. The potential within him built. The Creature of his bloodlust felt the time approaching.

Stepping through the motions of ancient sword masters, Bazrael angled his grip, allowing the flat of his blade to smack the balls against the nearby wall of the living room. He'd hit the targets with the specific sword strokes a few times before slicing through them with killing strikes. He bisected the tennis balls again and again. Finally, his human body relented into the exhilaration of panting breaths, heated skin, and sweat.

Then, Bazrael would move on from practicing his sword fighting forms to bodily ones, closing his eyes, slinging the tennis balls at the wall, then transforming into a different physique. Bones snapped into new shapes. Skin reformed. He kept his morphing eyes trained on the moving target. Bazrael's human form threw a ball that his serpent body caught in the loop of a scaled tail. He flung it again and slipped into angelic skin, catching with the concave cradles of his feathered wings. The ball bounced again. Grasped by a hovering bat. Plopped into a puddle of black tar. Fell into the grip of a shadow. More forms. Goat. Blood. Dragon. Composite creature. Fire.

Through each transformation, the Creature called out within him. It had been awakened, this bloodlust turned into sentience, this ache for violence now living and thinking inside Bazrael. Part of tonight's training was keeping the Creature bottled up. But Bazrael couldn't keep control for long. The time to unleash his purpose was soon, maybe even within the next few hours.

Once practicing his shifting and reaction time was complete, the tennis balls were very much ruined. Stained, pierced, singed, and melted.

Devastation to the point of ruin.

How this world would soon look.

Mark

Without waiting for the go-ahead, the kid closed his eyes and swung wildly. Mark's crotch managed to take the momentum before anyone else got hurt.

"You got to keep those eyes open," Mark groaned, clutching his groin.

As if it weren't humiliating enough catching a ride with Coach Boyfriend to the baseball fields, Mark spent all morning catching bats to his midsection. These kids had no business playing baseball, much less getting paid lessons from an All State hitter, but their dads probably had fond memories of being on a team in high school, so they'd be punishing their sons for it for the remainder of adolescence.

The pain in Mark's testicles radiated, turning his stomach and thickening his saliva. He was gonna hurl, pee blood, or both. His face heated, and his ears buzzed as the kid looked at him, asking something Mark couldn't hear. All Mark saw was the boy's reddened face, apple cheeks, and glasses until he got hit again, this time with a vision.

The apple-cheeked boy howled with suffering as the world burned. He called out to be saved, begging God, his parents, anyone to rescue him. Asking for someone, anyone, to help.

"Are you just gonna stand there, or are you going to teach me to hit a home run?" the apple-cheeked kid demanded as Mark snapped back to the present.

"Let's try the beach ball again," Mark grunted as he grabbed the teaching aid.

The kid complained as Mark pushed the inflated toy into his chest. Not only was it a way to get the kid to focus on form and improve his swing, it also kept him from nailing Mark in the nuts anymore today.

"Alright. Twenty swings, nice and slow," Mark said, limping even more gingerly back to the chain link fence to get a swig of water. "Hips and your thighs, not just arms. Pivot those feet."

The kid began, twisting his body as fast as possible.

"Slow," Mark repeated, channeling his crotch pain into the command of an unsatisfied coach.

"Hey, I'm paying you to teach my kid how to hit homers, not play at the beach," Some dad barked from behind the fence. Mark was already sweating from the heat; he didn't need to get chewed out in front of a field full of kids.

Immediately, Apple Cheeks dropped out of his stance and turned, waiting to see his dad get him out of this situation.

"Keep going," Mark told the kid before lowering his voice to the father. "He's too stiff for any power. He's got to learn to use his whole body, not his arms."

"You know what I think? I think you're showing up to lessons drunk or high..."

It was a fair assessment that may have been right a week

ago. But that was back when Mark wasn't restless and itchy all the sobriety, so mentioning it was infuriating. Immediately, Mark's mouth went dry. Even with another swig of water, he was only thirstier, and it wasn't for this bottle.

The dad kept complaining, slapping the chain link fence. "I think you think my kid's easy money instead of going out and getting a real job."

The sun cooked Mark's skin and stung his eyes. He splashed water on the back of his neck, but it wasn't even cold.

"So put down whatever booze you got in there and go do what I'm paying you for."

Mark wheeled around. The dad was about as old as Coach Boyfriend but more of a muscle head. Only on top, though; this guy skipped leg day every week. He was stretching a tee shirt from some local church while his shorts hung like lampshades. Designer brand, though. Just like his sunglasses and watch. Hell, the guy's shoes cost more than all the clothes in Mark's closet. Dad here had more dollars than sense.

"You're paying me because I've never hit under three fifty for a season in my life." A wave of light-headedness made Mark blink hard and focus on breathing.

"And you're not teaching my kid a damn thing."

Poor Apple Cheeks probably got his terrible work ethic from his old man, but Mark couldn't say that. The truth was that he absolutely did not want to get a regular summer job. Those had long hours that interfered with baseball. Regular jobs were indoors with people he didn't like, surrounded by food that gave him acne. So Mark focused on the kid. And on shaking off an oncoming vision.

"Keep it slow. Twist the hips, push off that back leg."

"Will you let the kid hit a ball, for Christ's sake?"

Another wave of foresight. *Heat and light. Fire and Brimstone. Everything was red.* He could see the baseball fields, the diamonds all fitting together at the infields, burn. *The Earth beneath gave way, breaking open. Mark lost his footing. Cracks in the ground opened, pushing up boiling hot air. The people playing screamed in panic, running, falling to the ground, some falling between the ground. The grass became a carpet of fire. The sky turned black. Somewhere above, a horse neighed.*

"Anthony?" Mark asked.

"Christ, do you even know my kid's name? Come on, son."

Apple Cheeks retreated off the field to his dad.

They got into a luxury SUV, the dad yelling out the window as they drove off, "This is our last lesson, and I'm not paying for this one!"

Dust kicked up from the parking area, floating through the fence to the field...the field where kids ran, batted, threw, and caught. Nothing on fire. No one screaming. No one dying.

Yet.

"Hey, you okay?"

Mark didn't have to turn to see Beth with her cringing smile.

"Fine." He took some sharp breaths and pulled at the brim of his hat, an old batting routine that was supposed to help him focus.

"You haven't been around your house for a few days."

"Avoiding Mom's boyfriend." Mark picked up the bats, rope, beach ball, and other teaching aids, resetting for the next kid due in twenty minutes.

"Still haven't found your boot?"

"My four o'clock will pay cash. I can go grab one on the way home."

"That creeper in the van ever knock on your door?"

It wasn't that Mark didn't believe Beth about her encounter with a particularly devoted man planning to seek him out for the visions; he just knew when a girl encountered any guy alone on unfriendly terms, her natural reaction would be to make him out as more of a threat than he was. And Mark couldn't blame her—there were some real bad dudes out there.

"No. Hopefully, you scared him off."

"I don't want to be a pest, but you ain't been returning my texts."

"My mom took my phone away until I cleaned up the yard. Her boyfriend's idea."

"Okay. Well, I was just wondering if you had any more insight. Anything new to Anthony's future?"

This was tough. Losing someone was hard, and Mark knew Beth had a special relationship with that horse. Though she never explained it, Mark figured that she somehow had a super-natural connection with Anthony, like they could communicate with their minds. He couldn't imagine being that close to anyone, much less someone he knew was dying. It wasn't her fault she was not giving up, but there was no news to tell.

Mark turned to see her, dressed for warm weather. He'd never seen her in anything except coats, sweats, or overalls. She wore a low-cut top showing off cleavage and jeans that revealed her curves. But now wasn't the time for checking a girl out, and Beth was like a sister to Mark. He got close enough to look her in the eyes, to shoot straight with her.

Then he noticed the necklace. A gold horse's head with a big red stone for an eye. The crimson gem sparkled in the sun, flashing and blinding.

One horse created in life. One horse formed by death. One horse was made by truth. One horse was made by lies. An unknown fact will raise them to the heavens. A shared certainty will bring them down.

"Mark! Mark!"

A heavy, calloused hand slapped him. Did that kid's father come back? No, it was Beth.

He caught her hand and stared into her eyes. Wild. Frightened. Crying. Mark must have zoned out with a vision. Beth had brought him back, looking at him, expecting to say something, to reveal some truth, to give her hope.

"Where did you get that necklace?" Mark asked.

Chapter 5

Beth

This was a mistake. Beth was putting Mark through too much. Less than a month ago, he'd been kidnapped, tortured, and heartbroken the day she met the guy, and honestly, it'd been downhill from there.

Now, it seemed like his visions of the future were breaking his brain. Her asking for ways out of a problem she created was unfair. Mark was physically injured, psychologically traumatized, in addiction withdrawals, and beaten down by his own magic.

"The horse," Mark stared at it, "the pendant, it told me something."

Dang it. She knew she shouldn't have been walking around with the demon amulet out in the open. Her hand immediately covered it up, then spun it behind her back so she could take it off.

"What is that necklace, Beth?"

"Nothing. Just a gift."

"It's not nothing. It *spoke* to me."

Crud. Beth never thought that others would be able to hear Puka. She shouldn't be wearing the amulet in public, especially not around someone as vulnerable as Mark. The amulet should be in a box buried again. Or at the bottom of Lake Erie.

He reached for her, for the necklace, and she retreated, tearing her arms away. Normally, she longed for his touch, to feel his strong hands on her neck. But not like this. Not when he was so vulnerable and she so dangerous.

His voice softened, "It told me a prophecy. Of horses. About Anthony, it could help me see a way."

"Ain't no way." She almost laughed, stepping back to head to her car.

"One horse created in life." Mark's words stopped her in her tracks. He'd said it in an accent. *His* accent. This was how the demon spoke. But now she let that damned thing taint Mark. "One horse formed by death. One horse was made by truth. One horse was made by lies. An unknown fact will raise them to the heavens. A shared certainty will bring them down." Mark snapped out of it and spoke like himself again. "If we can figure out what that means, we could stop whatever's coming."

There was no stopping it. Beth was the one who started it. She was the cause. She was the problem.

"Cecilia!" someone shouted from across the baseball field. A tall, lean figure jogging over. Mark was distracted enough for Beth to dash to her car.

"I think this guy wants to kick my ass," Mark said with a lighthearted chuckle.

But Beth was in no mood for humor or quips. She drove away before her mistakes could hurt anyone else.

Bazrael

Bazrael sprinted across the four interlocked baseball diamonds. Sure, other people were running, but that was exercise. This was excitement, a fresh breeze of exhilarating mint and pine needles. The closer he got, the stronger the sensation, the more uncertain he was of what to say to Cecilia or what Bazrael even wanted from seeing him again.

And that uncertainty made it all the more exciting.

What was it about the All-Star that dominated Bazrael's thoughts and emptied his mind? What power did the young man have to assert himself alongside Bazrael's purpose?

By the time Bazrael neared the All-Star, within the same infield, Cecilia had armed himself with a bat—not in the sporting sense, but a defensive stance.

"Are you here to kick my ass?" Cecilia called out when Bazrael was still across the infield.

"Oh, no," Bazrael assured him from second base. "I am not looking for a fight. Your teammates already addressed me with violence."

"They did what now?"

"They tried to kick my ass. At the pizza place."

"How many of them?"

"Four. And quite the athletes. Strong with great conditioning. No wonder your team advanced to the championship."

"Four of them kicked your ass, and you can still run like that?"

"They were not successful. But at no fault of theirs."

"So I handed you an L and knocked your team out of first place, my teammates jumped you, and you're sprinting like a banshee at me with my old ankle cast? For what?"

"Yes!" Bazrael had forgotten he still held the cast. He trotted over, hands up in a show of nonviolence, and dropped the medical device at Cecilia's feet. Bazrael backed up, hands still gesturing peace. "Though I am unaware of any banshee known for their running."

Mark squinted. "You're not from around here."

"I am not. I am Cuban. In a sense."

"Well, thanks for returning the boot. And not kicking my ass, I guess." He dropped to a knee, careful and deliberate with his hulking width, like a warrior in prayer, removing a sneaker, then wrapping the velcro straps of the boot around his foot and calf.

The All-Star was mesmerizing. Not just from his confident demeanor, it was the leftover mystique of how he had won their pitching battle in a way Bazrael still didn't understand.

Most ignorance was annoying to Bazrael, learning to navigate social customs with little experience or know-how. But this ignorance was different. This was a curious suspense that pulled at Bazrael's thoughts like gravity or magnetism. He wanted to savor the sensation, but he couldn't stop himself from asking the truth. "How did you do it?"

Cecilia didn't look up. "Lose my boot? I'm not the best at following doctor's orders, I guess…"

"I was referring to the game. You tricked me into throwing the pitch you wanted."

From kneeling on the ground, the All-Star looked up with a sparkle in his eye, not quite smirking, but mouth set like he was tasting delicious hard candy. "Is that what I did?"

His tone was infuriating and delectable. The confused reaction it produced within Bazrael was like gum stretched in different directions. But in a fun way. "Then what did you do? Read my mind?"

"What good would that do?" He stood, dusting off his knee before picking up his bat again, this time not in a threatening manner. The metal club belonged in his hand, an extension of his arm, like how some humans wore watches or rings; his hand looked out of place without it. "Your mind was blank the whole time."

"So you *were* reading my mind. You told me to throw a curve to get me to think of my next pitch."

Cecilia shrugged and smiled before heading back to a pile of bats, baseballs, and, for some reason, a colorful inflated sphere. Bazrael had never seen this child's toy associated with baseball, not even practice. Just more mystery the All-Star cultivated.

"Tell me what I'm thinking right now," Bazrael challenged him.

The All-Star Cecilia locked eyes with Bazrael, not with scorn, disbelief, or ridicule, but with focus. The twinkle in his deep brown eyes turned to steel daggers pointed into Bazrael's. Thrill pulsed through Bazrael, solidifying him into a statue. Thrilling. Bazrael wanted more. Much more. He wanted decades of this feeling. Bazrael was compelled to spend the rest of his short time on Earth with Cecilia. It wasn't long enough. And for the first time, Bazrael hated that his true purpose would end his lifespan as a human. He understood why so many people always longed for more time, for more life.

Cecilia regarded him and replied, "You're thinking of dying."

Mark

Mark found that talking to the tall pitcher was similar to batting against him; it required complete focus to keep a neutral face.

Something about the bright look of the boy, the softness of his expressions, the depth of his eyes stirred something in Mark. He felt himself blushing and smiling, forcing himself to furrow his brow and build a facade to hide his reactions. Just like some gameface against a pitcher playing mind games, Mark's glare was a defense mechanism to hide behind.

"Everyone is always thinking about dying, whether it's in the back of their mind or on the tip of the tongue. It's the reason we act the way we do because we got a big Grim Reaper looking over our shoulder. Death is in all our destinies."

The pitcher relaxed somewhat, his strong, broad shoulders dropping, his searching eyes growing gentle. Odd. Usually, whenever Mark brought up destiny or death, people tightened up. Nobody liked to talk about eventualities, and Mark learned to use the topic as another weapon to protect himself from awkward social interactions. But this goofy guy seemed to thrive in them.

"I'm Bazrael."

This guy must've been lying. Or maybe it was a nickname. Mark made it his business to memorize the names of all the ranked pitchers he'd have to bat against.

"Never heard of you. How'd you end up pitching for one of the best teams in the state?"

"Nobody else wanted to pitch against you."

Maybe he was telling the truth.

"I've never met someone who could read minds before."

Something felt rotten about lying to this guy. He was so open, so honest, and it was so difficult to keep him locked out. Difficult not to vomit the truth about how Mark read all the possible futures between himself and each pitch. Difficult not to open up and tell him about every truth Mark knew. To warn him about what was coming.

"I've never met a pitcher who could keep his throws a secret from me." He was already saying too much, even though it didn't feel like enough. Mark was laying himself naked here before this stranger, but instead of shame, he was dying to be viewed.

They sat in stillness for a moment, Bazrael towering over Mark with an accepting kindness, like a warm bed. Mark desperately kept his tough-guy face intact.

Bazrael grinned sheepishly, "So what are you going to do until the world ends?"

The facade fell. Mark could no longer hold a gameface. His eyes slackened, and his jaw dropped. How could this guy possibly know that? Maybe Bazrael was the mind reader.

Or maybe he was something else entirely.

Mark started an answer several times before his mouth and voice caught up. "The usual, I guess...play baseball. Spend time with friends. What about you?"

"I don't have any friends. But I am looking for one."

Mark's face reddened all over again. He wanted to be Bazrael's friend. Desperately. To know what he knew and how to keep so cool in the face of utter destruction.

"Aurora Marie Seitsinger." Bazrael said suddenly. "You know her."

This guy was something more than a mind reader, and Mark realized he was lucky to have come out on top during their last interaction. Bazrael was playing chess against Mark's TicTacToe. He'd be lucky if he could get away without spilling all of his most precious secrets.

He swallowed hard and managed a shrug. "Everyone knows that."

"You must still think about her. A lot. Her essence is all over you. You wear it like a cloak."

"Nah, that's old news. She barely crosses my mind." It was a lie, and it wasn't. When Aurora first broke up with Mark, it was as if he'd forgotten about him entirely. Then MaKayla Colfax reconnected him with her Fate power. But it wasn't the same. He didn't lust for her like he used to, but he still saw their destinies as intertwined.

"She's what happened to your leg, isn't she?"

How did this guy know all this? Mark didn't know if it was worth explaining Aurora's powers. Either it should have been her secret to keep, or this guy already knew, anyway.

"I don't even know what that means." Mark shrugged it off. "She didn't happen to my leg. I fell."

"What are you so afraid of, Mark?"

Deep in the tall pitcher's eyes, Mark saw it for a moment, a flash of the future, lifting a sword above this guy's head.

"Nosy people who don't mind their business."

Mark brought the sword down with all his might. The end of the world.

"Huh...you seemed tougher than that. I imagine a star baseball player has everyone in school in his business. Didn't expect it to rattle you so much."

"You couldn't rattle me from the pitcher's mound," Mark threw at him.

Bazrael didn't hesitate. "You took two strikes that left you dumbfounded."

"And it only took one to show you for the rookie you are." Mark took a step to get in Bazrael's face. He smelled like wood and maybe a cake baking. Was this his breath? Was it his aura?

"I need your help," Bazrael whispered.

Excitement jolted through Mark. Fear and excitement stirred and fizzed in his guts, his knees, and other places. Of course he wanted to help the tall, dark weirdo. He wanted to do anything he could to spend some more time with him, to feel this as much as he could. But he obviously couldn't admit that. The shield of high school socialization couldn't allow indulging of such desires.

Mark was sweating as a chill swept across his skin. Was he smiling like some goofball? Was he blushing? He set his feet, sniffed and hardened his face, pulled at his crotch to make sure it wasn't communicating anything else. Played it cool.

"Yeah, well, I'm pretty busy."

"I imagine so," said Bazrael. "I've been trying to find you for days."

"Days?"

"I need you to help me get to Aurora Marie Seitsinger."

There was nothing that Mark ever wanted to do more and, at the same time, avoid as much as this. He suddenly understood the concept of being between a rock and a hard place.

Beth

Beth's friendship was a curse. Knowing her, showing her kindness, was nothing more than a punishment for Mark. She pulled her car into the parking lot of one of the many abandoned industrial warehouses by the canal, sobbing. Shedding tears for Mark's misplaced hope, for Anthony's unavoidable destiny, for the pressure of Puka the demon's hold on her.

Tears streamed and blurred her vision. She didn't even see that same church van drive into the gravel parking lot, stopping to block the only way out.

The sound of the whining van door opening alerted her. She cussed aloud. Instinctively, Beth grabbed the pepper spray she'd started carrying on her, moving it to her lap, resting her hand to conceal it. She unhooked the work knife from her belt and slid it beneath her thigh closest to her window. She locked her doors.

She would be okay if she just stayed in the car. Just breathe. Be polite and short. Her window was already down, and Beth regretted pulling the keys from the ignition before rolling it up.

"Hello, little lamb."

Beth hoped the smile she flashed was as painful to see as it was to fake.

"The Lord brought you into my path again, praise be."

She just nodded, forcing herself to smile, comforting herself with the feel of the knife under her thigh. Ready to do what had to be done.

"I was driving along, taking the road the Lord leads, and I was thinking about our friend, the prophet." The words seethed out of him like a threat.

Beth was safe as long as she stayed in the car, though. She reminded herself she was strapped into a big machine of steel and fiberglass. A protective cage.

"Don't know any prophet, sir."

"That's right. Just 'some guy tore up his leg.'" The man leaned in, resting an arm on the side of the open window. "I'm starting to wonder if maybe the Lord sent me looking for His prophet just so that we could find you instead."

"We?"

"The Disciples of Gods' End. We learned about your town and how many blessings of the Lord have wound up here. I think you've been blessed, too. Miss...I'm sorry, I never introduced myself. I'm Pastor John Phillips Parker. They call me Parker. And you are...?"

He stretched out his hand, breaking the plane of Beth's protecting cage. The hand jutted in pointedly, completely still. Accusatory more than an invitation for a handshake.

Beth imagined grabbing the hand, not to shake, but to hold as her left flicked open the work knife. A slice across the soft of the wrist, and he'd be done. No more threatening girls. No more trapping people with a creepy van. No more of whatever the hell this scumbag was guilty of.

"Yesss," Puka hissed at her from within the amulet in her pocket.

Her eyes must have darted away, or maybe she made a face because Parker withdrew his hand and ducked closer. His head now broke the plane of Beth's cage of safety.

"Was that your blessing? Does the Lord talk to you, too, young lady?"

The smell of mint gum and halitosis billowed into the car, stinging her nose. The heat of his breath coated her face. The knife could slide into his neck from here. The vein showed beneath his perfectly shaved jaw.

"Do it," the demon Puka encouraged.

Parker squinted, studying her. "You need not fear me. I am here to do the Lord's work. Now, the Lord's work may cause suffering, but it is necessary. It is inevitable. Now. Does the Lord speak to you?"

"No," she whispered, resisting the instinct to recoil.

"Then maybe it's the Devil-" He moved lightning-quick. His head leaned away as his hand shot in for the handle. The door swung open, and Beth was exposed. He grabbed at her collar.

She swung the knife out.

He stepped away, and the seatbelt held her back. Once he'd dodged easily, Beth was stuck pointing the blade. Her hand whipped the pepper spray up to aim.

But he was already on her. One hand twisted the knife away from her. The other enveloped the pepper spray and pointed it into her own lap.

She sprayed helplessly, hitting her jeans. She punched with her now unarmed hand. He was so strong. Her wrist twisted. Her crotch burned.

His free hand grabbed at her, sliding over her shirt and pants.

What was this creep doing to her?

The hands continued wildly over her breasts, thighs, and hips. He pushed, twisting her wrist into her side, pushing her off her seat. And then his hand groped at her butt.

But he wasn't groping...he was searching.

And he found it. A finger dug into her back pocket and fished out the necklaces and amulet.

No.

"Now what have we here?"

The gem in the silver horse's eye sparkled, dangling at the end of the necklace hanging from his hand.

Chapter 6

Bazrael

There was an aspect of this conversation that Bazrael wasn't catching onto, a puzzle piece missing that made the entire picture impossible to understand.

"So if you know her, her family, and her friends, why don't you just go visit Aurora Marie Seitsinger on my behalf?"

Cecilia let out a big sigh and scratched his thick neck. "You can just call her Aurora..." He wandered off before he could answer the question, directing the next child he was teaching baseball to. "Fifty more swings, and you only step from one dot to the next. And make sure you follow through, because I'm going to be watching you like a hawk."

In no way did Cecilia continue to watch.

"If you got chased off by her little guard dog, I'm definitely not going to get close enough to talk to her."

The guard dog's witchcraft needled Bazrael's memory. Most likely, few American teens knew about the use of magic, and if they did, they definitely didn't talk about it openly. Either way, it wouldn't have been prudent to explain it to Cecilia, especially when Bazrael considered the guard witch's powers inexplicable.

That also meant not explaining to Mark he was an angel. Deception was already difficult for Bazrael as it was, but there was something about Cecilia that made him want to be open and honest. Something about the harsh, seeping stare of the All-Star compelled Bazrael to forfeit himself to it more, lay himself even more vulnerable under scrutiny.

"So we have to find someone else, like a middle-man, to ask Aurora about this...whatever this item you think she has..." Cecilia searched for the word.

"Summoned," Bazrael offered the term. "Aurora summoned an Ophanim."

More deception. Ophanim was Bazrael's travel form, the most comfortable way to move between realms and worlds, but that would be tough to explain.

"Cool. So I totally know someone who can talk to Aurora about this item, then we'll be even. You returned my boot; we'll return the o-fanny-um."

"Great. Who?"

Cecilia made a pained face. Again, there were pieces of this conversation Bazrael was missing. "Colfax. MaKayla Colfax. She's real tight with Aurora. But I'm fine with Colfax, I don't hate her at all."

Why would Cecilia hate this young woman? More social politics of the American teenager.

"I'm pretty cool with her boyfriend. They're weirdos, though. Not like you, but they're into some weird stuff. I totally bet they know what's up with Aurora summoning. I'm actually in group meetings, kinda...like a club, where we talk about...being nicer."

"Therapy?"

"Keep it down, man." The All-Star's strong grip latched onto Bazrael's arm. With the human contact came a skyrocketing heart rate and sweaty armpits. Surely, this was from any contact with any human, a sensation seldom experienced by Bazrael, and had nothing to do with the seemingly magic stronghold Cecilia had on him.

The All-Star looked around and leaned in until Bazrael could feel the heat of his breath. It smelled like mint and corn chips. Cecilia licked his lips, then asked in a whisper, "Who'd you hear I was in therapy from?"

This was a grave admission, a revelation of an enormous secret. Bazrael understood discussing emotions wasn't considered masculine in this society. Knowing Cecilia was in therapy wasn't just incredibly admirable for a lifelong athlete; it was also a sacred truth Bazrael knew not many shared.

"Oh, no, I didn't."

Cecilia released his hold on Bazrael's arm, leaving a cold vacancy where there had once been physical contact.

"Group's tomorrow. We can ask Colfax about the summoning, then."

But Bazrael felt his purpose arriving soon. It was on the way. Each second passed, each foot stepped, brought him closer to the imminent ending that was on its way.

"Tomorrow is too late."

"You really got in some deep trouble, huh, Baz?"

For a moment, Bazrael thought he may have to answer, to admit not only why Aurora Marie Seitsinger had summoned him to Earth but why he couldn't fulfill her request and what his true purpose was. The idea of confessing to Cecilia was a jolting, shuddering terror, but wouldn't it be nice to no longer bear this secret?

Luckily, before Bazrael said anything, Cecilia turned to yell at his pupil, "Step on those dots with each swing, Andy. You're only cheating yourself!"

"Can't see the dots if I'm keeping my eyes on the dang ball!!"

"Enough excuses, Andy. You know who doesn't have excuses? Bryce Harper."

"I hate the Phillies," the kid muttered as he returned to his swing.

Cecilia let out a frustrated sigh. "Baz, we're going to have to wait until group tomorrow night. If we had a car, we could swing by MaKayla's work."

The Creature within Bazrael stirred. As he quieted it down, he wondered whether Cecilia's given timeframe had upset the thing or if that was just another sign that Bazrael's purpose was approaching fast. Either way, the Creature was harder to keep at bay, and Bazrael needed to meet his summoner and reveal the truth to her.

But something about Cecilia was powerful beyond his humanity. He could read minds or look into people's desires, maybe even their futures. So he might be able to understand some of Bazrael's capabilities without asking too many questions.

"Cecilia?" Bazrael savored the name, using its power to make him brave enough to continue, "I might be able to get us there, but..."

"But what?"

As if an admission on its own, Bazrael asked in a whisper, "Can you keep a secret?"

The All-Star laughed. "Baz, you would not believe the weird stuff I know about that I keep to myself."

"Like what?"

Cecilia was silent for a moment, embattled within himself. Bazrael leaned in, seeing if he was trusted enough to learn more.

"Destiny. Fate. It's real. There's an unavoidable future for each of us. I can't exactly say how I know, but believe me, I know."

Knowing the words were more true than any human could understand, Bazrael had to stop himself from laughing. To a guardian angel, such a claim was a given, one of the basic governing laws of reality. But for a human living within the illusion of free will, this was an enormous step in thinking. A leap of faith. Another admission of Cecilia's most protected thoughts.

So maybe Bazrael could trust him.

"Well, in that case, I can get us there."

"Cryptic. I like that." Cecilia lit up like a lantern, glowing with contagious excitement. "You're all right, Baz. Andy! No! You're completely turned around!"

Once the pupil was aptly admonished, given homework, and sent on his way, Cecilia led Bazrael behind a sheltered dugout. There wasn't much room for privacy in the baseball fields, but unsurprisingly, the All-Star knew the exception. This was his territory. He ruled it as a deity commanded a realm with knowledge, competence, and dignity.

"There's a hiding spot over here I used to make out with chicks," he said, leading the way, limping along in his booted ankle.

It wasn't exactly private, but among the sounds of dozens of kids playing, the slap of baseballs caught in worn leather, and the ping of bats connecting with their targets, no one could see them. There was a safe, cool glow in a stolen space, free from all eyes.

The shadowed area was tight, open air caught between a couple of solid walls. Bazrael could smell the All-Star's minty, snack-scented breath, feel the warmth of it as well as the young man's body heat. Or was Bazrael just getting flustered by proximity?

Cecilia wheeled around, landing the dark brown eyes that somehow blazed bright right on Bazrael.

"So...what's the big secret, Baz?"

Wow, he loved that nickname. Or perhaps just the source of it. A vibration emanated from Bazrael's stomach outward, victimizing his joints with weakness and threats of failure. His secret had been watertight, revealed to no one thus far in his time on Earth. He stood on a precipice, uncertain what the reaction would be once he unveiled himself, a step forward into uncertainty that could never be taken back. Maybe this was destiny, though.

He savored the precious thrill until he shrank under Cecilia's pressure.

"Well?"

"I'm afraid I may have misled you, Mark. Not precisely a lie, but you believe I am a normal eighteen-year-old man of Cuban decent—"

"I do *not* think you're normal."

"—when in reality, I'm something else. Something greater. Or perhaps something much worse."

Cecilia's eyes widened, studying Bazrael. He was suddenly aware of how he may have looked, whether his clothes would be considered out of fashion or if his hair was kept. He was under a microscope examined by the expertise of such a specimen of humanity. The exposure was wild and freeing, a cool rush of wind or water on warmed skin. He longed to live in this space, this feeling of vulnerability with such a pinnacle of athletics.

Bazrael wasn't sure where to even begin, then realized maybe he didn't need to say much. Maybe there was enough trust to just experience it together. "I may not be able to explain what I am in terms that would make sense to you or that you would even believe, but I'd like to show you."

He stepped toward the muscular young man, so close he now definitely could feel the heat coming off the sun-kissed exposed skin of his thick arms. Their eye contact held in cooling relief while they got even closer. But the All-Star didn't waver, didn't flinch or retreat. And when Baz wrapped his arms around the human, he was met with heavy, strong arms holding him as well.

Their arms locked around one another as they fell.

Beth

Beth struggled to hear him, not being able to tear her focus from the amulet. Maybe she could tackle him or gouge one of his eyes, but then what? Could she get away from him fast enough to put the car in gear and drive off? And what about the others? And the van?

"...Diablerie, the work of the devil. I came across it many times in my life, often too young to realize." Parker paced back and forth in front of Beth, then leaned against the hood of her car, avoiding eye contact. Parker spoke as much to her as he sermonized to the others from his van, gathered around close enough to remain a threat. "And I'm not talking about wrath or sin or the evil of man. I mean the work of the enemy, the angel of God cast from heaven, destined to war against him at the End of Days. But how did such a pretty young thing like yourself come into possession of such darkness?"

"Just some stupid necklace my mom got me," Beth seethed.

"I see lies like smoke from a fire, little lamb."

"Don't know where it's from."

"Now, that may be true, but you know what it is. Otherwise, you wouldn't risk so much. The Lord brought me to you, I believe, for the purpose of relieving you of this burden. But you must tell me what form of devilry this is."

"Don't know what you're talking about."

"Don't lie to me." He rushed across the gravel to shove a finger in her face.

"What do you want from me? I don't know anything."

"Let me ask you." Parker's tone changed to melodic. "Was Judas performing the will of God?"

"What?"

"Judas Iscariot, betrayer of Jesus."

"I know who Judas is."

"Then answer me, was he performing the will of God?"

"I don't know."

"Well, isn't this just a conversation about things you don't know? I happen to believe that Judas did the will of God." Again, Parker paced while he evangelized to his audience. "Sometimes God employs evil men to perform evil deeds for a holy purpose, a purpose man is just too small to understand. Maybe I am here to perform evil deeds on you, Elizabeth. You see, I was guided by the devil here, to this moment, to this town. A devil offered me fulfillment of my wildest dreams in exchange for my soul. So I asked to be a rich man. And I was, for a time. But then I was not. So I asked to stay forever good-looking, and he delivered me to a secret society of great power who performed sacred rituals that transformed my physical vessel. But then, later, I was locked away from the tender touches I wanted my handsomeness to yield. And with one last desire granted me by the Beast, I asked to bring about the final days. And he delivered me unto you. But I do not serve that devil. I serve God. I thought I was brought here for the apocalyptic prophet. But maybe it was for you. For this. I've dealt with the devil, and I smell him on you. Now talk."

"You let me alone, or my daddy'll—"

He slapped her. Hard.

"Your daddy will what? Rise from the dead?"

She gasped. How could he know...?

Parker tempered anger with volume. "Is it unclear that you are in over your head, Elizabeth? Now tell me, is or isn't this necklace the work of the devil?"

"I don't know."

"I could write ten Bibles with what you don't know. Maybe we'll have to ask questions to the prophet. Maybe he can see things my way. After all, I could never bring myself to hurt a woman; perhaps, I could deal more plainly with that young man."

"I don't know if it's the devil, but it's a demon. From a river. His name is Puka, and he's a curse."

"Oh no, child. You just don't recognize blessings. Curses are just miracles we haven't bent to our favor. Tell me, what did Puka do to you?"

It was a betrayal to Anthony to give the secret a voice, something so sacred, buried so deep within herself, it bled as she tore it out and admitted, "He made me a bargain... He got me a horse."

Beth fell sobbing, hair and tears blinding her eyes, her body convulsing in surrender to helplessness.

Again, Parker was gentle, his fingertips barely touching her face. Everything within her screamed for her to recoil, to cringe, to run, to lash out, anything. But all she could do was follow the guidance of his rough, calloused hands, bringing her eyes to meet his. With the back of his knuckles, he wiped her tears and pushed the hair from her face, smiling sadly.

He whispered, "No, little lamb. He got *me* a horse."

And Parker left her there, sobbing. More alone than ever.

Mark

Mark had seen his own future played out in his mind countless times. He'd seen women fly through the air, swinging on invisible ropes. He'd even seen his ex-girlfriend blast him the length of a home run with nothing but the strength of her will.

But he'd never seen anything like this.

The world collapsed around them. Realities, as in plural, flew by like looking out a car window headed through tunnels. They were moving, they were falling, but they were also standing still as worlds ripped by them. Each new existence felt different, the smell of the air, the pull of their weight, the breath in his lungs. The only constant as they moved without moving was Baz.

And then, somehow, impossibly, they were back in Lockport, New York, behind a dumpster in the alley by a row of shops. Something so magic, vibrant, and reality shifting came to an abrupt end with the stinging smell of hot garbage and urine.

But that's how the supernatural went for Mark.

He got to his feet, wiping his hands after smelling them and confirming none of the alley grunge got on him. Baz stood above him, smiling patiently, eyebrows up like he expected Mark's reaction to whatever space-time travel had just taken place. Even Mark had to admit, the facial expression of such a need for validation was endearing, almost cute. If Baz had had a tail, it would be wagging.

Just then, the screech of tires pierced the air. Behind them, on the main drag, a van had slammed on brakes, then gone in reverse to pull into the alley, stopping traffic and inconveniencing loads of cars responding with honking.

Mark had been chased down before — cops, other jocks, dealers. This was obviously someone who'd spotted them and had a change of plans. Mark racked his memory for anyone he'd pissed off recently, anyone he might have owed money. That was the problem with drinking and doing drugs with strangers on a regular basis; sometimes he made enemies he didn't remember.

But Mark was in no condition to run. Better to stand and fight.

The van stopped, and the doors opened. Next to distressed and cracked name of a church, someone had painted an odd shape, a circle broken vertically to make a V. Maybe some kind of gang symbol tacked on to a junkyard van gotten at a discount. The men getting out were hulking masses of muscles and tattoos squeezed into collared shirts.

It was time to see what Baz was made of. Luckily, Mark saw some scrap wood sticking out of a dumpster. The men approached, staring directly at Mark, so he armed himself with a two-by-four, offering another one to Baz. But Baz refused, pushing the makeshift weapon away and stepping in front to face the danger.

One of the men from the van, marked with an adorable teardrop tattoo by his eye, held up a photo, looking back and forth, comparing it to Mark's appearance.

"Are you the Lord's prophet?" He asked with a thick southern accent.

"Sorry, I was raised Presbyterian." Mark attempted a tone somewhere between a threat and a condescending joke. He was just happy his voice hadn't cracked.

"It's him," Teardrop said, pocketing the photo. He told the other men, "This is gonna make Parker even happier."

"Get in the van," another said. The three men stood evenly spaced across the alley.

While Mark thought up a smart ass response, Baz spoke, stepping toward the danger. "You get in the van and leave. We're not here for trouble."

"But friend, we are the trouble."

"I don't have any friends," Baz said. Weird flex, but okay... "So put the trouble back in the van."

This guy was not good at trash talk. His mouth was about to get the two of them beaten up. Mark gripped the board as best he could, choking up his grip like holding a bat.

"Naw," Teardrop said, reaching behind his back and pulling out a handgun. "I keep my trouble with me."

Jesus, everyone involved was so bad at smack talk. Mark immediately tried to scout an exit. The alley dead ended, but maybe one of these doors would be unlocked. At least he could scream and hide behind the dumpsters, or maybe in them.

Teardrop raised the gun as he approached closer, the barrel right at Baz's chest.

Mark dropped the wood and threw his hands up, fighting to keep his lunch down. As tough of scrapes as he'd been in, it was always fists and knives, maybe a bat. But never guns. Cold choked his throat and squeezed tears out the corner of his eyes.

Then Baz moved.

At first, it was just a few steps toward Teardrop, still right in the path of the gun. Then it was a jump, a leaping step, right for him. Baz grabbed the gun and tore it away.

The men all backed away, their turn to put their hands up.

But Baz didn't aim the gun. He didn't even change his grip on it. He stepped forward fast, and all the men took off. He swung the gun, bringing it across his body just like pitching a baseball. He threw the damn thing.

The guys jumped in the van just as the pistol or whatever it was hit the windshield. It cracked, and the gun went flying.

Before Mark could even see where the weapon landed, the van was backing out the alley, tires screeching once again, swerving backwards into traffic, van doors closing.

Who throws a gun? Like of all the dangerous things that could be done with a gun, throwing was probably the most irresponsible. And yet it worked.

The piece landed behind another dumpster, but Baz didn't even seem to notice. He just turned to look back at Mark with that same expectant smile.

Catching his breath while rubbing away tears and sweat, Mark had no idea what to say. Not vomiting was a win at that moment. But somehow, Baz held a nonchalant air about him, a goofy smile.

And somehow, despite the threat of getting shot, not to mention the nonsense of colors and sensations that flew by while traveling magically, Mark knew he was safe.

Whatever Baz was, he was safety. Perhaps a little naïve or ignorant of the way things were, but that was part of his charm. There was a strength in him, a power beyond courage or his traveling ability. Baz was protection personified.

Mark realized he was back. This alley wasn't a dream or a vision or some alternate world Baz had taken them to. This was home. This was Lockport. This was where Mark was a baseball All-Star, not to mention an untouchably cool ladies' man.

The threat of strange men jumping out of a van to threaten to shoot them was a distant memory. No, something farther than a memory. In the warmth of Baz's smile, the danger had simply been an event that happened to someone else, like a news story, a rumor, or an exciting movie.

What was real was Baz, who was impossibly magical and unaccountably brave. Mark could have stayed in that moment, in the warmth of that unworried smile forever. He longed to continue falling through forever in those strong arms. But they were back.

Reluctantly, Mark shook it off, evoking his hardened game face, limping out of the alley and into the shopping district. As he passed Baz, Mark almost said something, asked for confirmation, asked what just happened. But instead, he cleared his throat and led the way to the art store.

Chapter 7

Bazrael

Bazrael couldn't help but laugh as Cecilia got more and more frustrated. His eyebrow furrowed, and his neck bulged as it turned red. But his eyes kept darting to Bazrael's, and then the All-Star would compose himself quickly before continuing to talk to the store clerk and lose his patience all over again.

"I haven't seen Aurora for days," he insisted. "She doesn't call me anymore."

"It's not like her to no-call-no-show." The clerk was worried. "You should tell me if something happened."

"I don't care, I'm looking for MaKayla."

"Wait. You're not two-timing Aurora with MaKayla, are you? They're best friends, for crying out loud..."

Bazrael wasn't certain what two-timing was. Perhaps a dance? But American teens didn't dance in threes, as far as he knew. But the idea of Mark dancing was interesting...

"I'm not. And MaKayla has a boyfriend!"

"And where's he been? MaKayla's been worried sick since

he stopped calling her back. Is he and Aurora in some sort of situation?"

"Lady, I have no idea."

"You kids with your drama. I try and stay out of it."

"Just tell me when MaKayla works again."

"I can't do that, Mark. For the safety of my employees..."

Bazrael had heard the art store worker use that name more than once. "Who's Mark?" Bazrael asked.

The clerk looked at Bazrael in a way that so many humans had in the past few days, although he was certain he hadn't said anything ridiculous. His skin grew clammy and itchy under her attention.

"*My* name is Mark," Cecilia said gently, placing a hand on Bazrael's shoulder. It was warm and comforting, like his words. Although his words were more confusing than the hand.

"I thought your name was Cecilia," Bazrael said quietly.

Unfortunately, the clerk heard and added, "And I thought I told *you* not to come in if you weren't buying anything."

Bazrael had come in earlier in the day, feeling the remnants of Aurora Marie Seitsinger's essence, but again, he couldn't find a socially acceptable way to ask to talk to her. And now he was embarrassed again, under the itchy glare of the clerk, finding yet another dead end in the maze to his summoner. Plus, the woman's comment made Mark withdraw his hand. The store was suddenly turning hot and a bit claustrophobic.

Thankfully, a bubbly and smiling young woman stepped in before Bazrael left or said something socially unacceptable to the clerk.

"It's okay, Melissa. I know this meathead," the young lady pointed a thumb at Mark. Or Cecilia. Bazrael was pretty sure the other lady was named Melissa.

"MaKayla," Mark gasped dramatically. "I'm hurt. I thought we were close."

Melissa, the clerk, scoffed at Mark as she walked off, making uncertain contact with MaKayla. The young lady, overflowing with a radiant positivity, had a complicated aura about her. Firstly, she was teeming with the residue of Aurora Marie Seitsinger, absolutely dripping with it. She and the summoner were close in proximity and emotional connection, similar to the guard witch protecting the Seitsinger home. Secondly, her unassuming appearance was practically a taller, skinnier copy of the guard witch. But there was something else about her...an inherent godliness that reminded Bazrael of his father. This young woman wasn't a human in the sense most were. But beneath the surface was something more. Something super-human. This MaKayla was no ordinary American teenager.

"Relax," she said. "My boss expects me to stick up for Ora in front of you. Is there something up?" she asked Mark quietly in an attempt to keep her words from Bazrael. "Did you see something?"

"No," Mark said quickly, eyes darting to Bazrael.

"Who's your friend?" She looked him over with a searching glare, and again the semblance of godliness flared within her. Her eyes settled on Bazrael's chest as if she were looking into him to study the walls of his heart. For a moment, she seemed puzzled, looking at his sternum. And Bazrael wondered if the contents of his soul had somehow surprised her.

"This is...Buzz," Mark said. Who was Buzz? Did Mark mean Baz? Confusion surrounding names was escalating. "We've got a few questions of a sensitive nature and were hoping you or Cain might have some answers."

"Questions about what?" She ripped her focus from

Bazrael's chest with what looked like a Herculean effort.

"Something we can't discuss here. But maybe, you know, *in group*? Something about Aurora and what she's been getting into?"

"I haven't spoken to Ora in days."

"Can you text her for us? We have a pressing question."

"She's not answering my texts. She's not even reading them. I'm telling you, I haven't had any contact with Ora since *that night*."

That last phrase carried a weight that Mark Cecilia acknowledged with silent thought. And yet again, Bazrael was witness to a conversation in which he was missing key information.

"Don't remind me," he said. "We're more interested in something she might have done."

"Well, I have to admit, I don't know a ton about sensitive subjects outside my lane, but Cain might know."

"Then we need to introduce Cain to Buzz." Mark must have meant Bazrael.

"Buzz?" She arched an eyebrow, drawing the name out onomatopoetically.

"Baz," Bazrael corrected.

"Don't you have his phone number?" she asked Mark, seemingly ignoring Bazrael.

"I don't have a phone," Bazrael said, expecting to have to explain why for yet another time in the past few days. But instead, MaKayla just continued with Cecilia.

"Cain's number."

"I don't have a phone either." Mark shrugged with his lackadaisical smile that warmed Bazrael so much, he wondered if the room had heated up.

"How do you guys not have phones?"

"Why are you here on your day off?" Cecilia threw back at her.

"I've got an art project and needed paint."

"MaKayla Colfax is in summer school?"

"It's art. I don't do it just for a grade. You play baseball when it's not for school."

"That's because I'm going to go pro."

"Sure about that?"

The suddenness with which Mark's face dropped ruined the light conversation. Their banter had been fun, humans who didn't want to admit they got along well. A smooth, easy exchange that was foreign to Bazrael. He would never be able to address people with such confidence as Mark had. But her words took the All-Star off his pedestal.

Bazrael knew that Mark Cecilia would never be a pro baseball player. He had to know that, too. In a few days, there wouldn't be any more pro baseball. There wouldn't be any more anything. But this Colfax girl didn't know that, did she?

"Cain hasn't been feeling well." MaKayla was now bristling, too. Bazrael yearned to see the humans return to their leisurely and fun back and forth.

"Yeah, so you said." Mark dropped his voice even more. They were getting contentious.

"The manager thinks Cain is cheating on you," Bazrael offered with a smile, hoping to either jumpstart the dialogue or ingratiate himself with new information.

"Buzz—" MaKayla started, searching for words.

"Baz," Bazrael offered, still smiling.

"Baz, you're not helping," Mark muttered. Oh, no. Bazrael had committed some social sin. Maybe Cain really was cheating, and the subject was touchy.

"He's just not himself." MaKayla sighed. "A little with-drawn."

"Well, the last time I saw the two of you, you were…" Mark trailed off.

More secrets. By now, it was obvious that what he wasn't saying in front of Bazrael was a purposeful secret. But Bazrael had secrets of his own, so he couldn't complain.

MaKayla shrugged sheepishly. "I was pretty high on myself, but believe me, I got taken down a peg."

"Girl, same," Mark concurred.

This was Bazrael's chance to recover. "I don't even have any friends." He shrugged, toning down the smile a bit.

"Dude, don't say that."

"It's fine, Mark," MaKayla said. "Baz—"

"Buzz," Mark corrected.

"It looks like you have at least one friend," MaKayla said, taking in the two of them with a genuine smile.

Bazrael liked her. She was bright, like one of those shiny balloons, an opposing copy of the Seitsinger's guard witch. What the two of them shared in appearance and inhuman prowess, they starkly differed in attitude and approach. He shrugged bashfully and dug his toe into the ground. "Not friends," he said. "I'm just his pitcher."

MaKayla let out a chuckle.

The All-Star stuttered for a word.

MaKayla smiled. "His pitcher?"

"He's a pitcher," Mark declared. "A baseball pitcher."

MaKayla's chuckle grew into a giggle. Mark turned red, starting at his neck.

Bazrael confirmed, "I pitched for you the other day. It was intense."

She snorted.

"That isn't what he means." Mark's voice cracked.

MaKayla was loudly laughing. Bazrael liked her laugh. He laughed, too. "It was my first time; I've never pitched for anyone else but Mark!"

Within that wondrous laughter, MaKayla pointed to Mark and said, "If he's the pitcher, then you're the—"

"Batter," Mark answered quickly. He was blushing hard now. A deeper, reddish tan that warmed Bazrael from here. "I was batting."

Bazrael was enjoying this. "He is skilled with that bat. He hit a home run!"

"Wow." MaKayla was laughing so hard she was crying. "I bet he did."

Mark seemed to be stifling a laugh of his own. "Can you just shut up and tell your boyfriend we're going to swing by?"

But Bazrael didn't want the laughter to end. "He loves to swing."

"Will you shut up?" Mark giggled, trying to keep up the appearance of stern anger.

"Does your boyfriend like to swing?" Bazrael asked MaKayla.

"Jesus, you two are hilarious. Thanks—I needed a laugh." MaKayla let out a deep sigh. Her eyes settled on Bazrael again, bouncing down to his chest and then back up to his face. There was something she saw that gave her pause. "Cain's a bit...shy about meeting new people. He's definitely not in the mood for it right now."

"Well, can I catch a ride?" Mark asked her.

Mark going to see Cain alone? That meant splitting up. Bazrael getting stuck by himself once again. Would he have another chance to spend time with the All-Star before the end of everything? Or to engage in easy and fun human conversation? There just wasn't enough time.

"Sure," MaKayla answered, "I can drop you off on my way home. But I'm giving Cain a bit of space right now."

"That's fine. I'm buddies with him. We don't have to talk about you."

This was starting to move too fast, things in motion outside of Bazrael's control. But only he understood what was happening, the importance of getting to Aurora Marie Seitsinger, and the waning time remaining. He asked Mark, "Are you sure you understand the summoning enough to—"

"Summoning?" MaKayla paled.

"Calm down; it's just a term he uses. Baz is Cuban."

"I'm not actually Cuban."

"You're not Cuban? You said you were from Cuba."

"My ward is from Cuba. I'm from...somewhere up North."

"Your ward?" MaKayla asked.

"Listen," Mark said. "I'm not abandoning you, Baz, I just need to warm up Cain a bit, and then we can come to you. Write down your address. Do you have any paper, something to write on?"

Bazrael did not.

MaKayla ripped a page from a nearby sketch pad and handed Bazrael a pen.

"Look at you," Mark said, impressed. "Goody-two-shoes defacing property."

"I work here, and they love me. They can afford one ripped page," MaKayla said with a dismissive deadpan that reminded Bazrael again of the guard witch.

He wrote down the address of his showcase house. The image of Mark standing in the furnished living room pulsed a thrill through Bazrael. Then he thought of Mark standing in his bedroom, and Bazrael could barely get the words down on paper. Suddenly this was a great idea, and Bazrael was sweating.

Mark

"So who was that Baz guy? Or Buzz or whatever?"

Mark rolled his eyes. He wasn't homophobic or anything; there were guys he played baseball with for years who were gay. And just because Mark immediately got along with Bazrael didn't make it romantic. The poor guy was clueless and happened to be in a position where only Mark could help. And sure, he towered over Mark and was objectively handsome, but Mark liked having him around, knowing he'd already gotten the best of Baz on the baseball diamond. And the guy was so clueless, it was endearing. What was annoying was Colfax's implication.

"Can't two guys be friends without everyone thinking they're gay? I honestly expected more out of you, Colfax."

"That's not what I'm talking about," she said as she drove. "Summoning? Wards? I can see the pathway of his lifeline; it's the size of my dashboard. What is he, a wizard?"

Mark thought back to falling through realities in Bazrael's arms and the way the guy knew about the end of the world. Yet Mark didn't know much about him. "It honestly hasn't come up."

"It hasn't come up?! You're helping him confront your magically endowed ex-girlfriend, but whatever supernatural powers he has hasn't come up?"

"He just said she summoned an O-nay-fum."

"What hasn't she summoned? Have you talked with her recently? Is she okay?"

Mark shrugged. "She's made it clear she doesn't want to talk to me."

"I think she's made it clear she's not interested in a relationship, Mark, but you're still connected. You were boyfriend and girlfriend for over a year. You've been through things together. I can see the heartstring attaching you to her. Don't make me read it."

"What am I supposed to do, show up at her doorstep? 'Hey, I know we used to smash, but now I want to introduce you to this cute guy who says you summoned something for him?'"

Why did Mark call Bazrael cute? He hadn't meant it like that.

"I'm just wondering why you're helping this guy if you just met him. I don't have to tell you that dangerous people have been showing up around Lockport."

Mark had had his fill of dangerous people coming to Lockport. A witch kidnapped and tortured him to use his vision. A guy with a face tattoo had come after him with a gun. All MaKayla Colfax had gotten was an upgrade to her Fate powers.

"No," he growled. "You don't have to tell me."

"Whatever you and Ora had might be over, but that doesn't mean you can't look out for her."

"That's funny. Your boyfriend told me that I was being sexist when I said I would look out for her."

"I'm just saying you can be a good friend without having to have her permission."

"Aurora summoned this O-fay-num, and that brought Baz into my life. What did you call her? Magically endowed? My magic lets me see the future. Aurora's magic lets her create the future. Something tells me I'm not doing anything without her permission."

"We all have free will, Mark."

"Do we? I thought you saw things, too? Pathways? Destinies? You said in group you saw what's coming, and there's no stopping it."

"I see things, but you don't know what can or can't be stopped. Maybe Ora is powerful enough-"

"Maybe your buddy 'Ora' summoned the damned apocalypse. Maybe this is all just another magic trick for her. The end is coming, Colfax. Fast. I don't know if there's anything that can stop it, so I'm gonna just live my life. This guy, Baz, came to me and asked for help. When we run into trouble, he sticks his neck out. And maybe he's the last person I get a chance to, the last friend I can make before it's all over."

That quieted her, but just for a second. Then she asked with seriousness, "What do you see when you look into his future?"

A deep breath was just enough to stop himself from mentioning bringing a sword down over Baz's head. "Same thing as I see for everyone these days. Death. Fire. A fight to end all fights."

She pulled up to the house and stopped the car. Mark opened the door when she said, "I think we should have a meeting. Something of our own outside of group, just the people we trust. There's stuff my mom left behind: pictures, notes in books, diaries. If it is the end of things, she was a part of planning it. They called themselves God's End, and they started all this, not Ora. We need to see if we can work together to stop it."

"Good luck, Colfax. Barely any of us are even on speaking terms—including you and Cain, if you don't mind me saying. If you want a team to gel, they need to spend time together, get to know each other, maybe find a rival they all want to beat. Right now, the most powerful beings in Lockport are all holding grudges they have to get over. And fast."

Mark got out of the car and shut the door.

MaKayla called out to him, "Do you really see death and fire for everyone?"

"I do. Why, what do you see?"

"A lot of threads cut short."

Mark turned and approached the enormous house. It took a second before MaKayla drove off as he got to the front door. He hated rich people's homes. He was always afraid he was going to break something more expensive than his whole house.

At the third knock on the oversized, imposing door, the lock clicked, and it creaked open. Except no one was there.

"Hello?" Mark called out.

No one in the darkened house replied.

"Hey Morrigan? It's Mark Cecilia!"

His voice echoed back to him from the emptiness. Who'd opened the door? A growl came from deep within the posh home. Human? Animal?

"Hey Morrigan, I'm here just to ask a couple questions, alright? The door just opened, I'm coming in."

Another growl, this one more aggressive. Or desperate.

"Put your dog away, okay? I don't wanna get bit, you know?"

The interior of the home was impossibly dark for a sunny afternoon. Not a cloud in the sky, but the big house with expansive windows was as shadowy as a tomb. It smelled of lemon cleaning supplies and sweet, expensive candles. Mark pushed the door open wider, hoping to see inside more. His hand shook as it reached forward. Only more empty darkness.

Closing his eyes, Mark took a deep breath and reached into

his own future to see what would happen if he entered. Flashes of himself limping up steps, a growling figure cowering from him, crying eyes desperately pleading with him, an altercation with someone much bigger, much stronger than Mark. But Mark would live. He'd walk out with his normal limp, no worse for wear. He'd even find a ride to Baz's. Images of Baz flashed: his calming smile, his awkward, funny ways. As brave as he was, Baz was still scared, still unsure about his purpose and place, still dependent on Mark's help.

Then Mark considered leaving now and saw the future of that possibility. Hobbling home from here, walking along the dark roads, he missteps, his foot rolls, and he busts his ankle up worse. Or he cuts through the woods, and his footing slides from under him, breaking the ankle completely as well as his collarbone. The idea of running home flashed across his mind, which was really limping into a skip. He would fall, roll down the hill, and drown in the canal.

So his best option was entering the house and getting in a fight with a bigger dude who was most likely crying. Great.

Each of his steps on the hardwood floor echoed. Once completely inside, the door swung closed behind him, just like some cheesy horror film. And Mark's part was obviously of the victim who was too stupid to leave. When he grabbed the doorknob, it opened easily, but going back meant more ankle injury or death. He tried light switches, but nothing would work. So he carefully walked farther into the dark, following the gravelly huff breathing deep within the house.

He tripped over chair legs and ran into a hard granite kitchen countertop before he slowly inched along with his good foot ahead of him. The growls were coming down from the carpeted stairs to the second floor, where it was just as dark.

"Morrigan? It's Mark Cecilia. I'm coming upstairs..."

As he ascended, the animalistic noises changed from a far-off hint of danger to a very real, very close threat.

Along the walls, framed photos too dark to see gave the eerie hint of a family home without the details of warm smiles. This house struck him as a fake shell, an impersonation of an expensive home of a perfect family unit, laid out with furniture and decor but hauntingly devoid of real humanity. No empty glassware, no piles of laundry. No clutter.

The second floor was hot and smelled of teen boy and breath, like a locker room, but less comforting to Mark.

"Morrigan?"

He was answered with snarls, heavy breathing, and a cough. At the end of the hallway, a shape moved. Grayish light filtered through a curtain, not enough to reveal the hall but enough to tease the outline of a moving pile of something a few feet away. Something shorter than a human, but wider. An upended chair, table, and strewn rug surrounded the shadow on the floor.

"Cain?" Mark's voice broke. He was sweating a hot, stinging, sour sweat of fear. A knot choked his throat with one in his gut to match. His legs protested with each hesitant step forward, knees jelly, muscles tight.

Mark cleared his throat. "Cain? It's Mark..."

The shadow jerked, reflective eyes like silver dots snapped suddenly to Mark's. His body went cold. His legs froze.

The growl from the shadow elongated into a groan and, finally, an identifiable sound. "Mark?"

It was Morrigan's voice, about two levels deeper, dried out with ground brick and wet with blood. Was he wounded, curled into the fetal position on the carpet? Mark took careful steps forward, fighting the urge to rush to an injured friend.

"Morrigan, are you alright?"

"You shouldn't have come. I'm...I'm..."

Morrigan rose to his feet. He was always taller than Mark, but now, the guy filled the hallway. And somehow much wider as well. Was he in shoulder pads? On stilts? But no, that was impossible as his back brushed against the curtain and his enormous feet stood bare on the floor.

Light cut into the hall, slicing blindness and revealing Cain, shirtless and swollen with muscles. His face wet with tears, as was a small burn in the carpet floor. His eyes still shone silver like an animal's in the dark.

Again, his rough, wild, and low voice pleaded, "I'm not myself, Mark. You need to leave."

"And you need help, buddy. What, are you, juicing?"

Mark had seen teammates experimenting with hormones and steroids, but not like this. Mark saw Cain Morrigan a little over a week ago. Even with aggressive pumping, he couldn't have made gains like this. And he definitely couldn't have grown a foot taller.

"I'm changing...it's not safe for you here."

"Morrigan, I hate to break it to you, but it's not safe any-where."

"What's going to happen to me? Can you look? Can you see?"

In the shadow of his now-giant friend, Mark managed to breathe and relax, allowing himself to peer into Morrigan's future.

Musculature. Veins. Sweat-slicked skin stretched over pecs and biceps. A hand gripping bladed batons, the knuckles turn white.

"You...your body is preparing. For a fight."

His wolfish eyes turned sad and scared, utterly human.

"Fighting who?"

Blade clashed against sword. Impossibly huge weapons, a glowing blue blade thicker than a man's hand was long. The silvery blue metal bit into a sword held by an equally muscled figure with tall, hairy ears and furry skin rippling and moving like a million muscle striations. The face angry, fierce, but handsomely chiseled. Fangs like tusks. Tears of blood. Wings like a bat's.

"I think it's a demon."

Chapter 8

Beth

Her arm ached, shooting pain when she moved. Her phone on the ground was stomped into uselessness. Her car lay next to her, just as beat up with tires slashed.

She dusted herself off, checked for bleeding. Bruises, mostly, she'd be fine. But the amulet with Puka was gone. And that bastard Parker was after Anthony. She had to save him, to warn him, to get him to safety.

She had an idea. Maybe it was just a silly thing they did in old Western movies, maybe it was an implied superpower of the Lone Ranger, or maybe it could work. She worked some spit into her dried mouth and raised two fingers to rest between her teeth.

It was a whistle she always used to call him, a way to let her horse know where she was in any field or farm, just to check in. But Anthony always came running.

The squeal of her whistle broke through the late spring air, cutting and echoing against the empty buildings.

Was Anthony close enough to hear? Was a horse's hearing better than humans? Was it good enough to recognize those two notes specific to Beth?

She waited. And waited. She listened. And waited more. She whistled again and waited longer. Again and again.

Nothing.

Anthony wasn't coming. And Mark, for all of his special vision, hadn't warned her of this. Not a month ago, she'd helped her town out in the snowstorm and had seen unnatural, wondrous things. Impossible things. She'd seen people she knew from school doing inhuman feats. But none of them were here to save her now. No one was going to.

She got the old tire iron out of her car, grabbed a utility knife they kept in the glove box, and started walking.

Luckily, after navigating Lockport on horseback, she learned the lay of the land. She knew where she was going. And she knew what she had to do. Beth was going to save the day.

Her home was closer than the barn, but Beth was gutted to see there were no cars she could use. She washed her face, changed clothes, and equipped herself with a can of bear spray she'd laughed about them bringing with them in the move from Tennessee.

In the back of her closet was a very specifically decorated box. A shoebox covered in magazine clippings of heartthrobs, movie stars, and boy bands. Hotties. Crushes. In a home filled with women, a box like this would be expected to exist, but for house frivolities, nothing of any grave importance.

It was Bethany's war chest. In it was the collection of all things supernatural (besides the amulet, which, of course, had to be kept farther out of reach and more well-hidden). Within was the little case the amulet came in, as well as the old family bible, complete with notations of at least two previous generations, Beth's own bible gifted to her on her baptism, a ticket to the county fair that Beth was certain she'd been followed by a shadow, a button that kept appearing even after she threw it away, a picture taken of her by the river the day Puka had first found her, and a simple buck knife with a ruby-red handle, the one that she'd used to trap the demon in the horse necklace. And finally, a picture in colored pencil, drawn years ago when she first met Puka. A portrait, a reminder of what that thing looked like to prove to herself it wasn't a fever dream or hallucination. She'd consult the drawing after each of her first encounters, confirming the slick skin, the handsome face, the strong limbs, and the tall, hairy ears.

She pocketed the Bibles, the button, and the knife, giving it a flicking flourish to jog her muscle memory of handling the blade. It snapped shut with a satisfying jingling sound.

Once equipped, she started down the road toward Anthony's stable. The afternoon was crawling toward evening, the brightness of the sky waning beneath a supernatural glow punctuated by swirling tufts of pollen. A beautiful night to do ugly things. Necessary things. After all, hadn't Judas performed God's will?

Bazrael

He'd never cleaned like this before. It wasn't a real home, so there weren't any helpful sprays or detergents, only air fresheners and polishes to make surfaces shine. But had a guest coming. A very important guest.

So Bazrael feverishly polished and freshened the air with an artificial scent designed to resemble dried linens. He swept. He wiped up crumbs and watermarks with wet towels. The main bedroom's walk-in closet easily held all of Bazrael's possessions: all of his clothes and sports equipment. The sparse cabinets housing little more than bread, chips, tortillas, and beef jerky reminded Bazrael how unprepared he was for a guest. This wasn't a home for living; it was a house for selling. And like it or not, Bazrael felt he had to sell himself to Mark Cecilia.

Maybe not himself, but the idea of helping him. Bazrael had no allies, no teammates in his quest to fulfill his purpose. And that's what this was about, the mission. He had to find Aurora Marie Seitsinger. Soon. Spending time with Mark Cecilia may have been nice, but it wasn't the goal. Making the All-Star smile wasn't the pressing issue.

Bazrael had a map of Lockport laid out on the kitchen table. Colorful hair elastics he'd found in the house encircled the baseball fields, the pizzeria, and his home. A small toy Superman stood in place of the Seitsinger house, representing Aurora.

Carefully, Bazrael placed another hair tie, this one a jellied magenta, to denote the craft supply store, fondly remembering the fun human banter Bazrael had witnessed and joined in on.

Then, the hairs on his extended arms raised. An imperceptible shadow flew over his home, and Bazrael felt the fires of angelic transformation heat within him. A steadying breath drew raggedly across his drying mouth. His eyes clenched shut against the angry orange warning within his mind.

The Creature stirred.

He had to fight. Instinct was taking over Bazrael's body, bloodlust pulling to the surface stronger than in the altercation in the pizzeria parking lot. His skin itched and glazed over with sweat. His bones burned as they extended. The tips of his fingers elongated. Bazrael resisted, pleading in his mind that there was no imminent danger.

A knock interrupted his thoughts. He paused, holding his body still through pain and transformation. A quick breath and reassessment confirmed that danger had passed.

Another knock.

Whatever was at the door now, it was a disturbance of another kind. Nothing supernatural to trigger the Creature. His hackles were raised, and the war drums within him thundered.

Another rhythmic series of knocks, some melody Bazrael didn't recognize.

So what intruder was this? What new enemy had found Bazrael? Was this a message from whatever threat had passed by? Had the supernatural entity Bazrael just felt to his very core left some calling card tapping at the house entrance?

He forced his body to return to its human norm, but suspicion prevented the transformation from completing. His skin was its normal warm tan, his bones their usual length. But one hand remained ready, inky black claws protruding from the tips of his fingers. This appendage was that of the Creature's, a body made for war. His hand flexed with strength and indestructibility. The rest of Bazrael appeared human—easy to underestimate to any threat.

In a crouch ready for attack, he stalked to the door silently and quickly threw it open, hoping to catch his opponent off-guard, baring spiny, murderous fingers and roaring an unearthly battle cry.

Bazrael's martial readiness melted immediately.

Mark Cecilia stood stunned, face blanched, pungent fear

radiating off him. His eyes, as big as saucers, dropped immediately to Bazrael's hands, the long, bony talons splayed. Mark stumbled backward down the front steps, and then he scrambled to his feet, breaking into a run.

"Cecilia, wait!" Bazrael reached for him, seeing with human eyes the fearsome sight of the deadly Creature fingers. With a disdainful shake, he converted his hands back to human as the All-Star ran into the night.

The dark outside was betrayed by drops of sallow street lights as the lone figure hobbled away, growing smaller and smaller. Mark Cecilia had just limped out of Bazrael's life as fast as he could.

But Bazrael needed him, needed his help, his insight into the social webs of Aurora Marie Seitsinger. Mark Cecilia was the only willing translator of human American teen-speak Bazrael had found. And even if Bazrael didn't need Mark in order to find Aurora and complete his purpose, he *wanted* him for selfish reasons.

So Bazrael ran after, trailing the off-kilter gait of the All-Star burdened by the plastic boot. Mark's figure winced with each step of the infirmed leg. This resulted in a wild, monstrous flight down the road. Bazrael sprinted straight, pumping arms, blowing wind, closing in.

"Mark!" Bazrael called out.

"Stay back!" Mark's words stabbed.

Bazrael ran alongside him, now panting. "Let me explain!"

"Leave me alone, you damn monster!" Mark veered away, cutting back through the empty neighborhood of abandoned lots. He stumbled over a curb, then back to his feet, his limp even more pronounced. He was going to injure himself further. Mark was killing himself in an attempt to flee.

Bazrael couldn't let Mark hurt himself more. Bazrael couldn't face what he had to do alone. And Bazrael couldn't imagine his remaining time on Earth without Mark's presence, or worse, the presence of Mark's hatred...even if that meant giving up his big secret.

With a sigh, Bazrael acquiesced. He transformed, but instead of giving into his baser self, the Creature, he reached back to the glory within him. His old grandeur. Wings sprouted, feathers snaked from his flesh, muscles burned in rapid growth, bones cracked to elongate. Yelps erupted from deep within Bazrael until he was changed completely. He took to the air with a leap and beat his wings.

In a simple arc, he sailed over Mark, making up the distance between them easily. Using an updraft to cushion his descent, Bazrael landed on his feet directly in the path of Mark's unbridled, manic escape.

The All-Star fell to the ground, looking up from the dirt to Bazrael with his wings outstretched, wearing nothing but humanity's electronic light in the darkness.

Mark swallowed hard and whispered, "What are you?"

Mark

Mark's ankle ached. He'd be lucky if he didn't mess up the tendon more. His leg throbbed in time with his racing heartbeat and panting breath. The pain radiating from his foot grounded him, a welcome distraction from the ridiculousness of his current reality.

Bazrael, this boy who he spent part of the day with, the pitcher he'd defeated only a few days before, was no boy.

Muscles and feathered wings, straight out of an ancient painting. Baz's stature was dominating, tall as a basketball hoop, looming over Mark, who was now sitting on the ground in forfeit of running.

But Baz wasn't threatening him; he wasn't even mad, it seemed. The angry monster who'd opened the door was gone. His features softened, framed by black hair somehow longer, curling at the ends, rounding out his impossibly soft bone structure. Bazrael was achingly beautiful in a way that Mark had never seen in a man. He wasn't hot or handsome but fragile and graceful. Kind, soft, and warm. He was beautiful.

Mark brought down the sword over that beautiful face, covered in blood.

Bazrael's eyes brought the visions, so Mark looked elsewhere into the night sky as he listened to Baz explain.

"You had to have known something, that I was different. We traveled dimensions together. You read minds, didn't you read that I was new to this world? That all I am is my father's failure coupled with this new purpose? What do you see when you look into my thoughts?"

"I can't read thoughts, Baz."

"But the baseball game. The curveball. You couldn't hit my pitches until you made me think about what I would throw next."

"I don't see thoughts, Baz. I see futures."

"A prophet." It was neither a question nor an accusation. The angel said it like he finally got a trivia question right. "You were given foresight and didn't prophecy my descent?"

"What descent? The pitch you threw?"

"My descent to Earth."

"From where, space?" It all made sense—how he traveled

across worlds, why he had such an odd name, why he didn't understand social customs, the way he had random excuses of why he was confused about so much. In that moment, Baz was both fascinating and terrifying. "You're an alien!"

"No, Mark Cecilia. I do not originate from space or another planet. Is it not obvious from my appearance?"

The muscled giant lifted his arms, thick and veiny, as he spread powerful yet delicate wings out wide.

"An angel? That's impossible."

"Says the man who thought I was a space traveler? Mark, you can see the future."

"That's different, though. This is... I don't believe... I don't believe in..."

"Angels?"

"God."

Baz gave a thoughtful nod, a smile creeping over his pointed chin. "The human idea of 'God' is pretty far off from what's real."

"So what is God, really?"

"Unknowable power. Somewhere between humanity's ideas of infinity and chaos. Entropy with a personality. Mathematics that loves you."

"And He sent you down here? Or He cast you out?"

"It's...complicated. I told you, my Ophanim was summoned, and I came."

"What, like calling a dog?" Mark had always had cats, so the idea of an obedient pet responding when called was foreign to him. But the strangest things were turning out to be true.

"I left Iowah's realm of my own volition."

"When were you in Iowa?"

"My father, Iowah, one of the beings most Westerners

consider God."

"So God's not even God? His name is Iowa?! We're just wrong about everything?"

"Historically speaking, humans have been wrong over ninety-nine percent of the time. I left Iowah's realm at the same time I was summoned. Do you believe in destiny, Mark?"

They were all destined to die. A rainy night turned red. They would all die as the horses landed on the crumbling earth.

"Yeah, destiny is one of the only things that makes sense to me."

"Such little has made sense to me since my arrival. Except knowing my purpose. And knowing you." The statuesque giant shrank, the blinding brightness of his form fading to the even dark of night. Shrinking until he was back to human size, peering down into Mark's eyes in a way that riled Mark. Like the moment after an aluminum bat connected with a ball. How was Baz somehow more handsome as a human than in an angelic body? How did Mark now feel completely naked when Baz was the one who was...

"Dude, put some clothes on!"

"I can do that. Can you come back to the house and tell me if your friend Cain will help me?"

The last thing Mark wanted was to disappoint Baz. No, that wasn't right. The last thing he wanted was anything to happen to Baz. But Mark knew that was a certainty. A secret he had to keep from the angel.

Beth

After knocking for the fourth time with no answer, Beth was ready to give up and leave. But then she heard the crashing and crying. It was coming from nearby, right behind this house.

Beth was nervous enough approaching anyone's house. She

knew MaKayla, but they were definitely acquaintances and not friends. The fact they did group together felt like an invasion of privacy, a glimpse into the secrets Beth knew MaKayla would rather keep quiet. Showing up at her house unannounced was like poking at an open wound.

A loud sound of breaking glass turned into an agonizing squeal, then more crying. Beth instinctively ran toward the hubbub, rounding the house, opening the gate, and following the sound of labored breathing behind the brick garage.

In the blaze of white work lights, a figure stood, heaving for breath, wearing a welder's mask, work gloves, and overalls over a long-sleeve tee. The sleeves were rolled up, however, and tiny cuts trickled lines of blood down slender forearms to the tan work gloves grasping a sledgehammer.

"Why are *you* here?" a slight voice, hoarse and out of breath, said from behind the welder's mask.

"MaKayla?"

With the back of a bloodied glove, the figure opened the mask, lifting it to reveal MaKayla's face, streaked with tears.

Beth's protective instincts kicked in. "Are you okay?"

MaKayla heaved a few slowing breaths, diverting it through her nose, "I'm fine, Beth. How are you?"

Beth realized how sweaty and red-faced she must be after crying tears of her own at the sight of Anthony's empty stall. Then she ran most of the way here. She must have been a worse mess.

"Been a long day. You're bleeding."

"Yeah, it happens. What are you doing here?"

"I just heard the breaking glass and the yelling..." Beth vaguely pointed back toward the front of the house.

"I'm working on a project." MaKayla started sifting through

the remains of a broken plate.

Set against the garage was a half-finished mosaic, a wild and angry piece of a woman in midair, hair whipping, a sunny day on one side, a gloomy blue night on the other. Beth didn't get it. But then again, art was never her thing.

"I need your help, I think," Beth said. "I need…I don't know what I need, but you live closest to the stables…"

"Beth, what's wrong?"

"It's Anthony. They got him."

"Okay, do you need to call the police?" MaKayla dug a phone out of her pocket and offered it.

The police, laughable. Whatever MaKayla was, whatever she could do, she understood the level of beings out there. The police were no match for real trouble. "They can't help! Nobody can help!"

"Beth. Breathe. Slow down. Whatever it is, we can figure it out." MaKayla sat Beth in a folding chard and pulled up a paint bucket to sit beside her. "Do you need some water?"

Beth shook her head no, then forced herself to speak, to explain why she was here, that she belonged here, that she needed help from something, from someone more than the police. "I saw you. Flying the other night. In a real pretty dress. I know you know there are things happening, people in this town who can do things I can't explain," she said, careful not to betray the trust Mark had in her about his gifts. But saying enough that MaKayla would catch on and maybe even trust her. "Spent a good chunk of my life thinking I was the only one who knew about the weird stuff with no explanation. Sometimes I thought I was crazy-"

"You're not crazy, Beth…"

"I know. Yeah, I know, but it was just so lonesome knowing

things all by myself." But Beth was no longer alone. And maybe whatever MaKayla was capable of, whatever she was, meant that she could help. That she wouldn't just blame Beth for being so stupid. "Then we moved here, and I discovered there were others, and... MaKayla, I released a demon."

"You what?"

"I didn't exactly release him. But he was stole. I had him trapped in a necklace. Stuck. And this creepy guy in a church van, Parker, he stole it. And he stole my horse, Anthony, too."

"And that's why you're on foot?"

"No, Parker slashed my tires."

"Okay. Listen, Beth, I don't know anything about fighting demons, but I can try. I'll stand with you."

"Wait. You believe me? Even though I'm talking crazy?"

"Beth, 'crazy' is mental illness. You're talking about difficult things, supernatural things. But I've seen enough of that to know you're not mentally ill. You seem stressed as hell about what you're going through. But not mentally ill."

"Thank you. But I don't know where to find them. Parker or Anthony-my horse."

MaKayla took a breath, then removed her work gloves. "I can help find him, Beth, but you have to realize that things will get weirder."

"Okay?" Whatever MaKayla was offering, Beth would take it.

"Okay." MaKayla took off the welding helmet. "I can see your connections. Your Earthly ties to others. Now, I see connections to friends, family, your Mom and sisters, and your Dad, even though he's gone."

"How'd you know all that?"

"We all have gifts. But I don't see any connections to a

horse?”

"Does that mean he's dead?! Oh my God.."

"No, Beth. I'd still see the connection, even if he were dead. It would just be different—like your connection to your father."

"Okay, good."

"I just don't see a strong attachment to a pet."

"Anthony is more than a pet. He's my best friend. He's a part of me."

"Oh. Oh..." MaKayla's tone shifted with realization. "So there's a weird loop, like less of a connection to someone else and more of a connection to yourself but..."

MaKayla reached out and closed her hands in front of Beth, holding tight onto nothing in particular. Her face quirked with confusion. "Oh. There he is. You're right; he's not a horse. He's not like anything I've ever seen before. And he's going to...you're going to."

MaKayla's face paled and went slack. She stood slowly and backed away, fear in her eyes as she looked at Beth.

"What is it, MaKayla?"

"You. You're trying to end the world to keep him alive."

"What? No! I wouldn't... listen, I'm not sure what I'm going to do, but first I got to find Anthony!"

"No, Beth. I can't help you do that."

"MaKayla, please."

"Beth, I'm sorry, but you can't. I have to stop you."

The knife was comforting in Beth's grasp. She stood. "You're not going to stop me."

Beth was built, strong from working horses. Ready to act after feelings of helplessness against Parker. She could take a city girl like MaKayla, no problem.

In the warmth of the white work lights, the two women stood

several feet apart. Crouched. Ready.

But then a glint of light from MaKayla's side caught Beth's eye. The reflection of metal. Did MaKayla have a knife as well? No, it wasn't a knife. A shiny pair of scissors.

What was this girl going to do with scissors?

Then the glint flashed brighter, nearly blinding, until Beth looked away.

The clutter of gear falling to the ground. A gust of wind. When Beth looked back at MaKayla, she was flying, hovering in the air, now wearing that pretty dress, a silken toga rippling in the air along with her long, loose hair.

The figure seemed to produce a cool light of her own, brandishing the scissors in a tight grip pointed in warning toward Beth.

"I can stop you, Beth. I can, and I will."

Chapter 9

Bazrael

All of the excitement of preparing his home for company was gone. Bazrael felt Mark's eyes all over him. Through him. Mark Cecilia's precious, godly vision of what was and what would be focused on Bazrael's physical form.

But he could put some clothes on if that made it easier for Mark to talk. Humans were almost always ashamed of their own bodies but absolutely terrified of others'.

"Can Cain help me?" Bazrael asked from the walk-in closet, slipping a shirt on.

"Yeah, old Colfax wasn't kidding about Morrigan going through things. He really wasn't himself." Mark sounded generally surprised. Rattled by things that night besides Bazrael's angelic form.

"What did he tell you about Aurora summoning me?"

"Not much. He'd seen it. He saw her, Aurora. She evidently can do it like ringing a bell. Just...call whatever she wants. But he didn't know much else."

"So, how do we reach her?"

"The old-fashioned way. I just go and talk to her."

"Mark, I can't go near her—"

"Listen, she's my ex; I'm not thrilled about seeing her either."

His ex? Ex-girlfriend? Aurora Marie Seitsinger was the former girlfriend of Mark Cecilia? The inside of the closet began to spin around Bazrael. The woman he was seeking, the woman who'd summoned him, had been in a failed relationship with Mark. Ideas snapped into place: why MaKayla Colfax was so incredulous of Mark's questioning, the subtext of their entire conversation.

But then...why had Mark agreed to help Bazrael talk to her? Was the angel being used? Was Mark using today, all the time they'd spent together, to regain proximity to his former lover? Did this mean everything Bazrael had been feeling, the longing and embarrassment, the biological instincts, all of that had been one-sided? Bazrael was seated in the closet, sweating ice cubes, freezing in embarrassment.

Bazrael had to know. It was difficult to talk with a dried-out mouth. "Has she woken up yet?"

"I don't know. I'll go find out."

"You'd go and talk to her?" Bazrael's voice cracked. "For me?"

"Sure, I'll ask about the Oh-Nay-Phim why she summoned it. And what else do we need to know, where it is?"

Lying was an obstruction in connection, a stone that sat at the back of the throat, making it harder to get words out during conversation. It was a weapon against a relationship but also a shield for one of the participants.

At that moment, Bazrael had taken a hit. He was wounded,

now entirely unsure of whether he'd been growing an association with the All-Star or not. Was this an ally or a human using him for selfish gain? Did Mark just want to rekindle a lost love with the Seitsinger girl? Or perhaps flaunt his association with Bazrael to enrage her? The wound festered with questions. He had to protect it. So he took up a lie for a shield.

Bazrael got himself off the floor, wiped away tears he hadn't realized appeared, and approached Mark in the bedroom. Tossing a tennis ball to himself, the All-Star sat on the bed, a position that should have evoked something within Bazrael. But now, it only left a bitter taste, a reminder of how easily humans could use one another.

Fine. Bazrael was human, or at least a close facsimile of one. He could use others, too. "I have the Ophanim somewhere safe." Bazrael lied. "It's hidden, but only I can give it to her; it's too dangerous for human hands."

Mark's eyes took Bazrael in, perhaps sensing dishonesty.

"Angel business, huh? Serious stuff."

"Yes." Bazrael took the tennis ball out of Mark's hands and put it in a bucket with the rest in the corner. This was no longer a time for practice. It was now a time for purpose and war. So Bazrael put away the toys.

"She may still be asleep," he said. "The very act of summoning the Ophanim probably drained her of all energy, supernormal and human."

"What, like a coma?"

"Something closer to human sickness. Lethargy, low temperature, low pulse, weakness."

"All from summoning?"

"The Ophanim is more powerful than you can imagine." Bazrael let the words hang like the threat they were.

"That night. The last night of the snowstorm. I saw her. It was the last time we spoke. She…" Mark blanched as he looked away. Was it shame that diverted his gaze? Cold feelings filled the room as Mark's focus left them, left the present. His attention left Bazrael back in the room and wandered off entirely. Was it so easy for humans to turn uncaring toward those who regarded them so highly?

"She cut me off," said Mark, "With magic. I don't understand it. Cain says she can have whatever she wants with just a word. That's how she summoned the…Ophanim. She 'summoned' me away. Out of her life. That was over a week ago."

Mark's pain was bittersweetness radiating off him. How glorious that one who hurt others so flippantly was saddled with a wound and betrayal he could not let go? But despite himself, Bazrael also bristled at seeing Mark suffer.

"She is a powerful being," Bazrael admitted. "But I must speak with her, no matter your history. If you cannot bring yourself to do it…"

"I'll do it," Mark said, attention snapping back to the present, to that room, to Bazrael. Mark held a steady gaze, standing and taking a step forward. "If that's what you need, I'll do it."

They stood feet away from one another but kilometers apart. Bazrael longed to embrace the All-Star, to feel the warmth of his skin, the strength of his arms, the softness of his lips. But he also wanted to punish and hurt. To beat Bazrael's pain into Mark through physical injury. To dominate helplessness into the cool athletic American teen so wonton with the feelings of others.

"Are you sure there isn't another curse keeping her asleep?" Mark asked.

"I don't think so, but I can't be sure."

"Then that's probably it. I'll go over there and check on her."

Again, Bazrael wanted to know why. Was Bazrael's focus on his purpose driving Mark into the arms of another? Did that even matter? They would all be dead soon enough. Bazrael would begin the fight to end all things. No human would draw breath. So what if Mark Cecilia's remaining time was spent with Aurora Marie Seitsinger and not Bazrael? He wasn't even truly a person; he was a weapon who simply resembled a human. Desiring more time, more contact with the All-Star had been folly. Bazrael had gotten caught up in emotions, humanity, and baseball—that was all. The only thing that mattered was his purpose.

Bazrael dragged his steady gaze to Mark's. The young teen burned bright red, the light of the moon and stars out the window dancing in his eyes. But Bazrael's stare was constant. Cold. Mission-oriented.

"Thank you for doing this," Bazrael stated simply, his voice low and threatened with emotions he hated. Then, without meaning to, he added, "for me."

Mark swallowed hard, holding eyes with Bazrael. He stepped toward the angel until their breath mixed. Bazrael's chest tightened. His pulse accelerated. His baser biology stirred. But he fought this, focusing on the bilious taste of Mark's secrecy and betrayal.

Mark swallowed hard and said, "I'm sorry I called you a monster."

"*It's what I am,*" the Creature inside of Bazrael replied.

"When I look at you, I don't see a monster. I see..." Mark's pupils danced back and forth to either of Bazrael's. Mark licked his lips as they curled up at the edges. He took a breath in to speak, leaning even closer.

Bazrael felt himself leaning in as well as if pulled by an invisible force. Bazrael had seen humans kiss. He'd witnessed the awkwardness of his ward Miguel's first attempt, all the way to the familiarity of parents long-married. But Bazrael's body thrummed as he leaned in to experience it.

Time stretched as emotions battled within himself.

Then Mark's eyes popped wide. He stood back, straightening his posture. Suddenly, Mark looked around everywhere in the room except at Bazrael.

"You know, I'm just going to go now."

"Now?"

"Yeah..." Mark retreated as he stumbled over his words while actually stumbling, backing away. "Serious business. Angel business. O-Nay-Phin and all."

"Ophanim."

"That's it. That's what I'm going to go ask about."

"You're leaving right now? How will you get there?"

"I can get there."

"With your injured leg?"

"I'll just look into my future..." He closed his eyes for only a moment, then began moving for the door. "Actually, yeah, I'm going to hitch a ride with an old friend."

Was it that simple for Mark to glance into the yet-to-be? Or had something scared the All-Star away? Bazrael silently cursed himself for letting his guard down, for not maintaining his shield of distance and deceit.

"Right now?"

"Yes, in fact, I have to leave right now while he's still within earshot." Mark turned and hurried down the steps for the foyer, leaving Bazrael in turmoil and noticeably unkissed.

"Okay, be careful, Mark!"

As Mark staggered out the front door, he called back in a strained, breaking voice, "Will do, pal!"

The absence of Mark hollowed Bazrael out. All of the betrayal, the pain, the longing, the hope... It all bled out immediately until there was nothing left but a vacuum.

That emptiness was immediately filled with the Creature. It fed on his suffering. It grew from his diminishment. The Creature awoke and grappled for control.

Beth

Beth was in no shape to fight. Her feet were practically burning from walking all over tarnation. When she squeezed the blade in her hand, she was reminded of the ache in her hand and wrist from getting disarmed by Parker. But Beth could throw a punch, and lord knows years in the saddle gave her legs strong enough to kick. Whether MaKayla could fly on the wind or hold some old scissors wouldn't matter much after a good wallop to the gut.

"I could never fight, you know," MaKayla said as if it were a grave warning, "Had never been in a fight in my life. Came close once but had no idea what to do. But then, I got these." She held up the scissors, polished to a shine. "Or maybe these got me. And it's not like I know what to do now, but these know what to do. They guide me."

MaKayla's hand flicked outward, the scissors flashing for an instant before flying at Beth. She flinched, the scissors hitting Beth's knife, knocking it from her grip. Insane marksmanship. The city girl just disarmed her from a good fifteen feet away by throwing scissors? Impossible. MaKayla could know exactly where the knife would be when Beth recoiled.

The old scissors gleamed in the grass as Beth reached to

snatch them. But her hands closed on nothing but dirt. Where were they? Where did they go?

"Go home, Beth. These are forces beyond your control; all you can do is make things worse. If I can, I will save Anthony, but you need to forget about saving the horse, or I'll make you."

And there MaKayla stood, once again brandishing her scissors as a threatening weapon.

Beth was wrong about her. MaKayla may have been a city girl, but whatever powers she possessed made her impossible to beat in a fight. Beth had to get out of there and quick.

She may not have been better in a fight than MaKayla, but maybe she was faster. She took a deep breath, then let her eyes drift past MaKayla, looking over her shoulder before popping them wide and gasping.

It worked. MaKayla glanced over her shoulder, and when she did, Beth sprinted in the opposite direction, back toward the front of the house and the road.

She got seven good running steps down when she was yanked backward. Like someone grabbed her by the rib cage and jerked her ten feet.

The ground knocked the wind from her lungs. Or was it the jolt to her ribs? She slid to a stop, thanks fully on grass and not the dang concrete driveway. As Beth heaved to fill her lungs and regain her bearings, MaKayla lorded over her.

"Seeing the connections between people was easy."

Beth tried to interrupt, to shut this prissy girl up, but her words only escaped as coughs and wheezes.

"Then I learned to look within them, to feel their motivations, their emotions. And once I mastered that, I was aware of their decisions, their next move, their path. And your path leads to the death of everyone, Beth. Everyone. Anthony isn't worth that. I don't think Anthony would want that."

But MaKayla didn't get it. She must have been looking into Puka's future. Or maybe the repercussions of Beth's past actions. This destruction of tribulations wouldn't be Beth's doing; it was Parker and Puka's fault. And Beth could stop them if this annoying little city girl would just get off her case.

"I have to stop you, Beth. This path of yours is nothing short of apocalyptic. But I won't imprison you. And you're lucky I don't sever relationships anymore, or else I'd cut you off from caring for Anthony at all. Please understand I could kill you with the snip of my shears, but I'm doing everything I can to find another way. So I'm just trimming your destiny." Again, MaKayla grasped at something invisible, wrapping a fist around air. She looked at the nothing she held intently, then, moving carefully and with exact strokes, she gave a few snips of her scissors. "When the time comes to decide what you're willing to sacrifice, you're going to find fewer choices. I'm not going to kill you, Beth. And I refuse to control you. But I won't let you kill or control others for the sake of what you love."

She turned to walk back to her house. "You're not going to watch the world burn alongside Mark Cecilia, not if I have any say in it."

Watch the world burn with Mark? Why would that happen? What was she talking about?

" And before you try something stupid, realize that my boyfriend doesn't have my sense of empathy. Or the ability to hold back a death blow."

Mark

Mark could see the approach, even if he couldn't hear it. He felt it, less of a vision and more of gut intuition. Anthony was coming.

And he couldn't arrive soon enough; things with Baz were getting weird. An angel from heaven? Sure, the guy was socially awkward and had some monstrous tendencies, plus he didn't exactly respect personal space, but was he biblical? Evidently, yes. And that meant helping Baz was suddenly this bigger thing, not just a distraction from the visions of the apocalypse. Helping Baz was doing something, something for good.

The night was cooling off, and as Mark awaited his ride, pulling down his sleeves and jogging in place to keep the blood flowing, he worked on problem-solving. Their problem was simple: Aurora was in an enchanted sleep state. That made the solution simple: true love's kiss.

He would kiss Aurora awake for the greater good of all mankind.

And even if Mark and Aurora were perpetually on-again-off-again, he still saw their intertwined destinies. One vision of Mark's future that remained constant was he and Aurora back to back, working together, taking on the whole world. Metaphorically, most likely. Like MaKayla had said, they would always be connected, even after a breakup, but the future would push them together once more.

But his mind kept wandering away from Aurora. He knew he had to kiss her to save the day, to figure out this whole summoning thing, but the moment he envisioned the kiss, it wasn't Aurora in his thoughts. It was Baz.

Which was ridiculous—Mark wasn't gay. It obviously had to do with seeing Baz in his angel body, all jacked and swole. It was just a mental manifestation of physical admiration. Like seeing a teammate making gains in the gym and saying good job. But Baz made it weird again, getting in Mark's face. So it was completely natural that Mark's thoughts copy-pasted Baz's close face into thoughts of Aurora out of her enchanted coma.

A high-pitched animal scream snapped Mark out of this bizarre train of thought. Good. His ride was close.

Mark put two fingers at the corners of his mouth and blew to whistle. A wet hiss was all that came out. He tried again, but this one was just a heavy breath. After two more attempts, Mark was getting light-headed. So finally, he just yelled out, "Anthony, over here!" as loud as he could.

The animal scream came closer, clarifying into an approaching whinny until Mark could hear the distinct *clop clop* of hooves on a road. There, in evening dark, stood Anthony, the big brown horse in the center of a pool of streetlight.

Crap, no saddle.

Getting onto the horse (Mark refused to use the word 'mount') was awkward and infuriating. Mark had excellent hand-eye coordination and was a champion-caliber athlete; he should have been able to get onto a horse no problem. And he did, by the sixth or so attempt, apologizing to Anthony for grabbing him by the mane. The horse didn't seem to mind as he took off as soon as Mark was completely seated.

"Wait! Anthony, we have to go to my ex-girlfriend's!" Mark called out as the animal jostled him hard enough to make his teeth chatter.

The magical horse heeded Mark's steering toward his ex-girlfriend's house, although riding bareback was nearly impossible. Most of the time, Mark hugged the horse's neck as his thighs gave out from squeezing so hard. Who knew that riding a horse was such a workout? And how much riding without a saddle punished the testicles. At least using all his concentration to stay on Anthony kept him from thinking too hard on the kiss ahead...or Baz.

The night was cool enough to balance the sweat from muscular exertion, though Anthony was hot and damp himself. How far had the horse run to meet up with Mark? What kind of shenanigans was the animal up to, roaming free in the night?

With proximity to Aurora's house came visions. The dark of night, which usually brought sleep and dreams, always brought Mark glimpses of the future. Man, he could really use a drink right now.

Standing alongside Aurora as they fought off the world. The Earth cracking open to fire, steam, and lava. Humans burning by the billions. Anthony flying across the sky next to a horse skeleton, a colorful winged unicorn, and a fourth horse so bright, it burned Mark's eyes.

But his eyes weren't burning. They were shut with his face pressed into Anthony's sweaty neck, thick with the smell of horse sweat, musty and sweet.

Anthony had stopped at the familiar sight of Aurora Seitsinger's house. Mark had been here dozens of times, maybe even hundreds. Picking her up for dates, dropping her off, sneaking in after her parents were asleep. Fueled by lust, love, and the inescapable desire to be near her, he had risked so much over and over again just to see her.

But now, he didn't really feel anything for her. It was concerning that she'd been asleep or sick for over a week, but his heart no longer fluttered at the thought of her. His pulse didn't quicken like it used to. His hormones didn't kick into motion.

And that was sad. It was a loss Mark had never confronted. Like someone had died, but rather than someone, it was the relationship between the two of them. Sliding, or rather falling, from Anthony brought Mark back to reality, back to this moment, where despite no connection to her, Mark was attempting to help Aurora. Not to impress her or to get sex out of it. Not to swoop in to be her hero. He was doing it for something else. For someone else.

With Anthony away from the house and out of the street, Mark mentally prepared himself for what had to be done.

"That's close enough," a husky voice warned from the darkness.

Mark froze. In the face-off between angels, witches, and prophets, he'd underestimated the trouble he could be walking into.

Instinctively, he dipped into his foresight to assess the threat. He saw a collection of powerful beings gathered around fire, surrounded by salt. He saw a hairy animal stalking him. He saw Cain flying through the air, locked in battle with a sword-baring demon. But he didn't see himself in any danger from the voice in the shadows.

"Visiting hours are over. Besides, I don't think she's interested in seeing you." Stepping out from the shadow of a tree, a figure stood, face covered by the hood of a cape that was dark but lined in white fur. She threw the hood back, revealing Ivy Skelton. Mark hated this witch.

"So she's awake?" Mark conveyed through his tone that he was rolling his eyes at Skelton's dramatics.

Her hesitation to answer was answer enough.

"I'm not here to visit," he said plainly. "I'm here to wake her up."

"You know how to wake her? You saw it? In a vision? How?"

"It's obvious. She's in an enchanted sleep state. The only thing that can save her is true love's kiss."

The laughter bubbling from Skelton first maimed Mark, then angered him until he had to shut it down. "These are forces greater than you can understand."

Her laughter halted abruptly. Good. Maybe Skelton could be reasoned with.

"So let's figure out how to get me in there..." Mark approached the house, pointing to Aurora's second-story window. But Skelton didn't follow. She stood still, eyes closed, talking to herself, whispering something into one of her rings.

"If you're not going to take this seriously, then fine," said Mark. "I'll just do it-"

"*Myself*," Mark thought without saying it aloud. The words didn't form to finish his sentence. He cleared his throat to say it again, but again, he couldn't. So he tried cussing. Nothing but silence. He came up with an insult to hurl at Skelton, but his voice box didn't work. He couldn't even whisper.

But Skelton could. She stood there, eyes closed, whispering into her jewelry.

Mark tried to scream, failed, then punched a nearby tree. Of course, that only hurt his hand, and nearby, Anthony appeared to laugh as much as a horse could.

So Mark forced himself to take some calming breaths and held out a rude gesture until Skelton opened her eyes to see it.

"I was weaned on 'forces greater than you understand,' boy. I know you can glimpse into possible futures, but that is a party trick compared to the power of gods I grew up studying."

Mark didn't even know what that meant.

"And if you think I'm going to let you non-consensually

sleep-kiss my girlfriend in your crusade for machismo, you're as clueless as you look."

That was a whole lot of words that Mark didn't understand, and he would have said as much if he could speak.

"I learned to shield myself from annoying boys before I learned multiplication. And that's without even dipping into the serious witchcraft I leave in my war chest. Now, if you want to be helpful, you can foretell Aurora's future so we can reverse-engineer whatever has incapacitated her."

Of course she needed his help, but Mark wasn't about to after all these insults. She'd have to ask nicely.

Mark tried to tell her that and still found himself mute. Fine. He'd suck it up and be the bigger man. He took a deep breath, ignored his fury at Skelton, and closed his eyes.

He was blindfolded but could see the world was against them. Violence in the sky, chaos under their feet. Mark standing with Aurora as humanity's last chance. Fighting as four horses descended to destroy Earth.

When he opened his eyes, Skelton was whispering again into her jewelry.

"I saw..." Mark's voice surprised himself. He could talk again. Now it was time to break the truth to Skelton, to let her down easy. Clearing his throat, he continued purposefully, "It's what I always saw. Me and Aurora taking on the world."

"What does that even mean, 'Taking on the world?'"

"Like Bonnie and Clyde."

"Bonnie and Clyde were murderous bank robbers."

"Who took on the world."

"They killed bankers and police officers. Is that what you and Aurora are doing in your visions?"

"No, why would we rob banks?"

"Why'd you bring up Bonnie and Clyde?"

God, this girl was frustrating. Was she playing dumb on purpose?

Mark slowed down his words and whisper-shouted, "It's me and her against the world!"

"What does that mean! Tell me what you actually see."

This chick, with whatever knowledge of the supernatural she claimed she had, definitely didn't understand the way visions worked. "Aurora and me, back to back. The world crumbling around us, the ground breaking open, and we're fighting everyone coming at us."

"Fighting with what?"

"Swords and, like, light beams and such!"

"Who's holding the swords? Who's shooting light beams?"

"Aurora."

"And what are you doing?"

"Helping."

"Helping what? Hold the sword? Shoot the lightning?"

"It's light beams and I tell her where to fire things!"

"So she's taking on the world, and you're just pointing? Mark, that's called being in the way."

"I'm not in the way... I'm not just pointing at things. I can't even see, I'm blindfolded."

"Why would you be blindfolded?"

He'd never considered that. "I can see the future better without distractions."

"Mark. Don't take this the wrong way, but I don't think you're destined to 'take on the world' with Aurora. You're a guide, maybe a disciple. Don't mistake me—it's incredibly important for somebody practicing thaumaturgy, for using the power of gods. She needs believers."

"What? Like I'm just some follower? I'm her boyfriend...was her boyfriend. She needs me, needs true love's kiss. I'm not just a believer."

"There's nothing wrong with devoting your life to a cause you believe in."

Mark got too loud. "What, like her slave?"

Skelton shushed him, took a breath, then explained, "Mark, do you see how she gets better or not?"

"No, not specifically. You don't think it's true love's kiss?"

"No, I don't, Mark."

Bummer. What was he even doing there? He was helpless, some spectator watching a game he couldn't play. This was worse warming a bench.

"There's this guy...Baz. Aurora summoned his O-Fay-Niss, and he's trying to get it to her. I'm just helping."

"Ophanus? Do you mean an Ophanim?"

"Maybe?"

"Do you know what an Ophanim is, Mark?"

"Something that has something to do with angels?"

"That's surprisingly accurate. But you may need to ask your friend Baz what exactly he means. I tell you what, if she wakes up, I'll give you a call. What's your number?"

"I actually don't have a phone right now."

"Then, I don't know... Maybe I'll see you at group?"

"Yeah...I guess..."

"Fine."

"Fine." They stood awkwardly for a long moment. Mark didn't want to leave without accomplishing anything but was relieved he didn't have to kiss his ex. As he struggled back onto Anthony, he wondered why he was so relieved. Kissing Aurora used to be all he ever thought about. But now he had a mission.

He was on the side of good. He had to help Baz. They were on the side of good.

Chapter 10

Bazrael

Pushing, struggling, battling the Creature was a war within Bazrael.

The Creature hungered for blood, energized with the potential of violence. The end approached. The future of this world waned.

Trapped within the Creature's mind, Bazrael railed. He was more than this monster, more than just a weapon. He was not an object to be summoned in order to bring forth the End Times. But there was no escaping.

His body tumbled across his room, mirroring the internal fight. Skin ripped. Bones broke. Teeth sliced their way through flesh. Wings bulged out against shoulder blades.

He poured his focus onto his hands, his human hands, concentrating to keep the fingers intact. His body obeyed, even when his vision blurred. The human form of his arm held, though he had no control of its motion. The hand reached onto the strewn objects across the floor, grasping the Bible.

The Creature found it. There it was, hidden within the silly book of human superstition, the blade. With a solitary singing note of metal grinding on metal, the sword pulled free of the pages.

Baz's body had fallen beyond his grasp. Its humanity slipped. Bone extended, transforming hands into claws.

The Creature felt complete with the blade. Purposeful. The sword disappeared within his talons as he absorbed it. It was inside the Creature now, in his depths, where Bazrael was, sinking within himself. He was smothered, falling away from his own body, where the Creature spread his control. Slick bat wings spread, sharp talons splayed. A guttural booming battle cry escaped his ragged throat and echoed through the house and into the night sky. An invitation to begin the end.

This wasn't who Bazrael was, not anymore. Yes, he was summoned to this world for a reason, but now that he was here, he was human. He loved being human. Laughing, crying, playing baseball. He was living a life in the final days of a planet. He was dancing and rejoicing as the light faded. He lived, and he loved.

He *loved*.

Bazrael was in love. Thoughts of Mark Cecilia filled his mind. Anger, jealousy, pain, uncertainty, and desire all accompanied the thought of the All-Star. This was love, the fibers of thousands of disparate emotions woven into one connection, and that connection created a warmth in his chest and a cool breeze along his skin. *His* skin.

Bazrael's skin had returned. The Creature was gone, stuffed back within. Bazrael took form now. His tall, strong, human body standing among the wreckage of his home.

On the floor, split in two, was the Bible where Bazrael had kept a sacred sword. That blade was inside of him now, along with the potential of angelic grace, demonic chaos, and the pitch-dark, wet skin of the Creature.

This was an escalation. The potential for violence, the machinations to set the end of time into motion, was all housed inside of him. These were not separate pieces to be assembled to make something terrible. They were now assembled, the means of destruction right alongside the Creature to push the buttons.

There was no time to meet with Aurora Marie Seitsinger, to explain to her that the reason she summoned him was moot. His purpose dragged him forward now, to his destiny. Each piece was in place. Each cog and wheel worked in time to manufacture the end.

Bazrael was the machinery now. And only the thought of love had delayed it from starting. He had to find Mark. He had to be with Mark. Because next time, Bazrael might not be able to fight off the Creature alone.

Mark

Seeing that the lights in his house were on was the first warning to Mark that his night was going in the wrong direction. Then, as Anthony approached, Mark noticed both cars parked in the driveway. This was going to be bad.

Even though he gripped onto the horse's neck as tightly as he could, Mark still landed too hard on his banged-up ankle, pain shooting up his leg, causing the joint to throb with each step. But before he walked through that front door, he took a deep breath to suck it up and walk like nothing bothered him.

"Where the Hell have you been?" his mom shouted before

he even saw her.

"I thought you'd be working and staying over," Mark answered meekly.

"Well, surprise. Where have you been?"

Mark fought the instinct to throw a smart remark in her face. It had been such a long day, and Mark didn't feel like playing these games with her. "Out."

"Answer her." Great, Coach Boyfriend was here for the assist.

Mark wasn't going to take this from him. He lashed out. "You know where I was?" Mark snapped. "Visiting Aurora because she's sick, bedridden for days."

Mom grew quiet. "Is that true?"

It stung to use Aurora as a shield, and Mark could only nod in answer. His mom had always adored Aurora, and the news would devastate her.

"For how long?" she asked.

"Like a week."

"Why didn't you tell me?"

"Nobody told me!"

"Well, we'll send flowers, or I'll make a casserole or something."

"Isn't she your ex?" Coach Boyfriend asked.

"Don't be heartless," Mom chided. "Even if they broke up, they dated for over a year. She's a sweet girl. We'll send something along tomorrow. But you're being punished right now, Mark. You're not supposed to be out."

There was no response to this that would help Mark's situation, so he just looked down at the thick carpeting. Brown accented with white and gray cat hairs.

"No more baseball games this week."

"But, Mom, it's the championship!"

"You can't even play with that boot," Coach Boyfriend said. "You're definitely not resting it like you should."

Mom pressed. "I don't have the time to keep an eye on you like you're a little kid, Mark. You knew you weren't supposed to be out this late, but you went anyway. This is what happens. Now go to your room."

"I would have called if I had a—"

"Go to your room!" Mom commanded.

"Stop talking back to your mother," Coach Boyfriend barked.

"Don't yell," she said to her boyfriend. "I can handle this."

"He's being disrespectful." He pointed an accusing finger at Mark.

"He's a teenager—of course he is."

"Don't let him talk to you like that!"

With their anger diverted, Mark sulked back to his room, throwing himself onto his bed. With each pulse of his heartbeat, soreness radiated in his ankle. Now that he was actually resting for the first time, he realized how tired and beat up he was.

The day was too much. Baz had just walked into his life with the changing of a relief pitcher, and now they were fighting for good together.

Whatever this Ophanim was, it meant the world to Baz and, most likely, Aurora as well. That was good enough for Mark. Even if it meant working with that maniac Ivy Skelton, he'd figure out how to help them. This Ophanim may even be able to prevent the apocalypse; it couldn't be a coincidence that all of this was happening at once. So of course, Mark would do anything he could to help.

So now he had to get out of the house without getting into any more trouble. This was so complicated, so much more difficult than it needed to be. Mark preferred it simple, like baseball: throw him a pitch, and he'd crush it out of the park. This was like playing chess. It made his head ache.

"That sounded pretty intense," a soft voice said from the edge of the bed.

Great. All Mark wanted was to be left alone to think and sleep. But he wasn't so lucky.

"Want to talk about it?" his therapist cat asked.

"No."

"I know you're going through a lot. And there hasn't been room to process all that you've survived in the past couple weeks. It's okay to sit in your feelings, but shutting them out won't help."

Mark unstrapped his ankle boot and pulled off his jeans. "Got it. I'm good."

"Well, you didn't exactly open up at group last week."

"Lower your expectations for tomorrow's group. I have a feeling we've got a lot for everyone to work out."

"So your feelings get pushed to the side for something more important again?"

"Big things are coming, Slider. Maybe there's no time for feelings."

"You can talk to me, Mark. This is a safe space. I won't betray your trust."

He chuckled under his breath. "Because no one would believe a talking cat."

"Because I care about you. Wanna talk about what happened today? Was it really important enough to break curfew and get in all this trouble?"

Mark collapsed back in bed. He thought back to surprisingly civil conversations with Skelton and Colfax, even busting balls with Baz.

"Yeah, it was all worth it."

Beth

The crunch of her footsteps on the sidewalk leveled off into a steady rhythm as Beth's aching legs went numb. The bottoms of her feet burned hot with every step. Her arms dangled lifelessly, jolting with her gait as she walked down the street aimlessly.

Her eyes darted to each vehicle, whether parked or driving, keen to find the white church van. She remembered every detail of Parker's van- white with rust spots behind the wheel wells, a broken grill like it was sneering with uneven teeth, and though she didn't recall the name of the church printed on the hood and doors, she remembered the logo of a cross in a circle, the vertical line of the cross split down the middle.

With each step, her body begged her to stop, to rest, to eat, to sleep.

No. Not with Anthony still out there. He wouldn't stop looking for her. To divert her focus from her fatigue and pains, she ran scenarios through her head: sneaking up on Parker by crawling in the shadows to slash his Achilles tendon. Wrenching an arm behind him while pinning the buck knife to his jugular and demanding they release Anthony. Cutting the necklace off Parker, then summoning Puka to destroy Anthony's kidnappers.

With every imagined attack, she gripped and regripped her blade, flipping it around from holding to stab, then reversing grip.

Headlights tore by from a rundown dark van spewing the smell of hot rubber, burnt oil, and old engine belts. It wasn't Parker's. But on the back windows, either painted over or tinted, a big logo stretched across the double doors of the van.

A circle around a cross split down the middle.

Adrenaline burst from her chest to empower her muscles. Without thinking, she broke into a run, sprinting after the van.

Her feet no longer ached as they slapped the pavement. She felt the powerful muscles in her legs flex and push as they propelled her forward. Her lungs burned a comforting sear. She moved as fast as humanly possible.

With the deep blue of the van coming in and out of visibility in the street lamp light, the taillights guided her onward. Like red eyes piercing the night, they glared at her as they retreated farther and farther away.

On she ran as her thighs burned and her feet grew heavy. She gulped lungfuls of cool night air that stabbed like hot needles.

Her body protested as she slowed. The red eyes teased her, growing smaller and more distant. Sweat stung her eyes as it poured from her forehead and temples. Tears streaked down her face, and snot ran from her nose. Hope dripped off her like all the other fluids down her face.

The van's red eyes mocked her until they were barely far-off pinpricks. Then, in a quick motion, the two eyes met, the right one sliding to merge with the other, then both disappearing to the left.

The van had turned. She calculated how far ahead, either two stop lights up or just past.

She picked up her speed, pumping her arms harder now. She had to catch up. If the van turned again, it would be lost forever. Anthony would be lost forever.

She ignored the pain and heaviness, driven by her own guilt. She thought of how Anthony's eyes widened and bulged when he was scared, how his whinny jumped higher and screamed, how he hopped backward and flinched from danger.

This was all her fault. She'd kept Puka the demon around too long. She'd been selfish not to let Anthony go sooner, to let the vet put him down, just because she didn't want to lose him.

And now, everything Mark had seen was coming to fruition. Those religious nuts were going to recreate the book of Revelations using her horse and that damn demon.

She had to stop them.

Pushing her legs harder and faster, knife glinting in the scarce light, she finally made it to the turn, leaning as she veered onto the side street.

But it was dark. No taillights. Fewer street lamps here on an old road of scattered industrial buildings. Rusty skeletal scaffolding that used to load boats towered around her. Silent, bulbous silos of concrete painted blue in the night's light stood guard along the abandoned street.

She ran to pass each building, then searched past it for those taillights.

Nothing. Empty lots divided by tall chain link fences surrounded every building, silo, and steel frame.

As she checked each lot, the possibility of finding Anthony dwindled.

Up ahead, she saw a yellow street sign marking the end of the road. She jogged all the way to the end of the pavement, past the final building. There was no trace of the mocking red glow of taillights. No trace of Anthony or his captors. Darkness owned this section of the city. Light was forbidden, giving into the bluish glow of the city sky.

At some point, Beth's panting gave way to sobs. Tears from physical exertion were now tears of despair. She didn't notice when she had stopped running. She didn't remember collapsing to the ground.

Her body throbbed with pain and fatigue. Beth bowed her head, humbled.

Funny. She used to think that she was psychically linked to Anthony, that their souls were connected in a way that would never be truly separate. But there was no doubting that Beth was utterly and completely alone now. There was no mental tether that she could use to find Anthony or even let him know that she was searching. She wished that she could tell him not to be scared, that she wouldn't give up until she was close enough to nuzzle him, to pat his velvet nose, to scratch behind his ears. But even if Anthony was nearby, even kept in one of these dozens of empty buildings, she had no way of communicating with him.

Unless... she raised her hands to her mouth. Placing a finger and a thumb to spread her lips wide, she whistled. The high pitch pierced the quiet night. Echoes bounded off the concrete of silos, bouncing off into nothing.

But there was no reply. No whinny. No desperate screech of a horse. He couldn't have been around. Anthony wasn't within earshot.

"You hear that?" a harsh, jagged whisper asked from nowhere in particular.

Beth froze, perking her ears to locate the source of the voice.

"Don't worry about it," someone hissed in response.

It was close, but Beth didn't know from where. She tiptoed to walk through an open gate and search behind the nearest abandoned silo. Whispers meant people hiding. And Beth was certain it was whoever was driving that van.

Bazrael

The night had been unbearable, fighting off the Creature within him. Bazrael felt his purpose even more clearly now that the blade was a part of him. He was no longer practicing transformations or rehearsing strikes for a later battle. The mission was within him now, as was the Creature and the sword. He felt their yearning.

The sharp edge of the blade desired to meet heavenly flesh. That image, the delicious sensation of slicing into the skin of the godly, played over and over in his head, not allowing sleep or any true rest.

Bazrael had given up halfway through the night and began walking. The air was heavy with dangerous possibilities, a forest of dominoes teetering on balance. He didn't gamble on transforming into a body capable of flight; the Creature could take advantage to seize control.

So he walked for hours.

There was a pull in his chest, as if his longing had a directional orientation. He walked and walked toward where he felt Mark was. His focus stayed squarely on the All-Star. Mark would help. If just the thought of him held back the Creature, surely his presence would fight the compulsion of transformation even more?

Even if Mark's allegiance was elsewhere, even if he lacked the same regard for Bazrael that Bazrael had for him, he was the only one keeping the Creature at bay.

Maybe this was the human condition, to long for that which couldn't be attained. Humans lived in squalor, desiring riches. They constantly moved toward death, praying for everlasting life.

But Mark had gone into the night to help Bazrael with his purpose, his dark mission. Bazrael had sent his champion forth, but in succeeding, Mark would only be serving the Creature.

Humans had it so easy. Even this close to the end, to the punctuation to close out the run of life and time, they had no concept of such pressure. No greater purpose weighed down human thought. No expectations from higher authority guided their every movement.

To be human was to float on air like one of Bazrael's feathers, to be guided by whim and destiny, and to choose to love it or to wallow in helplessness. Bazrael wished he could simply float along, but the Creature had to be held. Even in this body, Bazrael was less of a human than he was a cage.

At last, he came upon the small, unassuming home Bazrael immediately knew must be Mark's. There was a residual essence of Aurora Marie Seitsinger in the air here, weeks, if not months, old.

Around the one-story home, grass grew tall in spurts around muddy puddles. Two cars slept in the driveway, rumpled with use. Mark didn't have a car, so that meant adults.

Knowing Mark was already in trouble, Bazrael couldn't just knock on the door, especially not before dawn. He'd already had his phone privileges revoked. If Mark had a friend disturbing the sleeping house, his availability could become even more restricted.

So, Bazrael settled into a neighbor's tree shrouded in the darkness with a straight line of sight to the window of a darkened room. If someone turned on a light within, or if the sun rose against the far side of the house, Bazrael would gain some sight into the home. So he made himself as comfortable as he could against the rough bark of the lively green tree, seated on the hard round branch that accompanied the age and wisdom of old plants.

Time passed in that curious human way, slower when Bazrael focused on the inevitable future, faster when his mind wandered from his goals. Thoughts constantly fell to Mark, imagining him out in the world, either championing Bazrael's cause or begging for Aurora Marie Seitsinger's attention.

Mark was a historical holdover. He'd have done well as a gladiator. The All-Star would have made one hellstorm of a crusader. If he'd had a clear, noble cause, Mark Cecilia would have dominated in all aspects of life. Instead, here he was, a non-believer in the time of dead gods, filled with all the power a mortal could wish for. Mark's personal quest was selfish and naïve, clinging to the dreams of professional sport when he was assured there was no future in it, no future anywhere.

Bazrael awoke with a start. He'd drifted off to sleep. He also had drifted to his left, sliding from balance on the branch.

Instinctively, he gripped the bark. In his rash reaction, his body had partially transformed. Slick black talons protruded from his hands, digging into the tree's surface. The depths of Bazrael's mind had chosen between fight and flight.

The Creature stirred, summoned, dragged out into the light. Bazrael's human form sunk within himself weighed down in thick water. Submerged, plunging, drowning.

Lights came on in the Cecilia house.

A self-satisfied grin spread across the Creature's toothy face. Through the lighted window, the oracle awakened. This incompetent mortal would lead the Creature straight toward the conjurer who'd summoned him.

Perhaps the sticky pitch-dark magic of the guard witch only applied to Bazrael and not the Creature. Or maybe the

Creature's intention would be strong enough to break through such wards. But no matter what, the Creature understood his mission was at hand. Soon his dark purpose would fruit. The world would sow its end.

Bazrael's blade slid out of his arm into the Creature's grasp.

Chapter 11

Beth

When had she dozed off? Beth was weak and parched, her head foggy from just waking up or the exertion from the last day's constant walking.

Then she remembered the progress she'd made, the luck she'd had. She'd found Parker's minions, the van. She was staked out, ready to strike...

Her hand felt along the overgrown grass beneath the silo stairs in her hiding spot, searching for the buck knife. The morning was bright enough that she should have been able to see the blade glinting in the light, but she couldn't find it. She checked her pockets, but they were empty. She felt for her backup knife or her flashlight, but found nothing.

"Fell asleep on the job, little lamb?" Parker's voice mocked her in a teasing sing-song as his dirty, calloused hands wrapped around her wrists.

Mark

There was no use fighting. Any struggle, any opposing force would be shut down immediately, and the situation would go from hopeless to worse.

So Mark went on his best behavior; he cleaned. He vacuumed. He did laundry. He even mowed the mud patch of a lawn.

Maybe he'd be able to get out of the house for group if he played his cards right. Maybe.

He avoided Coach Boyfriend and dedicated time to brown-nosing his mom, washing her work uniforms, vacuuming out the car for her rideshares. But the strange thing was, he didn't hate it. He wasn't getting angry or fighting off visions constantly. Focusing on Mom helped. Helping Mom made a difference in her life, and it felt good.

In his downtime or when switching tasks, he saw that there wasn't much helping anything else. When he thought of what it took to wake Aurora, he foresaw the world turning on her, destiny betraying her. When he imagined what would become of Morrigan and his new roided-out state, the future showed Morrigan falling in battle with a demon.

But worse, when Mark thought of Bazrael, he saw himself bringing a sword down over the angel's head.

Bazrael's screams punctuated Mark's thoughts throughout the day. Each time he finished a chore, every time he grabbed his water. Going through his physical therapy exercises. A bright blue sword swung down over the angel again and again.

Mark pushed himself harder to fight through the visions. Deep down, he knew that Bazrael was the good necessary to stop the end of the world. So if Mark turned on Bazrael, somehow defeated him... Without booze or smoke to keep the visions away or calm his nerves, Mark only had physical exertion.

To keep pressure off his ankle, he worked his weighted bat and blasted his core.

"Do you think this is a wise use of your time, Mark?" Slider the cat mused from under a bush nearby. "Are muscles a priority when you see the end times approaching?"

"Strength, not aesthetics," Mark grunted the mantra that guided all his training.

"Oh yes, dreams of pro baseball once this pesky apocalypse has ended…"

In a flare of frustration, Mark wielded the bat like a weapon, only to see an impressed gray cat regarding him like she was bored.

"And what's better?" Mark growled, "Working through trauma and processing and internalizing and all that junk so I can sleep better once the 'pesky apocalypse' is over?"

"Group therapy can lead you to self-actualization, so you can use your powers to their fullest potential."

"I just see the future, cat. I'm not one of the ones strong enough to change it. You're mistaking me for the witches and wizards and angels."

"Mark, who the hell you talking to?!" his mom shouted from the back door.

Slider the cat yawned and began licking her crotch.

"Just…pumping myself up." Mark swung the bat. "Mindset, you know."

"Well, cut it out. You look crazy talking to yourself in the backyard."

"I'm not crazy, Mom. Just working through some stuff."

"Well, thanks for cleaning up around the house and mowing. You're still grounded, but if you want to go to group tonight, Bill will give you a ride."

Good. The plan worked, and now Mark had a shot at this whole convocating the magical people or whatever Colfax and

Skelton wanted to do. But it felt better to make peace with Mom, even if he had to put up with a car ride with Coach Boyfriend.

With a bit more energy, Mark went back to his Russian twists, working his abs until they felt like they'd start cramping. But no matter how hard he pushed himself, he couldn't shake the feeling that someone—or something—was watching him.

Bazrael

Bazrael could only look on as he and his body spied on the All-Star. As Mark worked around the house, exerting his body and showing his muscles, the feeling of yearning converted to a base lust. While Bazrael's feelings for Mark had once helped him overcome the Creature, these thoughts only strengthened the Creature. Animal instinct and desire were in the same realm as bloodlust.

That wasn't how Bazrael felt about Mark. Their connection was one of similar interests, shared experience, and ease of conversation. Of course, Mark was attractive, but he was also kind in ways other humans weren't. He'd initiated Bazrael into a society that had been so foreign and inaccessible.

Startling guilt gripped Bazrael. Tart and acidic, the feeling seeped into Bazrael's thoughts of the All-Star and the current situation until Bazrael could name it.

Regret.

Why hadn't Bazrael confessed himself completely to Mark? Why had Bazrael allowed jealousy to affect his actions?

If the Creature remained in control until the approaching end of time, Bazrael could never admit to Mark that he was the Ophanim, the summoned weapon, the fulcrum that would lever the fate of mankind.

Bazrael would never be able to declare his appreciation for all that Mark had given him, from laughter to competition, from lust to love. Bazrael wouldn't have the opportunity to confess his total infection of that most powerful human sentiment, love. His love for Mark was a bigger rush than falling from space through the Earth's atmosphere. His love was a greater thrill than unfurling wings, taking to the sky, and feeling the warm kiss of the sun's light.

Even if Mark didn't share the same feelings, they were a most precious possession for Bazrael. He loved Mark. And he loved that he had that love. That was enough.

Hidden from the shining sun in the tree's shade, Bazrael's Creature form watched and waited as Mark went about his day. The heat and brightness repulsed the Creature, and it sank into the drying mud. Finally, once the day neared an end, Mark and the adult male human got into a vehicle and drove off. The Creature dove into the ground, slithering through dirt beneath the human city as a worm possessed.

As he traveled and followed the prophet, the Creature felt the tickle of nearby immortal power. They were approaching magic, diablerie, and thaumaturgy. Supernatural energy pulsated and crackled from a source they neared. This was not the power of Bazrael's deity father, not of his angelic brethren. This magic wasn't bound to heaven nor Earth. It was unknown to the Creature and gave its appetite and ferocity pause. Mark the prophet stayed by this power source as the human vehicle left. The Creature remained hidden underground at a distance where he could smell and taste the sting of enchantment, but it could not detect him.

Within the Creature, an exhausted Bazrael could no longer

fight, losing the energy to attempt escape, to regain control. He sensed the essence of Aurora Marie Seitsinger, but not her presence. Instead, he, too, felt the thrum of an unknown sorcery controlled by mortals. Helplessly, he waited and watched.

Mark

Mark walked up to the entrance of the old church, ignoring the group gathering to the west of the building.

"Mark, where are you going?" Colfax called out to him.

He waved her off, limping to the door. "I can't hang out. Just here for therapy."

"Don't be daft," Skelton barked at him, not looking up from setting something out on the ground. "Come over here!"

"Sorry, guys. Can't hang." And Mark walked into the church's side door. He slid into the empty kitchen and meeting room, smelling of dust and losing light along with the day. Peering out the corner of a window, he saw Coach Boyfriend's SUV circle back out to the leave the church parking lot.

But Mark wasn't dumb. He waited longer.

Sure enough, Coach Boyfriend paused before pulling out onto the road, then drove slowly as the church was still in sight, making sure Mark stayed inside. In fact, Mark stayed another minute or two until he was convinced Coach Boyfriend wouldn't drive by to check on him again. Once he was sure the coast was clear, Mark limped back outside to see Colfax and Skelton squabbling.

"If it's not a big deal, then you'll tell me where you got it from." MaKayla Colfax was hunched over, pouring a box of salt onto the ground, leaving an arcing white line and coming around to finish a big ten-foot circle.

Within the circle, Ivy Skelton sat with an old cookie tin in her lap. Placed on the ground around Skelton were objects, presumably from the cookie tin: a colorful little children's eraser, an old ceramic mug, a bowl, two candles, and bell, and a pair of fancy scissors.

She held a piece of bread to her forehead and whispered something, before barking at Colfax without looking at her or even opening her eyes. "It's a big enough deal to pop you in the mouth if you don't shut up about it."

"Cool," Mark said with a grin. "Cat fight. You two were supposed to go at it in the parking lot before the end of last semester. Finally, a rematch."

Colfax rolled her eyes. "Thanks for joining us, Mark. Although you could have left the sexism at home."

Lighting a piece of incense from a candle, Skelton gave commands again without looking up from her task. "Enter the circle before it's complete."

Mark stepped inside the dumped salt, careful not to knock over the knick knacks being placed in some kind of order. Suddenly, a streak of gray out of the corner of his eye approached, and Dr. Slider stood there in her oversized-sweater-and-jeans therapist uniform.

Skelton blew out the flame of the incense stick before stabbing it into the ground. "You, too, MaKayla. Inside the circle."

"Should I go get Cain first?" MaKayla paused with a gap of salt about a foot long to pour and finish the circle.

"Morrigan's here?" Mark asked, remembering the horrible, muscled-out, and miserable state he'd left his friend in.

"Waiting in the car."

"Is he still…?" Dr. Slider's question trailed off, leaving Mark to wonder if the cat knew about the guy getting roided out, or if this was more about his emotional unavailability toward Colfax.

"Yeah."

"He's not invited," Skelton said matter-of-factly as she poured water from a pitcher into a bowl and a cup. "We can talk to him after we conduct our business. But I'm not inviting a masculine energy so dominating to my own into this circle."

Whatever that meant, Mark felt there was an insult aimed at him somewhere in there…

"Finish the circle and we'll begin," Skelton commanded.

Colfax continued dumping salt on the ground as Skelton whispered to herself while lighting candles.

"Now, we commune." Skelton sat cross-legged. The other two did the same, so Mark followed suit, careful not to sit on a flame or scissors.

"Do we have to sing?" Mark snickered. "I need to do my vocal warm-ups."

"Even if you don't share Ivy's beliefs," Dr. Slider chided Mark. "You can keep comments to yourself out of respect."

"Sorry," Mark said, "I literally don't know what we're doing."

"Casting a circle," Colfax answered.

"What does that mean?"

"We're doing witch stuff," Skelton said, annoyed. "Now, we'll convene by sharing in water and food." She sipped from an old mug, then passed it around. Everyone took a drink. Even Mark did so without comment. Next came the bread, which was admittedly delicious but dry. And not at all magical tasting.

Skelton spoke loudly. "We are here to awaken our sister,

Aurora."

Mark didn't want to think of Aurora as a sister, because that would add a different light to their history of physical activities. And Skelton as well, from as much as Mark could tell about their relationship.

"I thought we were here to stop the apocalypse," Colfax said.

"We'll have a better idea of what to do with Aurora with us. It's important that everyone within the circle believes that. We know what Aurora is capable of. She's the world's best chance of survival."

Mark understood. Skelton had told him that Aurora needed a believer, that his visions of him and Aurora taking on the world meant that he had to support her. If that's what it took to save existence, then that's what he'd do. He'd seen her power. He'd seen Aurora float in the air and toss him across an interstate without touching him. He believed.

He stood with her, leg throbbing, eyes burning in pain, guiding her as she filled the night sky with light beams. The ground lurched and crumbled beneath them, but Mark and Aurora wouldn't quit. She wasn't shooting at things in the air; she was herding things— people. She was guiding women and horses flying overhead. The light she shone moved them away from the rope crisscrossing the air, kept them from landing on the earth. Between the ropes, beyond the horses, two figures fought across the sky. Larger than human, one shining brightly, the other sucking in light, the two clashed blades that sent sparks exploding like fireworks. The night was too bright to see, and Mark felt grateful he had no eyes.

"I believe," said Dr. Slider, her low, mewling voice snapping Mark back to the present moment in the salt circle, smelling the patchouli smoke.

"I believe," Mark agreed.

"I believe," Colfax reluctantly admitted.

"I believe," Skelton said firmly, a confident period on their agreement. She continued, "Repeat after me: awaken, awaken, awaken."

They all joined in, clasping hands.

Dr. Slider's grip was dry and tight. Colfax's was soft and well-moisturized, maybe a bit sweaty.

Mark felt silly. He was the only one with his eyes open as they chanted in unison. He hoped nobody would drive by and see this. If a teammate caught sight of the ritual, Mark would be done for.

But then again, maybe there'd be no more baseball if they couldn't wake Aurora up.

So he said it like he meant it. He closed his eyes, reached out to her with his mind, and begged her, "Awaken."

He felt a cool breeze pick up. Mark couldn't help but open his eyes again to see the candles flicker, the nearby trees sway, and the human flying through the air right for them.

Beth

The knife she'd once used to summon a demon now pressed firmly on her wrist.

"Loner girl found dead." Parker pronounced the words like an article headline. "Little lamb, your body will be found and labeled a suicide before the end of days even begins."

"Whatever happened to thou shalt not kill?"

"Even Judas performed the Lord's will. Now summon the demon."

"Summon him yourself."

"Believe me, we've tried, lamb. But our rituals are godly. They bring us, as His believers and disciples, into the light. They don't work for the darkness of the likes of you and your company. None of our prayers, liturgies, or sacrifices managed to bring out your little friend."

Sacrifices? Were they killing to summon Puka? Surely this was just bravado to intimidate her. Immediately, Beth worried for Anthony. Not only was he obviously not here, but neither of the church vans had a trailer hitched. And there were no hoofprints in the mud or dirt of the abandoned manufacturing area. Maybe they had him somewhere else. Maybe these sickos crucified him.

But they needed something from her. They obviously hadn't made any progress if they needed her to summon Puka. And she wanted Anthony back.

But she couldn't reveal that she didn't know Anthony's whereabouts.

"What I get if I help you?" she asked.

"You get to live to see the end."

"So I die either way? But if I don't help you, God's gonna be pissed. At y'all."

Another of the guys, politely overdressed in matching polo shirts that showed peeks of very ugly prison tattoos, said, "I say we sacrifice her."

Parker smiled. "That may just do it. The blood of the little lamb might get us the demon's attention."

Shrugging as best she could without adding any pressure to the blade on her wrist, Beth said, "Maybe. Maybe not."

At this, Parker's smile melted, showing a glimpse of the face he most likely showed the world before he got the cult bug up his butt. Crooked teeth lined up like mismatched soldiers in his sneer. He threw Beth down to the gravel face first.

Rock smacked her in the lip and already-hurt eye. Heat told her that her face was bleeding somewhere. Getting herself back up, she smiled brightly for effect.

The men in polos cringed and looked away uneasily. But not Parker. He held that sneer.

"Little lamb, you are one lost soul, incorrigible to your own salvation. I may not be a patient man, but I'm a resourceful one."

He held out a hand to help her up. Beth considered spitting on it, but the throbbing heartbeat she felt in her face let her know how messed up and swollen she already was. So she accepted his offer, took his hand, and grunted to her feet.

Parker twisted her wrist back and slashed her across the palm, pressing the horse amulet into her bloody hand.

"Elizabeth," the demon hissed in her mind. But the men surrounding her showed no sign of hearing Puka.

Bazrael

A surge of supernatural force battered the Creature as Bazrael screamed within. Whoever had just arrived brought with them a form of magic that, when in proximity to the energies of the other people met, multiplied everyone's energies tenfold.

The power was like the focused presence of a god, waves of boiling hot ocean water pummeled the Creature, weakening his physical form and battering Bazrael's psyche.

Instinctually, the Creature scrambled, clawing out from beneath the earth.

From the surface, the gathering was visible. Mark Cecilia,

MaKayla Colfax, and Ivy Skelton, the guard witch, were meeting by an old church with two other women, strangers. Sorcery poured off three of the women in all directions, amplifying their auras, their potential, even their voices.

"Again, we sisters are united in purpose!" the one stranger shouted, the sound echoing from all directions at once. "We shall now form the true Gods' End!"

Three of the female humans glowed, the younger ones placing hands onto the shoulders of the stranger to form a triumvirate, a shape sacred to so much human ritual. The stranger held onto a wire, taut and wrapped around another nearby human. Mark Cecilia.

The prophet was tied up, held captive. Imperiled.

Before falling to Earth, Bazrael had been a guardian angel. He'd looked over Miguel Munoz, a smart kid who loved anime and baseball. It was a fairly easy assignment, and he didn't get in much trouble—no more than any other adolescent boy. He didn't seem to be destined to affect many lives from his grandmother's living room. But destiny had matched Bazrael with Miguel. And so the angel experienced growing up: knowing the love of a family, discovering the love of a game, and navigating an awkward first romantic love. It was not an eventful upbringing, but it had instilled the power of love in both Miguel and Bazrael. Then, when Miguel was eighteen, thieves broke into his abuela's home. She hid money in a cookie tin, and somehow, someone had found out. Three men, one with a shotgun, entered the home. They took Abuela from her bed, pressed a barrel to her chest, and asked for the location of the cash. Miguel came up behind them silently, baseball bat in hand. This was it; this was the moment more than all moments when Miguel needed his guardian angel. Seeing Abuela in danger, helpless, at the mercy of nervous, hungry, and angry thieves stirred something deep within Miguel. Bazrael felt it too. But unlike Miguel, Bazrael also was thinking of the boy; one creaky floorboard could get him killed, and one well-connected thief could send him to prison. One fast reflex would prevent Miguel from ever picking up a bat again. So Bazrael acted. A thief lost balance, making too much noise. The others got spooked. One saw Miguel who, in the darkness, appeared to have a gun of his own. The thieves ran. Bazrael saved Abuela. Miguel didn't have to do a thing. The Munoz home was safe again.

And now, seeing Mark at risk, Bazrael acted. He took over his body from the Creature as if he flipped a switch. The pitch skin of the Creature burnt away, leaving a vulnerable human beneath. The flow of hot liquid magic poured over his now-human flesh, burning and pressing him, pushing him back.

He put a foot forward and then the other, attempting to stride against the tide, but the waves of magic were too powerful. His footholds slipped.

But he would not be stopped. So he leapt. In the air, he changed form again, now driven by a new purpose and no longer fearing the power of the Creature. Wings sprouted and pushed against the air, swimming against the flow of magic.

MaKayla Colfax, Ivy Skelton the guard witch, and the stranger in her flowing dress lit up like streetlights as Mark struggled against his restraints. The other stranger, a woman without overflowing magic, attempted to free the All-Star, tugging at the cord and shouting at the triumvirate of overpowered beings.

The kidnapping stranger's voice reverberated through the thick current of sorcery. "We shall awaken the conjurer and take hold the reins of destiny!"

Bazrael's bright wings beat on. Without force or askance, the sword formed in his hand. Feeling the updrafts and swirling chaotic winds, he arced through the air, aiming to land within the white powdery circle that surrounded the humans,

His intense focus on the gathering of people veered suddenly. Pain burst in his side. The trajectory of his flight abruptly turned. He'd been hit by something. Something powerful enough to move his angelic form. An attack.

The Creature within Bazrael emerged. Talons emerged through fingertips. Pale skin blackened like burning wood. Wings darkened as they shed their feathers.

"Baz!" Mark yelped. Below, he kneeled, the line tying him up, pinning his arms, his eyes shut tight.

His eyes had been closed. He wasn't screaming for Bazrael to save him. He wasn't calling because he had seen Bazrael; Mark was in trouble, and his first thought was of Bazrael.

He hadn't yelled for his mother or absent his father. He wasn't calling out for his teammates. Mark screamed for Bazrael.

So Bazrael fought for Mark, pushing down against the Creature. His skin stayed mottled, caught between forms, flying wildly in the cloud of fluttering loose feathers.

Thick arms wrapped around Bazrael's torso and squeezed. His attacker. As the two careened through the air, Bazrael brought down his elbow into the heavy musculature of his assailant. The ground came up at them fast, Bazrael twisting and desperately flapping wings to land atop his opponent.

"Oof!"

The breath rushed from him as he bounced, freed from the strong grasp. His wings steadied him so Bazrael could land on his feet. Bazrael was mostly angel once more, tall and muscled with bright hair. Both his oversized human hands gripped the hilt of his sword, tip of the blade pointed and ready, facing his adversary.

The combatant, a giant figure just as tall as Bazrael, had porcelain white skin thick with heavy shadow and long flows of lightless black hair. His wings, also avian, seemed so dark that they absorbed ambient light. And bared in each hand was a baton, shy of a meter long with an arcing blade at the end.

Bazrael immediately recognized the weaponry and the type of creature wielding it: Sickles. An Angel of Death.

The Creature roiled within.

The dark Angel of Death charged. Bazrael stepped in to close the distance, stabbing the sword out before swinging it around. His hands had become talons, and he gave in to the violence of the Creature.

Blade met blade. Sparks flew.

The humans broke away from their sacred circle and holy triumvirate. Several shouted curses.

The battle had begun.

Chapter 12

Mark

He was tied up again, helpless again. At the mercy of someone else again. It was happening again.

Mark's vision flooded. He tasted the bile of vomiting up forced water. He felt the heat of a car aflame. He was crammed into the claustrophobia of a car trunk once more.

It was happening all over again.

"Mark, stay with me. We'll get you out of this..." Slider's voice was somewhere, maybe outside the car? Was the car burning or driving? Wait, was this even happening, or was he tied up back in Skelton's circle?

He tried to clear his mind, to remember where he was, to free himself of the mental prison within a car trunk, or a fire, or drowning. But he couldn't save himself. He was tied up and utterly defenseless.

So he imagined being saved. He thought of Baz's soft smile, his kind eyes, his strong hands pulling him from danger. He imagined Baz in all his angelic glory and pictured the monstrous hands he could summon. Mark cried out for Baz to save him.

The only answers were disembodied voices. Noises barely heard from underwater.

"Let him go!"

"MaKayla, call your boyfriend off."

"No, sisters, this is the way. The beginning of the end!"

The words drifted around him as he struggled helplessly against the rope. The world was closing in. His lungs filled with water.

The voices stopped.

A cat hissed and mewed.

A woman screamed.

Mark's bindings loosened. Hands scrambled over his body, pulling at his bonds.

Water receded, fire went out, and Mark was free. He gasped for air.

A hand petted his hair as a soothing voice purred at him, "You're alright, you're alright."

Slider. But a human again.

Nearby, Colfax struggled with a strange woman in a toga, grappling near the church. Frantically, Ivy Skelton adjusted the circle of salt strewn about in the chaos.

But in the street, against the fading light of the sunset, two winged figures fought. Sword clanged against some kind of ninja weapon. When they connected, fireworks.

"Cast them out!" Skelton pleaded. "Quick, you two, we have to cast them out! Cast them out! Cast them out!"

Mark was still getting his bearings, catching his breath, orienting himself to the mayhem unfolding.

"Cast them out!" Dr. Slider joined in the chant as Skelton linked hands.

They held fast to one another, and Mark joined their human chain.

"Cast them out! Cast them out!"

Skelton quickly caught Mark up. "The circle is new; we must cast out MaKayla and Lachesis. Cast them out from our circle! Cast them out!"

Uncertain of the situation, Mark at least understood to focus his thoughts. He resumed chanting with their goal in mind. "Cast them out."

The two winged fighters took to the sky, blades clashing, sparks flying.

"Cast them out!"

Dr. Slider squeezed Mark's hands. Skelton gave a firm nod.

"Cast them out!"

A few feet away, Lachesis, who'd been a mentor to MaKayla a few weeks back, flung the goody two-shoes into the side of the church and ran for Mark.

Lachesis cried desperately, "No man can see the destinies we will control!"

"Cast them out!"

The woman made it to the salt circle, wielding a thin chain like a whip. Then she hit an invisible wall, and crackling light blasted her back. She lay still on the ground.

"It worked!" Skelton announced. "Now, let's stop the boy fight. It's in their destiny to clash, but a destiny can be broken off by a Fate."

The image of a destiny shattering like ice flashed in Mark's mind. It would happen. It was someone's future.

Dr. Slider offered, "That lady seems to think you're a Fate, Ivy! You can break his destiny!"

What all had Mark missed? He remembered Lachesis flying

at them within the circle, then he was tied up. Something, someone had freed him.

"I'm just a witch," Skelton argued. "Fatehood is inherited by blood."

"Well," Dr. Slider said, "you certainly know a lot about them."

"I've got a book."

Mark offered, "Get Colfax to do it. She's a Fate."

"Right." Skelton raised her voice, "MaKayla, you have to stop Cain! Break off his destiny!"

Colfax struggled to her feet, holding herself up against the church. "I can do that?"

"First, we have to find a way to get them down," Dr. Slider said, taking in the fighters in the sky.

"No, we don't," Mark corrected.

Suddenly, Colfax lifted into the air. A bursting flow of fabric encased her and then settled into a newly formed flowing silken robe. Her hair was braided into a crown, woven with greenery, and she wore thick jewelry of gold. She glided upward, one sandaled toe pointed to the ground, ascending straight for the fighters.

"No!" A ragged screech came from Lachesis, who took to the air in pursuit. "This is the way we regain our hold!"

"We got to stop her," Mark desperately pleaded from the confines of the salt circle.

"Hey, Doc," Skelton asked, "can you transmogrify into anything except a house cat?"

"Yes," said Slider, who was now a giant eagle, launching herself into the air. She flapped enormous wings to gain altitude, to fly after Lachesis.

Skelton knelt to frantically gather the objects within the

circle and stuff them in her backpack. "Listen to me, Mark, because this may not make sense. I think the Fates are finishing, like capital F Finishing. Their Fate instincts are taking over to complete their charge."

"'To complete their charge'?"

"It's their purpose to control destiny. And their purpose may be overtaking their sense of humanity. If I'm right, then MaKayla won't be in control anymore, just the charge of the Fate within her."

"What do you mean?"

"They're working to kill God. To use Aurora's summoned weapon to usurp control of this world. Because their purpose will force them, like mindless robots."

"Like terminators," Mark said.

"Maybe? Listen, we're not safe here, and I don't know how much that eagle-cat can do. I can try some spells to cool off the fighting, but I need you to take this and run." Skelton shoved the backpack into Mark's arms. "There's books in there that the Fates must not find."

"What books?"

"Books about how to start an apocalypse. How to end a god. The Book of Fate."

Skelton shoved Mark away, out of the broken circle. "Run," she commanded.

Mark obeyed.

Beth

Answering stupid questions with spite and sarcasm was easy. Ignoring the demon no one else could see, however, was proving a challenge for Beth. Puka whispered into her ear so closely, his breath moved the hairs on the neck. As she sat on the gravel, Parker played with the knife in his hands, walking back and forth in front of her.

"I can see the fear filling your eyes with tears, little lamb. Just command the imp to reveal himself to us, and it'll all be over."

"Do it!" his henchmen demanded in agreement.

"Command him!"

"In the name of the Lord!"

Parker's minions punctuated his every attempt at breaking her with moronic interjections. Beth would love to plan her attack, to work out in her mind which person to attack first, how to move among them. But she was outnumbered four to one and unarmed against much bigger guys. That didn't mean she wasn't willing to fight; it just meant it wasn't going to end well.

The voice hissed in her ear again, "They're going to kill you, Elizabeth."

The breath on her ear made her flinch. She plotted out the strongest guy, three strides away from her. They wouldn't be expecting an attack.

Parker crouched before her and said softly, "You don't have to bear this burden, little lamb."

"Yeah, you don't have to do it."

"Praise."

Parker resumed pacing, spinning the knife in his hand. His goons kept their eyes on him, nodding and agreeing. "We, disciples of Gods' End, will relieve you of this terrible demonic presence. We will relieve you."

"It's terrible!"

"Take him in the name of the Lord."

She leapt to her feet, planting one foot on the gravel, and launching herself toward the biggest guy. Another of the men slapped her hard on the back, swatting her to the ground and knocking the breath out of her.

"Why must you be so contrary, little lamb? Has this demon poisoned your thinking with useless hopes of rebellion? Freedom? That's not how this ends for you. That's not how this ends for any of us. This is God's End. We are God's End. We are the mortals charged with preparing the world for the Lord's returned glory."

"Amen."

"You can stand among us, in the Lord's good graces, welcoming him back."

"Welcome back, Lord!"

"Amen."

Drool leaking from her mouth, Beth breathed heavily in dry, coarse rock dust. A rough whispered laugh echoed. Puka was amused. Beth would be too if it didn't hurt so damn hard to breathe.

"Okay, fine. I didn't want it to come to this. I try to be a gentleman, gracious with my dominion over the animals, but you left me no choice." Parker called to one of his henchmen, "Harry, make the call. Kill the horse."

Her chest tightened as she gasped in more dust. Coughing racked her body as she scrambled to her feet. One of the men caught her as she sagged into his arms, tears burning her eyes. With one word, she summoned him:

"Puka!"

And the demon appeared.

Bazrael

Centuries of sword training dwelled in the young angel. Any armed human who died in the name of Bazrael's father would pass along their knowledge to His angels, and then the acumen of fallen crusaders was collected and distributed in the heavens. The teacher of all angels in combat, Michael, preferred the sword. And Bazrael was an exceptional pupil.

But the Creature wasn't present in those lessons. He was nothing more than a glimmer of an instinct then. The Creature had no practice, not in Heaven and certainly not in the physical world, not understanding practical motion affected by gravity, friction, and inertia. The being of rage had received Michael the Archangel's training secondhand by simply viewing Bazrael practicing swordplay during the few days he'd been on Earth.

And now Bazrael could only watch this fight from within as the Creature engaged his opponent.

Hulking swings and screaming strikes over and over with the sword were easily dodged or blocked. Sparks cascaded down with each point of contact. His combatant wasn't much better, the dark angel of Death reacting more than fighting. Panicking, flinching, ducking. But his massive strength and double weapons evened out the match.

Both giants swung about on clumsy wings, fighting to stay aloft as much as they fought one another.

With his body, his training, and his weapons, Bazrael would have made short work out of either being. Instead, he could only watch and wait. But he also felt. The muscle strain of swinging the heavy sword, the heat of too tight of a grip on the handle, the vibrating sensation each time metal struck metal.

And then there was panic in each reaction. The Creature

could not anticipate moves, so each block was a last-moment attempt to prevent injury.

One of the opponent's combination moves of one sickle after the next glanced off the biblical blade and skimmed the Creature's arm. Another time, when blades were locked, the dark Angel of Death kicked into the Creature in the gut. If they'd been on land to brace their bodies, the blow would have knocked him to the ground.

Bazrael understood they were losing, inch by inch. The Creature had nothing to fight for, merely lashing out. His purpose was not to win, but simply to fight. The opponent made up for what he lacked in training with dedication. He was relentless.

One sickle came down. The Creature brought the sword overhead to block it. Then the sickle turned, locking the sword in. That's when the other sickle swung in horizontally.

It was a perfectly clean stroke, slicing through the air for the torso, aimed to slide between ribs. The sickle would slip into the body and do unbelievable damage. A killing blow. A battle ender.

The sickle landed.

Suddenly, impact knocked both combatants back, flailing through the air. Some unknown force had struck.

The sickle had only touched the Creature's skin before getting flung away.

Spinning out in free fall, Bazrael could only make out gray feathers of the being who'd broken up the fracas. Who or what had dared attack two dueling angels?

The accomplishing strike was short-lived, for as soon as the Creature regained control of his flight, the sickle blade swung, and he barely raised the sword in time to block. The Angel of Death was upon him again, and again, the gray-winged interloper arrived. A bird of prey, glorious in wingspan, noble in ferocity, scratched at both fighters with razor talons.

Burning stripes of wounds opened on the Creature's forearms, similarly on the opponent's. He withdrew his sickle to swipe at the enormous bird, and the Creature took advantage, swinging his sword to slice the unprotected Angel of Death from groin to throat.

Just as the biblical blade made contact, sinking into the shadowed nether regions of the Angel of Death, the two were ripped apart once more. But this time, it wasn't chaotic. Neither combatant tumbled or fell. They were cleanly separated, parted aloft by an invisible barrier. The Creature was firmly held by the torso a good fifteen meters from the dark angel. Neither needed to exert their wings to maintain their altitude.

All were frozen in place.

Another party ascended, a human female floating in a gossamer aura of fabric. Bazrael recognized MaKayla immediately. She clenched her hands solidly, holding something invisible that controlled the duelists.

The enormous bird landed on her shoulder, settling its wings. Bazrael may have suspected a power within MaKayla, but nothing like this. She floated effortlessly while restraining the two aggressive celestial beings. Plus, it was impressive that the giant bird perched on her.

She addressed the dark angel. "Cain, listen to me."

Cain? Cain Morrigan, Mark's friend and MaKayla's lover? He was a Grim Reaper?

"You have to stop this, Cain. You have to listen to me. We're going to figure out a way to stop this. We're going to get Ora's help and put an end to this before things get out of hand."

But this Cain Morrigan wasn't having it. He startled and struggled, slashing his sickle against invisible restraints.

"Cain, please," she pleaded. But he did not abate. "Then I have no choice."

She bent the invisible grasp she had on them, wringing and cranking her hands.

Bazrael felt it immediately as the Creature howled in agony. The restraints tightened, squeezed, slicing through flesh. The Creature jerked and convulsed, flinging the sword away. Something deep within him wrenched and loosened, something physical and emotional. A pain down in his core, his very essence made pliable and vulnerable. What was this attack?

Tears gathered at the edges of MaKayla's eyes. The confident, funny young lady Bazrael had met the day before was now missing. Her grip twisted and pulled as she struggled with some invisible material. With each distortion, Bazrael's beastly body spasmed. As did Cain Morrigan, who'd dropped one of his weapons as well.

So when MaKayla Colfax was diverted by her boyfriend's struggle and the Creature was occupied with his own injury, Bazrael made his move, pushing to regain control of his body. With whatever strength he had left, the Creature resisted.

"I can't break it off," MaKayla grunted as her hands squeezed. "They're holding tight to their destinies!"

The more she worked her invisible control on them, the harder Bazrael pushed.

"Get ready," Ivy Skelton called out from dozens of meters below. "I've got a calming spell. It won't last long, and it'll affect you, too!"

Witchcraft flowed around the woman on the ground, swirling and gathering until it exploded out in fuzzy, soothing feelings.

Immediately, Bazrael's need to regain control ebbed. At the same time, the tightening restraints of MaKayla pinched. Something deep within him broke, shattered. Instead of being caged within himself, Bazrael was now surrounded by emptiness. The urge to fight, the need to vanquish Cain Morrigan, even the desire to fulfill his purpose all vanished. He wanted… He was compelled to…do nothing. There was no desire, no fight, no ambition, no mission. There was only Bazrael.

And all he wanted was to make sure Mark was okay.

The Creature himself went slack, his head lolling. Cain Morrigan also visibly relaxed, dropping his other sickle. MaKayla Colfax also went limp. Her hands lost their grasp on invisible restraints.

The trio plummeted.

The ground rushed up at them, gravity in firm control. Bazrael couldn't bring himself to care about impending death, though. He just worried about Mark.

The bird of prey screamed, wings beating wildly. This must have awoken MaKayla Colfax, who abruptly stopped her own fall, grabbed at the air, and yanked. The three of them paused mid-fall.

Bazrael took advantage of the lull, seized control of his body, and flew away.

Chapter 13

Mark

Running, gripping the straps of the backpack, not allowing himself to check behind him, he ducked into the woods by the old church road. But as soon as he left the witch's circle, the visions hit.

Screaming horses riding across the sky.

Humanity cut off from a god.

The Earth cracking open.

He shook the images out of his head in time to avoid tripping over a log.

Where was he even going? What could he do? He needed to see if they'd awakened Aurora, but she was miles away. He had to find Baz.

Mark and Aurora, united again, fighting three Fates.

A sword coming down over Bazrael.

Looking into Bazrael's eyes for the last time.

He picked up the pace, limping along on the slick ground. He had to do something. He couldn't depend on finding someone else. He had to come up with a plan of action. He slid to the forest floor, his back tucked against a tree trunk. He checked the sky; no sign of anyone flying overhead. He stilled his breath and listened for following footsteps. Nothing. Ahead of him, he could see the ground pitch down toward the old abandoned warehouses along the canal.

He unzipped the backpack.

A scratched-up old blue tin, promising cookies on the outside, but inside was just a collection of junk: hand-written papers, necklaces, rosaries, and some old photos. Held out to the light, the pictures were of some group of older kids back in the 80s or 90s. He rifled through the bag, finding the items from the witch's circle: a half-empty box of salt, some candles, a canteen, a bowl, a mug, a unicorn eraser, sticks of incense, an old bell. Everything except those fancy old scissors.

The only things left in the bags were books. One was a notebook, old and worn, thick from continual use, each page crinkled and heavy. The other book was hardback covered in wrinkly leather. In the cool moonlight, Mark ran his fingers over the material that somehow left him uneasy. In the center of the cover, a squishy little button which, as Mark held up and discovered, resembled an eye. The sensation set off nausea growing in his gut.

This book felt genuine, felt real. This eye was probably real. It was real, powerful in a way nothing Mark had ever touched was. This was knowledge, ancient and dangerous, bound in leather. A textbook for the magic that truly governed the universe.

A third Fate surrendered to her sisters.

A friend sacrificed herself to buy time.

Horses fell to the ground.

"Should you be looking through that?" Dr. Slider asked evenly, standing only a few feet away.

"If I'm risking my neck to keep it safe, I think I have a right to know what it is."

"You agreed to take the bag without knowing. Do you think the witch gave it to you thinking you'd snoop?"

Mark knew it wasn't worth fighting the shifter over it. "So what happened? With the whole angel/demon fight?"

"It's over. For now. Those two are destined to battle, so MaKayla may have only bought some time. What do you see in their future?"

"Just more fighting." Mark kept it to himself that he foresaw himself fighting Fates alongside Aurora.

"Did you try writing down visions?"

"I don't think now's the time for therapy. Group's canceled for tonight."

"I'm not talking about therapy. You have unique powers, Mark. Noting them in clear detail could help those fighting to save this world."

"*I'm* fighting to save this world! I'm running errands for angels and smuggling enchanted artifacts for witches."

"Do you think your ability to run errands and smuggle bags is what makes you special?"

"What?"

"You are an Oracle, Mark. You affect the world around you through prophecy. As much as I love helping people through therapy, I didn't break up a flying supernatural talk with a Rorschach test."

"What's a Rorschach test?"

"The point is, the way I can help the most, the unique way only I can contribute, is by shape-shifting."

"So?"

"So how can *you* help using *your* gifts?"

"I'm not going to sit back in a trance while the world falls apart."

"That's an oversimplification."

"No, it's not. You just want me to watch these visions and let my friends fight and die."

They were quiet for a moment. Mark watched the lights blink on the big domed tops of the old warehouses that dotted the canal. He couldn't see or hear the water from this far away, but it was there, always moving. Relentless.

"You know," Dr. Slider said, sitting on the forest floor beside him, "I've never heard you use the word 'friends' before."

"What?"

"Even when I was just your house cat, and you'd talk out loud. You'd refer to your teammates, guys at school, your dealers, girlfriend, ex-girlfriend. But never just 'friend.'"

The lights near the canal blinked in the cool blue dark.

"I like that. That you have your people you call friends now."

"Well, a lot of good it does." Mark began loading the items back into the backpack, putting away the letters and old photos back in the tin. "I haven't been able to find anything out to help Bazrael, and every time I look into Beth's future, all I see is doom."

Lights moved across the warehouses. Headlights and tail-lights, even though they were long abandoned. Nobody was supposed to be down there. All the teens in Lockport had been warned about hanging out in the old shipyards.

"I imagine it's better to be doomed with your friends."

If someone was down in the warehouses when they weren't supposed to be, surely it had something to do with this apocalyptic fight, right? Yeah, maybe there were still small meaningless crimes happening like trespassing or squatting, but him seeing movement, people where there weren't supposed to be, that couldn't be a coincidence, right?

Mark had to do something.

"Hey, do you think you can find Skelton, the witch?"

"I should be able to; I've got excellent sight and can fly over the whole town."

"It's a city. Lockport's a city."

"Okay."

"But you can turn into a bird again and do that?"

"I am exclusively a bird shifter now. Already, my feline traits are fading away. I can only transform between a human and a harpy eagle from now on."

"You...permanently changed yourself? To break up the fight between Cain and that demon?"

"Yes. I had one chance to change my animal form, a gift from a sorcerer who was honestly, pretty toxic."

"And you used that one chance just now?"

"These are apocalyptic times, Mark."

"Well, if you find Skelton, tell her I'm laying low for a couple hours. I'll meet up with her at Aurora's later."

"I will."

And then, with the sound of flapping wings and feathers stirring up wet leaves, Slider was the harpy eagle. A large bird with fierce, intense eyes and a crown of gray feathers. She beat her enormous wings.

Mark stopped her, adding, "And if you see a horse wandering around anywhere who responds to the name Anthony..."

Slider the eagle twisted her head, listening intently.

"I don't know...tell him to meet me at Aurora's, too. No, that's too suspicious. Tell him to meet me by the baseball fields."

Slider the eagle took to the night sky, silvery feathers blending in with the darkness.

Mark slid the backpack back on, then trotted downhill, keeping one eye on the sky and the other toward the abandoned warehouses below. He was headed either to lay low for a couple hours or to find more trouble.

Bazrael

Bazrael flew without urgency. He found himself circling above the empty Cecilia house, confirming what he already knew: Mark was not here. The All-Star was most likely still under the control of those witches. Bazrael had to keep busy. Even if the need to fulfill his purpose no longer guided him, even if the Creature within slept, he stayed alert to remain in control of himself.

It wasn't lost on him that he'd been disarmed and had yet to retrieve his weapon. It'd flung off somewhere in the night, maybe lost in the canal, maybe wrecking some family's roof. He wanted to search for it but could not risk getting close again to MaKayla Colfax or her dark angel boyfriend. Bazrael refused to allow himself think on it for too long. If he thought of it, he'd have to do something, maybe go back and get it. Face the fight ahead of him. That would happen soon enough. Too soon.

Just like the vacuum he felt when MaKayla cast the spell on the Creature and allowed Bazrael's escape, some part of him was missing without the sword. After all, Bazrael was nothing if not the arm to wield the weapon. That was his purpose, his reason for even being on this plane of existence.

And poor Mark knew none of this. For all of the All-Star's

foresight, he existed without understanding all of the current circumstances. He stumbled forward in life with only pieces of the picture to guide him.

An acidity bubbling up from his gut reminded Bazrael that he was the reason for Mark's ignorance. Mark was willing to help, to brave the world and whatever dangers, for Bazrael's mission. And in return, Bazrael repaid him with jealousy and dishonesty.

Of course, Mark had used him for personal gain. Bazrael had done the same right back. There was no time for relationships now, no opportunity for an equal back-and-forth of feelings. But Bazrael still loved Mark, understanding it wasn't reciprocated. And his own lying actions disgusted him. The sour taste reached up to Bazrael's throat until he was afraid of what would happen if it escaped. Bazrael descended from the airstreams.

He pried open Mark's unlocked bedroom window and pulled a blank sheet from a notebook. He wrote. He confessed. He unburdened himself, not just of secrets, but of feelings.

Since meeting Mark, Bazrael had experienced the thrill of competition, the burn of defeat, the anticipation of a crush, the warm comfort of acceptance and friendship, and finally, the unnerving anticipation of unrequited love. Bazrael hadn't truly been human before his day with Mark. Yes, he had a human body: soft, locomotive flesh, but it was just a machine to get him around, to play baseball, to bring him nearer to his ultimate purpose. That was before Mark.

Mark made Bazrael a human. Specifically, a teenaged human in love. So in accordance with societal rites of passage, Bazrael wrote an embarrassing love letter.

Mark,

I've been keeping things from you. I was summoned to Earth by Aurora Marie Seitsinger to kill a god. But she doesn't know my true purpose is to fight in the final battle to end the world. I am the Ophanim. I am the weapon. I'm not a Cuban American high schooler who plays baseball. I am the catalyst to bring the biblical End of Days.

And I love you.

With the little time we have remaining before Earth turns to nothing, I'd like to spend it with you. I must warn you, that the creature inside me, my base instinct to engage in combat, is consuming me from within. The light is fading. And I'd like to utilize it to see your face.

Love,

Bazrael

fallen minor angel, son of god Iovvah

He folded it and clenched it in his hand, as he had no pockets in this angelic form and didn't dare risk transforming again. Then he leapt to the skies once more, determined to seek out the love of his life.

Beth

She had them. Beth confidently held all the cards, as she knew she had one last request of the demon she'd held onto for all these years. And when she made her final wish, Puka would be released unto the world.

And Parker and his goons were just standing around in awe at the beast. It's one thing to spend a life, or maybe just a couple years, believing in angels and demons. It was something else entirely to face one and try to think of something to say. Beth knew the sensation well and experienced at least a degree of it each time she encountered Puka.

Now the imp was before them, breathing in the air greedily like a starved man at a buffet. His long, hair-tufted ears flicked and twitched. A low, wet chuckle rumbled and jiggled his furred flesh.

Before Parker's minions could recover, Beth commanded. "Puka, my final demand is you to release my horse and bring him here."

A wide row of sharp teeth, mismatched in shape and color, spread across the demon's face.

"Then your hold over me ends, Elizabeth."

And with that, the evil little imp rocketed into the sky like a firework, instantly disappearing into the night.

All gathered humans stood in silence, lit only by a distant streetlight and the flashing red atop a nearby silo.

One goon exhaled in disbelief, shaking his head with a crazed smile, until he finally said, "I can't believe it."

Beth reveled. She'd beaten them. Whatever they wanted from the demon, they weren't getting. And whatever they did to her, at least Anthony would be safe. She'd won.

"It worked, Parker," the goon continued. "Exactly like you said."

What? Exactly like he said? What'd he say? Why would Parker spend so long forcing her to summon Puka if he planned on her releasing him? Unless... All Parker wanted was Puka's release, not his subservience.

"Of course it worked. Believe in the Lord. And there comes the fruits of our labor."

A clopping crunch in a slow, steady rhythm grew louder and louder. Beth recognized the sound; it was horse hooves on dirt and gravel. At last, she'd see Anthony, at least one last time.

"Amen," another of Parker's followers whispered as a white figure turned a corner.

Everyone stood dumbfounded.

Beth couldn't believe her eyes. This wasn't Anthony. This animal was taller, broader, maybe a draft horse, and completely dead. In glowing white, covered in flowing tatters of sheer ribbon, cloth, or flesh, walked the skeleton of a horse. Grotesque bones grinded with each jerky step as it approached with unnatural motion.

A hand wrapped around Beth's wrist, but she couldn't tear her eyes away from the horse skeleton.

The sharp, long face with the uncanny smile of a naked skull stared into Beth's soul with dark, empty sockets. No, not Anthony. Something worse.

The hand grabbed Beth and pulled her away from the bony beast. She turned to see Mark, crouching with a finger over his mouth to keep her silent, backing her away. Either he didn't see the apparition or he was somehow unfazed. But she followed him back, creeping slowly until they sprinted around the building across the darkened grass.

Mark limped along slowly, but Parker and the goons hadn't seen them escape. Beth could see a hole in the fence ahead that could get them to the trails along the canal and to freedom.

They hurried as fast as they were able, the weeds sprouting through gravel thankfully kept their footsteps hushed. The triangular exit within the fencing promised safety. Then she could find Anthony. Then she could stop all this. Just a few feet away...

"Ask, and the Lord shall provide," Parker's voice boomed from behind them. Beth turned to see how close he was, how much distance was there to still allow them to escape. He was pretty far back, silhouetted at the corner of the building. He wasn't chasing, wasn't pursuing them. They could do this. They could get away.

Then a shadow appeared ahead of them. A figure standing in the way of the parted chain link fence. One of Parker's goons.

"Amen," he growled, closing in on them.

Mark

They kept him on his knees. Trapped. Helpless. Once again useless. But if Mark fought back now, he'd get himself and Beth both killed.

One of his captors, most likely the leader, paced back and forth, admiring the ghost horse as he spun a knife in his palm.

The horse was terrifying, bones bleached white with flaps of see-through flesh dangling off like broken netting. Its face, without any skin or eyes, seemed to be in an intense sneering stare, looking into Mark's soul no matter where the skull faced. Its hoof pawed at the dirt.

Horse hooves galloped, touching nothing but air as the four horses neared the ground.

His breath quickened as he swallowed hard and fought to control the visions.

The ghost of a horse followed Anthony as they flew down to Lockport.

The leader of the kidnappers was talking, but Mark couldn't follow. He knew once the horses in his vision landed, it meant the end of all life.

They weren't alone in the sky as rope and twine cross-crossed, directing the limbs of flying creatures fighting with weapons.

Mark jumped as he envisioned blade crossing blade. The final battle.

Manipulating the ropes and controlling the fighters, three women pulled and twisted. MaKayla Colfax, that weird lady Lachesis, and Ivy Skelton.

Were their ropes attached to the fighter's wrists or wrapped around Mark's body? He was soon out of breath, gasping to fill his lungs, sweat streaming down his face in rivers.

The car trunk was so hot, the sweat and smoke stung his eyes.

That wasn't right. Mark was outside, with Beth, on his knees.

No, he was drowning.

No, he was watching angels and Fates fight to destroy the world.

He couldn't breathe. Each time he opened his mouth, more water poured in.

The snow soaked his socks and needled his feet. But it wasn't snowing.

He couldn't see where he was going. He was never going to see anything again. The ghost horse's empty black eyes looked through him.

He was going to die out here.

"Hey, are you okay?" a voice called from somewhere. Beth.

He answered. Or maybe he couldn't because he was drowning.

Or was he in the snow?

Or was he in the car on fire?

Or was he riding through the air to bring a sword down on Bazrael?

"Mark, are you okay?"

Her hand fell on his arm. He wasn't in danger. He wasn't dying. He was here.

"Tell us, Prophet!" the head kidnapper was roaring, arms up to the heavens, his co-conspirators all kneeling around him in prayer with eyes closed.

"Tell us the way to find the horsemen!"

No men, just horses.

"Yes, Prophet! Tell us how to summon the horsemen!"

"Summon them!" another cried out, clasping his hands.

The warhorse when the three-sided battle begins.

"Amen!"

Was Mark saying these things out loud or just envisioning them?

Conquest when the Earth breaks.

"The Prophet speaks the word of God!"

Famine is already among us.

With one hand up to the sky and the other held out to Mark, the leader of the kidnappers asked, "And what will the Lord have us do to prepare for His coming?"

Mark looked into the futures of the gang of men but only saw blood. Lots of blood in a short amount of time.

"Tell us, Prophet!"

"I see," Mark began, squinting through the blood and screams, reaching farther into the vision. "I see all of you dying."

"Yes!" the leader boomed, "We will die in the final battle for His glory!"

"No," Mark said. "You die way before that."

"Wait, how long before that?" Mark recognized one of the henchmen as Teardrop, the guy who'd pulled a gun on Baz in the alley.

"How long until the end is upon us?" asked the leader.

"The final battle happens," Mark said as he came to the

realization, "in a few hours."

"So, when do we die?" The assistant kidnappers were no longer kneeling, praying, or closing eyes. They stood around Mark, barking questions.

"We don't get to see the final battle?"

"Do we even see the Lord?"

"Brothers," the leader scoffed, regaining control of his crew, "Fear not, for we have a righteous charge. The Lord decides what and what not to reveal to His prophet, and we know we are crucial to that final battle, and we shall be validated as the apostles of Gods' End!"

"But he says we die first."

"Don't believe him," the leader said. "And open up that bag of his. Let's see what other truths and falsehoods he conceals."

They did so, dumping out the contents and then rifling through the books and artifacts.

"It's just his school bag," one of the kidnappers grumbled. "He's just a kid."

"Do not be fooled. The Lord's message to us is everywhere. All around us, He brings us news of our glory to come!" The leader approached the ghost horse with arms open in victory and showmanship.

While they rifled through, not noticing the ancient leather book of witchcraft, the leader convened with the skeletal beast. He stood admiring it with the dead animal's sick grin while Teardrop scooted over to Mark and Beth, whispering, "How do we die?"

Then Mark saw it, clear as day, like it was approaching that very minute, "You get hit by a winged car."

Chapter 14

Bazrael

The town was so peaceful from above, warm lights across a puzzle board broke up with streets. Sloping hills diced up by road and highway. An artery of a canal running through it all.

From this vantage, Bazrael's fight with Cain, the dark Angel of Death, seemed years ago, the threat of the Creature overtaking him again hundreds of miles away. The only imminent danger was to Mark. The crumpled paper in Bazrael's fist comforted him, gave him courage. He would relieve himself, reveal his honest feelings, bring each part to light. And of course, Mark would accept the news in stride. That was how Mark dealt with everything—with a coy smirk and sly joke. Then they could face the end together. Maybe not as lovers, but friends. Baseball rivals. Humans who just did their best when selfishness got in the way. Bazrael wouldn't be alive for much longer, but with Mark, he could truly be human for a few moments of ecstasy before everything went dark.

He just had to find the All-Star.

Keeping low within the treeline, Bazrael checked the scene of the battle by the old church. He could still feel the ebbing stickiness of magic covering everything, coating the ground, hanging off the church. There was even the sensation of Aurora Marie Seitsinger, but it was just the faint whisper of an aura.

The night was quiet and cool, trees mocking and shushing him with each gust. The broken and remade salt circle was there, but no humans. No Mark.

Bazrael took off, finding the baseball fields empty. He moved on. Thanks to the ward still in place, he couldn't get too close to the Seitsinger house, but no sign of Mark anywhere else.

Fine. Bazrael would search as long as it took. Again in the sky, this time following along the roads. It occurred to Bazrael that he wouldn't recognize Mark from above. Hopefully, Bazrael could identify him from his hobbled gait. But just in case, Bazrael would have to land, hide, and get a good look at anyone he saw walking.

And then he felt it. That familiar surge of magic. The waves of incredible power that had drawn out the Creature. Back in his first encounter, the overflow had stemmed from a circle of witchcraft. The circle cast around Mark and the triumvirate who held him captive. Did they hold him still? Was it possible that power was Mark's now?

Bazrael felt it along the road until it grew and grew, and he saw the headlights sliding across the town. This had to be it. Mark had to be in that car.

Bazrael flew ahead and hid in the shadow of a tree, keeping an eye as the car drove by. Adrenaline and blood pumping. The crumpled paper damp in his sweaty fist.

But there was no Mark in the car. Just a girl, the witch. The bodyguard. Ivy Skelton. A sharp stringed instrument playing an independent tune. She drove right past.

For an instant, relief cooled Bazrael's tense joints. Then the creeping idea hit him that he may not find Mark until it was too late. Maybe he wouldn't see him before the end. Maybe he wouldn't see him before the Creature took back control.

A screech pierced the night's shushing silence. A car door creaked open. Footsteps grew louder: curt, direct tapping approaching, purposeful strides on cement. Bazrael retreated further into the shadows, spread his wings, crouched, and launched himself into the air.

"Oh, no you don't," quipped a voice of gravel and fury.

He was jerked out of the air and pulled to land with an ungraceful thud on the ground. A flash of red filled his vision. Air crushed from his lungs. Rust stung his tongue.

"I knew it was you. Your strings are different!"

It was her, Ivy Skelton, though in full, colorful makeup. Colorful as in pink and black. A patch of blush like a cloud of sunburn over her nose and cheeks. Heavy black eyeliner, dotted drawn-on freckles, and lipstick. She was pink and black and steaming angry.

"Where's Mark with my bag?" she demanded.

"I don't know."

"Where's Cain Morrigan?" she pressed further.

"I don't know."

"What is that blue sword sticking out of your chest?" she asked with surprised curiosity.

"What sword?"

"What do you mean, 'what sword?' That giant sword sticking out. That oversized anime blade!" Ivy Skelton brushed hair from her face, almost stabbing herself with the scissors she gripped.

"I know many ancient swords, but I do not know Anne-ee-may."

"Anime."

"Like the cartoons?"

"The sword in your chest right below where all those ropes and strings are coming out!" She sounded crazed, voice cracking, pointing wildly at him with shears, double blades her own, in hand.

He put his hands up in surrender, one still clutching the note. His wings folded behind him. "I don't have any sword or any strings," he said slowly and gently.

"Then you have the strangest Fate I've ever seen," she replied.

Beth

It would all be over soon. They had no use for her anymore. They had that abomination of a horse cadaver. They obviously never needed Puka, who was off wreaking who-knew-what havoc on Earth. And they had Mark, who was somehow their endgame in whatever messed up apocalypse cult plans they had.

She couldn't help but think of Anthony. She hoped he was safe. She hoped he wasn't in any pain. Anthony obviously didn't experience the world exactly the same as a horse would, nor with the complete understanding of a human. It must have all been so confusing. He shouldn't have had to live like this. It was wrong to do to a horse. Wrong to do to a friend. She'd been selfish. Yeah, lonely and isolated, but that was just when she'd made her wish. She'd kept it up for too long after that. It must have been so scary for Anthony to live like that.

She deserved this. Being held captive by these ignorant goons was her punishment for a life of confusion she'd given the one thing she loved. The one friend who loved her back.

Parker's goons picked up around them, stuffing candles and trinkets back into Mark's bag. But there were also books: a spiral-bound school notebook and an antique red leather-bound hardback. That book was special, different. The cover was wrinkled and creased, the reddish leather miscolored and splotchy, and in the center, a glossy eye. It appeared focused, alive. But these goons tossed it into the bag like it was her chemistry text.

What was it that Mark had in this bag? She knew all too well how innocuous-looking items could house powerful witchcraft, just like Puka's amulet. Over the past few days, while Beth was deeper and deeper in trouble with Parker's cult, was Mark gathering weapons to fight off the apocalypse? Had he come to save her armed?

She looked to him, to grab his attention with a stare, to silently ask about the book. But Mark was out of it. It was like seeing him slip into one of his visions, only more desperate, feverish. Sweat soaked a ring around the neck of his shirt. His eyes were wild, open, but unfocused. His usually conceited smile was pulled back in unbridled agony.

"Famine is already among us..." Parker paced around the skeletal horse, muttering to himself. When he reached out to pet its skull, it retreated. Good to know Beth wasn't the only one sickened by his touch. He still held her knife in one hand, and with the other, he withdrew her necklace from his pocket, the gem-eyed horsehead amulet.

"The final battle," Parker said to himself, considering the

two items as if they held an answer. Then he placed them both in one hand, gripped the knife, and sliced the tip of his finger. Beth winced, either from imagining the sensation or flinching from the power he was summoning.

Parker pushed a red bead of blood out of his finger, whispered some prayer to himself, and smeared the horse amulet.

Beth braced herself. Was this how Parker gained control over Puka? Now that Beth was no longer necessary to whatever plan their little cult had in store, she was certain any summoning would end with her demise. She prepared herself.

Silently, she said goodbye to Anthony, trying the failed mind link once more. Goodbye and apologies.

With a shaking, shuddering breath, she whispered, "Thank you for being my friend, Mark." though he seemed unable to hear anything.

And she reached out with her very being to send love to her family, sorry that she'd failed them on some level and had been unable to be the daughter and sister they expected.

Parker exhaled and opened his eyes. He searched the skies around them. His goons joined, all looking toward the heavens. But nothing came. At least, nothing from the heavens.

A little gray sports car with a wide-reaching wingspan of white feathers tore through the fence and plowed over several goons.

Chapter 15

Bazrael

The blood spraying up from the impact riled the Creature in Bazrael. He stuffed it down, dividing his focus on chaining the entity within him while navigating the chaos in the old, dusty parking lot.

He leapt from the roof of Ivy Skelton's small now-red car into a throng of stunned humans. In his periphery, he saw hostages on their knees.

A surge of excitement rose within him as he identified Mark.

Ivy had been correct that one of the invisible ropes she sensed from Bazrael's chest would lead them to him.

Fist clenched around his confessing love letter, he flew into punches, knocking men to the dirt. Each impact, every hit and kick, invigorated the Creature within him. The kidnappers fell easily, even as they fought back. One pulled a knife, drove it into Bazrael's chest, but the tip of the blade chipped off on contact.

That man was repaid with a backhand that sent him flying five meters away. "Get the righteous armaments!" he yelled from the ground.

Bazrael launched himself, tucking his feet in midair, then landing them squarely on the human's chest. He flew back too many meters to count, tumbling to where the two hostages remained kneeling.

A searing pain sliced into Bazrael's shoulder. Human pain that Bazrael hadn't felt before. Freezing air stung inside his flesh while his skin burned at the rip. Blood trickled down his arm. Bazrael followed the trajectory of the object and then saw an arrow whiz by and ping off the concrete of a building behind him.

The human who fired the projectiles shook as he reloaded a crossbow decorated with crosses and various religious imagery. The Creature surged. He would kill the man with the crossbow. With each step forward, he was more assured he would destroy the physical body of the puny human. The Creature smiled his rows of teeth as his talons enveloped the man's delicate head.

"Be warned, enemy!" Behind, the leader of the humans stood once more, now with the chipped knife to the neck of the human girl. "For I am an agent of wrath!"

The Creature had never laughed before, but this new sensation overtook his physical form, grinning wide, stretching his face to agony as he shuddered uncontrollably. It was funny.

The human whose head he clutched behind had managed to reload his crossbow and fired. A dart of sizzling agony ignited the Creature's chest.

The Creature, still mesmerized by the sensation of laughter, had let his guard down just enough to allow for his own demise. Pain scorched from within his body. Enraged, the Creature squeezed the human's head in his hand until his talons met his own palm with a satisfying, wet pop.

The leader human's eyes grew wild. He was now the only opponent standing and the only possible target for fury. The Creature pulled the sacred bolt from his chest and tossed it aside, though the pain within him spread. He was losing strength fast. But even if the Creature wouldn't live to fulfill his destiny dueling over the End of Days, he could at least end this human.

Panicking, the human threw the woman down to land on her face before grabbing Mark.

The hostage-taker now had his knife on Mark.

Bazrael burst through, on top of the human leader before even completely shifting. His hands still a collection of elongated black talons, Bazrael grasped the man and ripped him in two.

Mark fell.

Blood splattered on Bazrael's naked torso.

Thunder roared in the distance.

Bazrael, no longer feeling the injury to his chest, scooped Mark up. Mark caught his breath, blinking away at the blood sprayed on his face. Bazrael cradled him in his enormous angelic arms as if holding an injured child.

"Oh my God, thank you so much!" the other hostage sobbed.

"Alright, everybody in the car," Ivy Skelton said before throwing a piteous glance at Bazrael and adding, "Everyone who can fit. We've got to see if we woke Aurora."

Mark gazed up at Bazrael blankly, as if he couldn't quite see. His face, usually brimming with expressions communicating his thoughts, was now frozen in slack neutrality. A mannequin's face. Lifeless.

"No," Bazrael said defiantly. "He's been through too much."

"Well, I'm going to check on her," Ivy Skelton announced as

she grabbed and shouldered a backpack.

"I've got to find Anthony," the other hostage said before clarifying, "My horse. He's got a part in this apocalypse."

"Well, the gears are turning fast now," Ivy Skelton said as she opened the car door of her bloody and dented vehicle before addressing Bazrael. "You've got to avoid any fights. Maybe hide for the rest of the night until Mark is better. We need time to devise a plan to stop all this."

"'The warhorse when the three-sided battle begins,'" the other hostage said.

In Bazrael's arms, Mark stirred, shaken awake by the woman's words. His eyes darted to her.

"What?" Ivy Skelton asked from next to her red-streaked and spider-webbed windshield.

"It's something Mark said." The hostage paused, looking at each of them before seemingly deciding to continue. "From his visions. The horsemen of the apocalypse."

Mark put a hand on Bazrael, strong and steady. Determination clenched in his eyebrows as his face and body revived. Bazrael released the All-Star to stand on his own.

"Horses," Mark said. "Not horsemen. Four horses of the apocalypse will gather in the sky. When they land, it's over."

"Already summoned one." The hostage looked down at the dirt, as if ashamed of something. "A zombie horse. It ran off when your car crashed in."

"Beth is right," Mark said. "We have to find her horse, Anthony. He'll be the leader of the four horses."

Ivy didn't move. "We have to get Aurora and see if she can stop this."

Mark paused, taking in Ivy Skelton with intense scrutiny. The world stopped and waited for Mark. "Why are you dressed like an anime girl?"

Suddenly embarrassed, Ivy Skelton may have been blushing, but it was difficult to see with her bright pink makeup. "Nothing. No reason. I'm just headed to see her."

"Dressed like a Tokyo goth chick?"

"Enough. I was just... I wanted to look nice in case—"

"In case you had to join a Japanese death metal band?"

"In case I had to give her true love's kiss!"

The idea hung in the air.

"Is that a thing?" the hostage Beth asked.

"No," Mark and Ivy Skelton answered with finality.

Bazrael steered them back to their problem. "If this Anthony is the key to the apocalypse, we should all focus on finding him first. I shouldn't hide when I can search from above, and with our only car, you can go to Aurora Marie Seitsinger *after* we locate the horse."

"I can't," Ivy Skelton insisted. "She's...she's my girlfriend. I need to check on her."

Bazrael immediately understood, though he lacked the words to say so. The social connections of American teenagers were exhausting.

"There are more ways to find Anthony," Ivy Skelton said, like an admission. "A summoning spell. If you three can follow instructions and start it. But you have to believe."

Mark softened, putting a hand on Bazrael's arm. "And we can keep you safe while doing it."

It was a tender moment that took Bazrael by surprise. And judging by the looks of it, Ivy Skelton, too.

Beth broke the silence. "So, what's the plan?"

Mark said, "We need a ride to the baseball fields."

"Fine," Ivy said. "I'll drop you off on my way. On the roof, big guy."

Mark

Mark repeated it back as best as he remembered, "Bowl of water for water, candle on fire for fire, a bloody blade for life, and for some reason, bread for Earth."

"Don't mock," Skelton scolded as she sped along the empty streets. "Belief is the most important ingredient. And you'll need a blade."

"Why can't we just use yours?" Mark wanted to say more, to point out the pair of scissors that Skelton was white-knuckling even as she held the wheel to drive. Those scissors acted as the blade in the circle earlier cast.

"I've got one," Beth said quietly. She hadn't been talking too much, and Mark didn't blame her. He'd been held against his will before. Captive. Helpless. It messed with your head.

"Good. It should have special meaning for you, though. There has to be an item someone in the circle has an attachment to."

Beth chuckled. "Don't worry. It does," she said, as if she'd expand on how whatever blade meant something to her. But Beth didn't say anything else, and nobody pushed.

Mark looked up out the moon roof to confirm Bazrael was still firmly attached. He was. A layer of safety for the car, a badass killer keeping a lookout.

Mark wished Baz wasn't stuck outside as it started raining, but not much could be done for that. But, who knew? Seemed as though everybody had some kind of magic these days. Maybe there was a weather wizard or a water bender in his friend group somewhere.

"Good," Skelton confirmed again. "Beth, you'll have to lay down the salt. You can't complete the circle until we're all there, and it needs to be big enough to hold all of us plus Aurora—"

"And Slider," Mark added.

"Dr. Slider?" Beth asked, "Our therapist?"

"Yeah," Mark said. "She's also a shifter. A hawk, I think. She's out there searching for Anthony, too."

"Good."

"Give me the notebook out of the bag," said Skelton.

Mark rummaged through and handed it to her.

"I'm trying a new spell to keep the Fates off my tail. I'll refresh it, maybe add another ward, but that might mean no one will be able to see me when I join up with you guys later."

"But we'll see Aurora."

"Hopefully," Skelton said. "Then she'll summon a solution to everything, and we won't even need the circle."

Aurora was the answer to all of it. Mark had witnessed his ex's powers, had felt the brunt of it himself. Aurora's magic was the grand slam that would save everyone and everything. But like Skelton had said, she needed believers. Mark took a breath.

"Okay," he declared, "before this goes any further, there's something I need to say, to get off my chest."

"Here it comes..." Skelton rolled her eyes.

Why would she give him crap when he was about to speak based on her own advice? Did she think so little of him? Was he just a joke to her?

"What's that supposed to mean?"

"Look, Mark, you're a nice guy. You've come a long way since

I met you. But is now the time for a big coming out speech?"

Mark wasn't considering what he was saying was a coming out speech. Unless… Did she mean that she thought Mark was gay? That he'd be announcing it *now*? Like Mark would take the time in the middle of an attempt to save the world to have some touchy-feely sit down about his sexual identity? What an insult. He wouldn't even dignify it with a response. Besides, Mark wasn't gay. Why would anyone think that?

Then Mark looked up at Bazrael, at his angelic physique, remembering his raw power while killing men with his bare hands, and how safe Mark felt when Bazrael held him.

No, Mark wasn't going to dignify Skelton's jab with an answer. Instead, he went forward with his proclamation, moving to kneel in the cramped car, wedging his elbows between driver and passenger as he clasped his hand in a solemn gesture. He wasn't quite sure what to say, so he let his heart lead.

"I, Mark Cecilia, being of sound mind and body, do hereby pledge allegiance to the…idea of Aurora Marie Seitsinger, as a powerful…magical girl. And to her mission, for which it stands, I pledge myself, three time All-County and two time All-State baseball player with a career batting average over four hundred, as a follower and true believer of her power and might. This is my solemn promise. With liberty and justice for all."

Relief lifted off him like removing wet catcher's gear. He nodded to himself, proud of such a personal and spiritual gesture.

The others were most likely being quiet out of reverence, like seeing a death row inmate be baptized or an athlete swallowing his pride to sign to his original team. It was a powerful moment radiating throughout the car.

"What in hells was that?" Skelton scoffed.

"I also don't understand," Beth said quietly.

Mark struggled for words to describe the obvious. "That was...a pledge! Skelton, you said Aurora needed me as a follower! Well, that was it. I'm finally ready to dedicate myself to her. And hopefully, my unshakable dedication is enough to revive her."

His words hung in the car as they continued on.

The two girls burst into snickering laughter. Mark's face flushed with heat.

"That's..." Skelton managed through her laughter. "That's real sweet, Mark, but a declaration doesn't really do anything. You have to act, you know? And I don't think one guy's...pledge of allegiance can break a magical spell."

Beth added with a faint smile, "And the baseball stats were a bit much."

"You know what?! Screw you guys. I was being vulnerable and open and honest."

"No, that's good." Skelton stopped laughing. "Thank you for being honest. But belief isn't based on things you say—it's your actions. Your willingness to act for good."

"I released a demon!" Beth blurted out like she'd been holding her breath.

"What?" Mark and Skelton asked.

"There was a demon I found trapped in a river or a creek, and it spoke to me, and I made a deal with it to bring Anthony to life, and I trapped it into a necklace, then when the cult captured me, they made me set it loose, and it's all my fault."

"The necklace?" Skelton was confused.

"I started all this!" Beth gestured wildly around her. "The tribulations. The end of days. It was me."

"You didn't start it, Beth," Skelton reassured her. "No one person starts an apocalypse. Many, many people set this into motion. Myself included. But it goes back to my grandfather and his occult friends trying to get control over the gods. Listen, all of us try to control things we aren't meant to, try to subject the world to our desires. And we tipped a complex system of balance into chaos. But now, things are moving beyond us. And maybe Mark's onto something. Maybe the best thing we can do now is dedicate to control ourselves, our own actions, and maybe all together, we can...not control this thing exactly...but at least slow it. Negate our own contributions toward it."

"Oh my God," Mark exclaimed, jaw hanging in disbelief.

"What?" the girls asked suddenly, searching out their windows for danger.

He smirked. "I can't believe Ivy Skelton admitted I was right."

Beth

The baseball fields were quickly becoming a mud pit. Rain poured in steady, unrelenting sheets with intervals of lightning cracks flashing in the dark, wet world.

Beth saw no sign of Anthony or Dr. Slider. And no black demon wings circled overhead. But she couldn't sit around and wait. She couldn't stop acting to see if what she wanted worked out. This was bigger than her. The witch Skelton was right; they had to control what they could in order to reverse the damage they'd done. So they picked a spot in the parking lot, empty of cars, hoping that the blacktop would hold the salt without it dissolving into the grass. She focused on the task, helping Bazrael unload each item from the backpack and handing them off to Mark. The witch drove off on the hope Aurora could help.

Overhanging trees gave enough shelter to allow them to light the candles, and she handed Mark each item to place. Once he had all them out, she found something else within the bag, not the creepy wrinkly old book, but a photo.

Faded colors of people in their twenties or thirties, dressed in black, some in religious vestments, others in gaudy jewelry, standing in front of a homemade sign that read 'Scholars for Gods' End.' That was Parker's cult, but these weren't the religious goons who'd taken her and Mark. This must have been the occult group of the witch's grandfather. All young adults, maybe a decade older than Beth, full of smiles and joy. Dedicated to what they thought was a noble cause.

Not so different from what Beth, Bazrael, and Mark were doing.

Lightning flashed, and Beth took the opportunity to search the distance for friends or foe, a glimpse of people or animals, some glimmer of hope. Something did glimmer from the point where several baseball fields met. Some shiny fencepost, or maybe it was an aluminum bat, standing up straight, alone in a field of rain and mud.

No one was coming. There was no hope on the way, just the lone hope they had. A little metal post in a stormy field trying to catch lightning.

"There they are!" Bazrael the angel's voice ripped Beth's attention away. Squinting, she fervently scanned in the direction he pointed for a sign of a loping horse or soaring wings. Nope. Just people. Two figures walking along in the rainy night. Walking straight for them.

Beth knew it wasn't help coming. She knew they could only help themselves. She handed Mark the lighter for the candles.

"Hurry," she said. "Before they get here."

Bazrael

Bazrael bristled at the approach of the two women. Even from this far across the fields, he felt it. Waves of magic, stronger than Ivy Skelton's but not as strong as the triumvirate's had been. And within the wave was the residue of Aurora and the feel of the dark Angel of Death.

Where these women walked, Death followed. There would be no stopping the end now.

Mark just kept on working. He may have derided Ivy Skelton's instructions while she recited them, but he was moving with reverence now, carefully placing each object just so. Such a curious specimen, this human who could evoke such emotions in Bazrael. The simple act of adjusting the bowl, placing it just right, sliding it a little farther, ensuring it aligned perfectly with the other objects. It stirred something in Bazrael. Confirmation.

I love this man.

And time was running out. Time to spend together. Time to tell the truth. The women kept approaching, slowly plodding from a hundred meters away. Counting down in their approach.

This knot in his gut, this spiked heaviness, grew with each of their footsteps, hurting Bazrael, piercing him from within, weighing him down. Destroying him before he could begin his final battle.

"Mark, I'm the weapon."

Mark didn't look up from adjusting where a colorful little eraser sat within the circle. "What weapon?"

"The Ophanim. The weapon summoned by Aurora Marie Seitsinger to slay a god. It's me. I must fight Cain Morrigan, the dark Angel of Death, to bring about the end of the world."

"Baz, slow down. What are you talking about?"

"Aurora Marie Seitsinger summoned me. To end the world."

"Wait." Mark looked confused. "I was there. Aurora summoned a weapon to kill a god."

"My father-"

"Sure?"

"-is already dead. Or at least not alive as humans think of life. There is no god to kill. Just a dark angel and a fallen angel to fight."

"Cain doesn't fight you." Mark shook his head as if to shake out confusion. "He's fighting a demon. Beth's demon. I saw it in a vision. We all saw it."

"That was me. Another form, the part of me that's pure anger and bloodlust, the Creature within me, but it's me."

Beth's voice piped in, "The warhorse when the three-sided battle begins."

"What?"

Beth, small and unassuming, meekly answered, "That's what Mark said. He was in a trance. He said, 'The warhorse when the three-sided battle begins.'"

"So?"

"So..." she said, "Puka, Cain, and Bazrael. A three-sided battle."

It made sense, but Bazrael had never even considered the fight he prepared his entire existence for would be three-sided. An all-out war of millions he'd imagined, letting so much blood that the air would taste of rust. Then, recent events made him think the competition would be a duel, the dark Angel of Death's sickles against his own blade.

But a three-sided battle would be trickier, more complicated. Especially without his sword.

The voice breaking Bazrael's sequence of thoughts was gentle and meek yet sewed havoc. "Why did you lie to me?"

Bazrael staggered back, the question landing as a blow more powerful than any sickle or sword. His only defense was asking, "What?"

"I thought you were one of the good guys. I thought I was helping the side of good win," Mark spat the words. "You're on the wrong side of all this."

The spiked weight within Bazrael flared, cutting deep and dragging him down. Depth and pain.

"Mark," Beth began, but Mark wasn't having it.

"I helped you. I ran all over town for you on a bum leg. I got kidnapped helping you. Twice."

The Creature rumbled within. It smelled a fight.

"That wasn't his fault—" Beth started.

"You're the one doing this," Mark interrupted, pointing an accusing finger at Bazrael. "You're the one we have to stop. You're the key to this whole Armageddon thing."

"I can't help it," Bazrael stuttered. "I'm an angel; I was created to fight in the final battle. It was what I was made for."

Mark flew to his feet, suddenly right in Bazrael's face. "And I was made to play major league baseball!" Then he added with disgust, "I put my body on the line for you."

All at once, Bazrael had to struggle against the Creature, navigate his wild feelings, and fight to hold Mark's hateful gaze. A cornered animal, scared and suffering, with no other options, Bazrael fought back. "What baseball, Mark? Are you going to be a baseball player when everyone is dead? When the Earth burns to ash? Heaven forbid anything gets in the way of Mark Cecilia's future as a baseball player! Humans are selfish, but you're willfully ignorant. You'd rather be blind to reality than face the fact that you will never be a pro baseball player!"

All three of them gasped. Mark took the insult like a cut to his body, Beth an appalled onlooker. And Bazrael himself smarting in immediate regret, shocked that he could lash out with such venom against a man he loved. How could he hurt Mark? Especially when he knew what Mark endured: the physical agony, the stress of having been kidnapped, and the burden of trauma. But without thinking, Bazrael had attacked the softest spot on this most vulnerable human.

Mark swung his arm in a wide arc, a punch of full force with all Mark's weight landing perfectly on Bazrael's jaw. He felt each bone in Mark's hand break in a percussive cascade.

Chapter 16

Beth

Beth put her body between the two guys. Bazrael the angel stood aghast, towering and statuesque, with his perfect mouth fallen open, his enormous, deep eyes wide in disbelief. Mark, cradling his hand, crumpled to the ground, seething as tears streaked his face.

How were they going to fight the apocalypse if they couldn't stop fighting each other?

After a moment, it was obvious the two boys weren't going to talk or fight any further, so Beth set to task.

A candle had fallen over, as had a few other items. So Beth stood them back up, arranging each item as it made the most sense. She lit the candle, silently asking for it to stay lit as the rain continued.

She fished the chipped buck knife out of her pocket and placed it across the circle from the little colorful horse eraser.

Lightning flashed, giving the blade a dazzling silver shine smeared in blood. Something made it seem like the lightning wasn't random, but rather a sign that placing the knife had empowered the witchcraft in the area. Beth felt it. The air crackled and pressed against her skin. Despite the thick rain, it suddenly smelled of earthy olives and crisp, clean plant leaves.

The boys stayed silent, brooding and pouting like ridiculous children not ten feet from each other. Beth continued, emptying the backpack. She held the photo of Gods' End upside down so the rain wouldn't damage it. There was also a book, the hardback with thick, soft leather. She cracked it open by the candlelight. Maybe there was an indication of how to harness the power of these enchanted items.

But the book was blank. Empty page after empty page. Useless.

As she closed it, lightning flashed again. Set into the cover, a glass eye sparkled in the instant of visibility, and Beth was certain the eye's pupil shrunk.

Beth whipped her head around for any sign of the demon or Anthony. Instead, she almost jumped at the sight of two women standing over her.

Something was different in their presence. The wind picked up, tossing Beth's hair around. Only...the wind was an updraft, seemingly coming from the ground beneath. And the rain had stopped. Or at least, in the radius of the women, the path of each raindrop veered away so as not to touch them. The light of the candle flared, casting dancing shadows and illuminating sinister features.

"Tell us where Ivy is." The two women spoke with one voice, declaring out loud to no one yet, at the same time, forcefully interrogating each of them.

"You cannot keep our sister from us. We cannot hold the Angel of Death at bay for long."

Bazrael visibly flexed at this, squaring up toward the women, clenching fists. Mark, defeated in a way Beth had never before witnessed, stayed on the ground, hugging an injured hand to his chest.

"Don't know where she is," Beth said, as it was obvious the boys were useless. "What y'all want with her?"

"The wheels are in motion," the older woman announced. "Only the Fates can steer our path from here."

"You can't stop it," Mark muttered from the ground. "I'd see it if you could."

"My dear," the older Fate said, "we don't want to stop it."

"Once God is dead," MaKayla said softly, almost in a trance, "we can rule with fairness. Justice. Balance."

"God?" The angel Bazrael asked. "My father? He is already dead."

All eyes shot to the winged figure, jaws hanging open.

"God died?" MaKayla asked.

"One god. The last one left. Iowa," the angel sang the vowels of the name.

"Iowa?" Beth asked, saying the name of the state, not singing it.

"The one from the Bible?" Mark asked.

"Humans don't get many things right about my father. But He is no more."

"But you're the weapon to kill him," Mark said, pained eyes reaching toward the angel.

"You're the weapon?" the two Fates asked simultaneously.

"I am the weapon to strike against His side in the final battle."

Lightning flashed. Black wings outstretched in the night sky, diving for them. Beth pulled her knife, ready to fight.

Mark

There was no future with the Fates in charge. Mark searched each of their destinies. In an instant, he fell into the lives to come of Colfax and Lachesis. They would stand together with Skelton against him and Aurora. Sure, they could spin thread, measure it, and snip it, but only to fight, not to rule. And only until the end, when the battle in the skies was over and the horses landed on the grass of Lockport.

Then the Fates, along with everyone else on Earth, died.

So not only were these women wrong, they were also unable to see the future he could. But why did they want Skelton? Why was *she* their sister?

"You do not have to fight, Bazrael," Colfax said, calmly. "None of you have to stand against us." She knelt among the items of the circle, placed perfectly yet incomplete. She pulled out the leather-bound book with the eye in it, then handed it to Lachesis. Then she looked at the old photo of Skelton's grandad back in the 70's.

"I have this picture," she said. "How did you get it? Who's holding hands with my grandmother? I know him..."

But before anyone could answer, a black blur fell upon them, bowling everyone over. In the lightning, Mark could see a slick, ink-black figure with leathery bat wings and tall hairy ears, pounce on Bazrael. Before Mark could jump in to separate them, Beth leapt, stabbing a pocket knife into the demonic figure's back, stabbing over and over. With a quick backhand, he knocked her off.

But there, beyond them, stuck in the nearby infield, Mark noticed Bazrael's sword sticking up from the ground. Bazrael needed it to fight Beth's demon.

Mark rushed toward the nearby field when someone grabbed his arm. Pain shot into his broken hand. Colfax had him by the wrist.

"Don't do this," she pleaded, her eyes furious.

She didn't understand. Maybe she was thinking like a Fate, like Skelton said, only working for a chance to gain power. But maybe she could understand this as someone who risked everything to save Cain Morrigan.

"I've got to help Baz," Mark pleaded.

But her hold on him didn't budge. And MaKayla Colfax was somehow stronger than any other high schooler Mark knew.

"Mess with him, you mess with me," Beth growled at Colfax, the knife flashing in her hand.

Lightning burst through the sky around them, alive with violence. Beth brought the knife down onto Colfax's arm.

Instinctively, Mark grabbed at her to stop the blade. For an instant, the three of them were locked.

Light flashed, not lightning, but magic. The ground fell away. A high-pitched whinny broke through the air. When Mark regained his bearings, he found himself a good ten feet from the circle. Colfax and Beth had been thrown equal distances in different directions.

And shooting upward from the circle, leaving behind a streak of rainbow. A horse. White with a main of every bright color, tail, wings, and a horn. It looked just like the little eraser from Skelton's backpack.

The warhorse when the three-sided battle begins.

The winged unicorn from Mark's visions was the warhorse from the apocalypse, which had been an elementary school supply. And it was now flying into the air.

The sight was evidently just as unreal to everyone else. They all stayed where they were, looking up slack-jawed as it flew upward. Everyone except Baz and Beth's demon, who were still tussling, a mass of wings rolling on the ground.

So Mark took off, limping onto the baseball fields in the pouring rain. Pain jolted him with every step, pulsing up from his foot, radiating with each jostle of his hand. But Mark pushed for the sword, not letting injury slow him, not looking back.

It was the only way Baz would live.

Lighting flashed. Rain cascaded. His steps were uneven, shaky, and sliding.

But he got there. The sword stuck into a pitcher's mound at an angle. With his good hand, Mark grabbed the handle and pulled. The ground released the sword easily. Yes. He could see the future, Bazrael turning the tide of the battle. *Blade against blade, glowing with power as three winged figures chaotically battled. And Baz's glowing blade was the most powerful in the fight.*

But all hope drained from him when he turned.

Cain flew into the fray, and the three went airborne, one sickle sunk into the shoulder of each of the other two. Up, up, high into the sky.

And Mark helplessly held his sword on the ground.

"Hang on, Baz," Mark said. "I believe in you."

Beth

Beth searched the grass around her as torrents of rain poured. There wasn't enough light to see, and when lightning flashed, only slick grass shone, making it impossible to find her knife.

It had bounced out of her hand when she was blown back. And with flying horses, angels, demons, witches, and Fates converging, Beth had to be armed with something. Everything was happening, and so fast. Anthony would be here soon. She had to survive long enough to see him one last time.

The flame from the candle in the incomplete witch's circle was impossibly high, a torch taller than her, casting shadows. Bazrael and Puka were tussling in the sky, or was there another with them now? Mark had turned and ran, limping into the darkness. Beth didn't blame him. He was the only one who could see how this was going to end. Considering he dragged his injured body into the night, things probably weren't going to end well.

The women, the Fates, MaKayla and the older woman, returned to the circle to sift through the artifacts from the witch's backpack. Whatever they were searching for would help them end everything. And they had to be stopped.

Beth had bested MaKayla once, she could do it again. Even if one conflict was an art project and this one is biblical, Beth would do what she had to.

Headlights washed over them as a car screeched to a stop. The witch Skelton.

Did she know the Fates needed her for their heinous mission? The witch seemed like a smart lady, so hopefully, she knew what she was walking into.

The Fates stopped their searching of the circle, standing to face the woman emerging from the parked car. Beth's hand, raking the wet grass, came upon the knife handle. She pulled it into her grasp.

"I'm not one of you!" Skelton the witch called out to the Fates.

"You just don't know it yet," the older Fate replied.

"How did you get this photo?" MaKayla asked, holding up a picture from the bag. "And why is my grandmother holding your grandfather's hand?"

Everyone looked intently at the photo, the three women frozen in a standoff, sharing some deeper meaning between them. But Beth didn't care. She didn't need to understand. She needed to act.

She bolted, keeping as low as she could to sneak up on the older Fate, blade in her hand. She closed the distance quickly and stabbed forward.

Something caught Beth's chest, holding her back like a harness encompassing her torso. Behind her, MaKayla had her hands clenched on something Beth couldn't see.

She struggled, swiping the air with her knife at the older Fate, jerking to get free from MaKayla's invisible grasp.

"Is the horse at the other end?" the older Fate asked MaKayla.

At the other end of what?

MaKayla closed her eyes and placed both hands on whatever invisible item she held. "Yes."

"Then call him," the older Fate said.

No. Beth sent out the thought with her mind to her Anthony.

Without opening her eyes, MaKayla spoke, barely audible, "Come on, Anthony. It is time."

"Let her go," a voice boomed, so shockingly loud, even the chaos in the sky appeared to pause.

The passenger door of the witch's car opened, and out stepped Aurora in a long bathrobe, hair tied tightly back in a bun. Even the rain seemed to pause to behold her power.

"Stop before you get hurt," Aurora commanded.

"This won't be like last time, Ora," MaKayla warned. "We've grown too powerful and you're weaker."

"You don't get to call me that anymore, *MaKayla*. If you stand with her, we're not friends anymore."

The older Fate backed up to stand beside MaKayla, facing their opposition. "Transformation is uncomfortable, Conjurer."

She then placed a hand on Beth's invisible lead-line, which MaKayla still held tightly. She gave it a small tug Beth felt in her chest, and then the woman clucked her tongue, calling the horse.

Nobody calls my horse but me.

"Then stop," Aurora said. The sheets of rain continued down on the witch and the conjurer Aurora as she slowly walked up to rest an arm on Skelton and, with a wry smile, said, "Before I have to hurt you."

Mark

Why'd Mark hit Baz? Why did it matter that Baz was the weapon? Of course he had to keep it a secret; he was probably ashamed of what he was, of who he was. Now Baz was going to die thinking Mark hated him.

Lightning flashed, revealing a tangle of wings in the sky, the three fighters impossible to fully see. Baz could already be dead, shredded to pieces by Cain Morrigan's blades. Or ripped apart by Beth's secret demon. This wasn't good vs. evil. Angels, Reapers, Demons, Fates, and witches. This was so much more complicated.

The demon lifted the sword, chopping into Baz's shoulder. But it wasn't Baz, rather the unearthly presence that dwelled within him. Mark couldn't shake the vision of the future, of Baz getting chopped down. *Morrigan's blades landed in a solid impact into Baz's back.*

This was all Mark's fault. He had to do something, but he was just a mortal standing around on the ground. Watching the game from the dugout.

He'd been so selfish, always protecting his precious career, always putting baseball before everyone, before Mom's feelings, friendships with teammates, keeping Baz at arm's length, not letting himself give in to what he felt when he saw Baz. Not just Baz's strong arms, his kind eyes, the safety of his embrace. But the way Mark saw himself when Baz was around. Mark could see how Baz saw him. A badass, a hero, a friend, maybe more. Mark could never live up to the person Baz saw in him, but when Baz was around, he felt like it. Baz made Mark feel closer to being that better person.

But he was only a person, a mere human in this fight of immortals. Mark couldn't fight back. All he could do was believe. What had Skelton said? A declaration didn't mean anything—he had to act.

Mark had to act with his belief, with his support. Mark had to devote himself entirely to Baz. No half-measures. No holding back and hoping that one day he'd get his baseball career. Mark had to dedicate himself to Baz's cause. That was the only way to help.

Pain stung his shoulder. He'd rested the blade of the sword up by his neck, the edge biting easily into his skin. The blade was unbelievably sharp. Of course it was; it was a weapon of an angel.

Mark knew what to do. He'd give up on his own selfish

thoughts of a future entirely. He'd sacrifice his only power, the damn visions, at the altar of what he truly believed in. Something he knew to be true. Something he never thought he'd admit to.

"Bazrael," he said, tears joining the downpour of rain. Then he took a deep breath, bracing his body for the pain to come, and screamed, "I love you!"

Mark lowered his face to the blade. His breath hitched in his throat as the godly weapon sliced across his open eyes.

Bazrael

Searing agony, cold and biting, froze each limb as Bazrael took hit after hit. The two adversaries were mindless monsters: the dark Angel of Death wildly flailing with his sickles, the animalistic demon clawing, biting, and whipping his barbed tail.

It took everything for Bazrael to keep track of which way was up, to control his wings and catch currents in the tempest.

Claw and blade sliced into him, burning his arms in lashes. Just as soon as an injury came, it began healing, but by then, another assault cut into his leg, dug into his back.

Deep down, his injuries were worse. The Creature inside his mind wielded weaponry of his own, flashing memories of Mark's anger and disappointment. The scorch of Mark's words tearing apart his psyche.

Each attack from the other winged entities landed as Bazrael simultaneously relived Mark's connecting punch.

"*I helped you!*" The Creature growled Mark's words in a searing echo, clouding Bazrael's thoughts and slowing his reactions.

He barely got a forearm up to block a sickle just as his other hand grabbed the demon by the throat.

"I put my body on the line for you." Mark and the Creature railed within Bazrael as the animal demon's barbed tail stabbed into his neck.

He threw the demon back in time to block the Reaper's other blade. How long could he keep up this fight? How could he continue to stave the both of them off?

"Why did you lie to me?"

Why was Bazrael even fighting? Why was he putting his every essence, every ounce of strength, into surviving? Why survive if Mark Cecila hated him?

Claws raked across his back, causing Bazrael to let his guard down. The sickles buried into his chest before the Reaper tucked his wings, diving down, anchored by his own weight. The two of them plummeted, the demon following. Wind screamed as Bazrael grasped at his aggressor in a panic. Then the Reaper's wings fluttered, spinning them both into a roll, the world somersaulting around them. The dark angel's blades released. The world continued spinning. Bazrael fell farther, farther, faster, faster. The world spun around, from ground to rainy night to closer ground to rain, to even closer ground.

The impact burst within Bazrael, banishing air, electrifying his nerves. Pain ate at his muscle and bones.

There was no reason to fight back. There was no life Bazrael could have as a human that was worth fighting for. This world was only pain.

The ground beneath him swelled. Grass of the outfield rumbled and burst, cracking all around. A hot orange fissure broke open, revealing deep within the earth where falling rain hissed into steam.

Lightning crackled, not flashing and vanishing but building and coalescing. From the canyons developing around Bazrael came a swell of light, a convergence of the bolts of electricity, ever-moving but combining to take shape. Forming legs and a mass of light for a body. Forked bolts for ears. Bulbous light for eyes. Lightning forming a horse, galloping up and into the sky.

Meanwhile, Bazrael's body remained racked with pain, unwilling or unable to move. The ground beneath him shifted, and he slid as dead weight along mud and wet grass, falling into a hellacious crevice.

Someone stopped his fall, then reversed his course. Something had prevented Bazrael from descending into the ravine of melted earth below. Some force had grabbed hold of Bazrael's body and catapulted him into the air back after his aggressors.

The Creature. Flying to his purpose. One final battle to sate his bloodlust. Bazrael didn't care or didn't know, drifting off into the void deep within himself.

Chapter 17

Beth

The flashing had steadied. Not just the flashing of intermittent lighting showing winged warriors brawling in the air. Not the silver-white horse made of pure electricity circling in the clouds. Emergency vehicles had come.

Beth almost laughed to herself. What were they going to do? What use were firehoses, guns, and the jaws of life in a battle that was ripping the world apart beneath their feet?

Cruisers, firetrucks, and ambulances stopped not a hundred feet away, just adding to the chaos. In the distance, Beth heard the whinny of horses. Was it coming from the sky? Was the ghostly skeletal horse nearby, coming to join the others? Was it Anthony?

She prayed to see him one last time. Gripping the knife so hard that her hand ached, she understood what had to be done. Anthony was lost. He would either die a painful death as his stomach ate him from the inside, or he would bring about the end times. Just this once, she had to act selflessly.

Amid the hubbub of fights, storms, and emergency vehicles, women spoke calmly within the incomplete witch's circle.

"You are one of us," the older one explained. "You belong by our side as the balance of power tips forever."

"If we are cousins," MaKayla said to Ivy Skelton, "That's how you got your powers. You can see the connections and paths of mortals. The scissors have latched onto you. If you ignore your destiny, their call will drive you insane."

As the women talked out their family drama, the ground continued to rumble. Cracks spider-webbed out from the baseball fields, forming barriers between the first responders and the broken witch's circle.

"You killed Dineen Arkady," Aurora accused, "for trying to do exactly what you're doing now."

"Because mortals cannot wield this power!" The older Fate raised her voice. "We can't simply cut humans off from gods without something, someone to keep reality together."

Of course, nobody but Beth was paying attention to the sounds of horses. They were definitely not coming from just the sky. She searched for the sight of Anthony, scanning the fields where Mark now kneeled with a sword in his hand, beyond the firetrucks employing their ladders to scale the cracks in the ground. Then she saw it. In a deeply unsettling clockwork, the machinery of bones galloped toward them. The ghost horse.

Still, Beth looked for Anthony, catching a glimpse of wings, not from the airborne fighters, but an enormous bird, sailing across the parking lot, skimming the tops of the women, landing as a human woman in front of the scrambling fireman.

A woman in an oversized sweater and jeans, keeping the other humans away.

And sure enough, from where the bird shifter had flown, a familiar sight: the chestnut brown horse Beth's wish had brought to life barely a decade ago.

Anthony.

Beth took off toward him.

The women scattered.

Beth held the knife ready.

The Fates snipped at the air between Aurora and the witch Skelton.

The ground shook.

Just as Beth was about to reach her horse, to cut the life from him, her footing tilted.

The earth lifted. Beth fell, sliding on the uneven grass. Around the baseball field, an enormous circle of land had broken off, rising up in tiers like a lopsided wedding cake.

And Anthony used the shifting ground as a ramp, galloping up before leaping into the air.

Across the fields, the ghost horse ascended as well, joining the circle of horses in the sky.

Bazrael

There was no up, there was no down. No sky. No ground. There was only violence. Blood. Pain. Hate. A demon and an angel, both deserving of his brutality.

Bazrael could barely experience it, curled up within the Creature, each slice of a sickle barely a nudge, every bite from the demon's fangs a whisper from kilometers away.

The end was here. The battle had begun. But it was already over for Bazrael. His world had already gone dark. He surrendered his every bit of energy to the consuming monster raging.

Bazrael would miss his time on Earth. He would miss the frustrations of being a teenager. He would miss baseball. He would miss Mark.

Mark

He stumbled across the field, dragging the sword behind him, following the sounds of Aurora's voice.

"Ivy, no!"

Mark could feel her presence, power emanating from her. Aurora was awake, more than ever before. He'd seen a glimpse of her power before, tossing him off a snow hill like he was a rag doll. But now...now, she was a force of nature. It was time to work together, to save humanity, to save the world, to save Baz.

His perception narrowed, grew more acute without the use of his eyes. He sensed Aurora's magic but also the combined power of three Fates, now with Skelton among them. That was the reason for Aurora's cry. Along with the fight to save everything, there was heartbreak. Mark understood all too well.

Floating above, the Fates pulled at strings, puppeteering the winged gladiators. They drew in Morrigan's weapons, tugging while flying their deadly kite. And Morrigan's sickles came down, sinking into the flesh of both the demon Puka and Bazrael. They howled in agony.

"Ivy!" Aurora raised a hand to the sky and pulled at the girl with invisible force. But as powerful as Aurora was, she was no match for the trinity of Fates working in tandem, Skelton now held up among them with their web of connecting threads.

At the disruption of their puppet strings, Bazrael and Puka lunged at Morrigan, tearing into him with sharp teeth. Blood fell with the rain.

All the while, the ground continued moving. Mark climbed onto another raised section of ground, aggravating his ankle. It was a crawl, sword in his good hand while keeping his broken right hand curled in on itself.

Above, the horses circled. They weren't descending. That's when Mark realized his earlier vision had been incorrect; the horses weren't galloping down to land. The land was rising to them, and when the dirt pyramid reached them, it would all be over.

So on Mark climbed as Aurora threw wind and rain at the Fates.

"You're cut off from Ivy!" He screamed as he reached Aurora.

"What?"

"They cut you off from her," he explained, "but not from MaKayla. You two are connected. Reach out and grab that connection!"

Aurora did, wrapping her hand around the invisible cord between her and the Fate.

"Now what?" Aurora asked.

"Zap her," he explained.

Aurora's other hand reached for the heavens and summoned lightning. A bolt twisted down from the clouds, spiraling around Aurora's hand, chasing up the connection to strike Colfax.

She began to plummet, but not for long, as her fellow Fates grabbed her.

Meanwhile, the fighting grew more intense, Bazrael and Puka overcoming Morrigan. They bit and clawed, Morrigan's body striped in blood as he dropped one blade, then another. The demon ripped a limb. Bazrael, in a bloodthirsty rage, bit into his neck.

As he wailed, so did MaKayla and all the Fates. They drew his puppet strings taut. Fists, headbutts, eye gouges. A winged bloody mess. And the earth continued to rise, now a mountain overlooking their city.

Mark panicked, "Take their scissors!"

Aurora threw another outreached hand forward and pulled. The Fates struggled to hold onto their blades. The center of the baseball fields was now a spire, reaching up to the circle of horses.

"I can't!" Aurora grunted as she struggled.

What could Mark do? He saw no more future, could reach into no further vision to guide her. "Throw them at each other!"

With a twist of her hand, the Fates flew into a clump, knocking bodies. With a flick of Aurora's wrist, the mass of winged fighters flew into the mound, creating a sickening sound as bodies collided and bones cracked. Then, they all fell. Bouncing and sliding from the growing mountain, they tumbled lifelessly onto the ground below. No movement. No signs of life.

"No!" Aurora screamed, punctuated by lightning. The flash lit up the sky just as grass came up to meet hoof, and the world shattered. All went to dark, and then, nothing.

Chapter 18

Mark

Mark gasped to catch his breath, reorienting himself to reality once the vision had passed. His eyes still throbbed, his actual vision a bloody mass of red, dominant hand still useless and jarring pain, which at least distracted him from the torture of his wounded ankle.

"Ivy, No!" He heard Aurora call out over the sound of the swelling ground.

She had to be the key; Aurora was the only one powerful enough to stop this. But it couldn't be the way he'd thought. For so many years, Mark knew his destiny was with her, the two of them against the world. Now he knew that led to the end of the world, whether they were victorious or not. The answer had to be something else. Had to involve someone else. But who? Bazrael and Morrigan were in a dogfight with Puka overhead. Colfax and Skelton were under the control of that other Fate, Lachesis. And Anthony was a tool of the Armageddon now.

Was Beth still around?

"Beth!" he yelled into the night, tipping his head around to listen for a response. "Beth, where are you?!"

Aurora's own screams for Ivy paused. Maybe she'd heard Mark. Good. Perhaps Mark only needed a little butterfly effect to change the future he foresaw, but it was doubtful. Forces stronger than he could possibly imagine were at play, and he had to stop them without punching, running, or seeing.

"Mark?" Beth yelled back from somewhere.

Mark carefully limped in the direction of her voice.

"Beth!" He wandered blindly, feeling along a drop off in the dirt. He had no idea what to do whenever he found Beth, but he had to do something. Maybe Beth knew what to do. Whatever it was, Mark wasn't going to be caught looking. When his chance came, he'd take it.

Hands came to rest on his shoulders.

"God, Mark, what the hell'd you do?"

"I...acted," Mark said. "I blinded myself. For Baz's cause."

"Ain't Baz's cause ending the world?"

"No. It's to live. Even if he doesn't know it. Now what do we do?"

"What do we do? Mark, we're human. These are angels and Fates. What do you expect to do?"

"We have to do something!"

"Do you? Mark, this ain't baseball. There's no home runs to hit. You don't have to risk yourself. You cut your damn eyes out by doing without even thinking."

"I'm not going to give up."

"I'm not asking you to..."

The ground rumbled as it lifted more.

"Don't give up," Beth said, "just don't do anything stupid. Help me. I have to undo my mistake."

"What's that?" Mark asked, feeling her hand slide down over

his on the grip of the sword.

"I kept that bastard Puka on Earth. I released him. My fault he's here."

"Beth, he'll destroy you."

"I ain't afraid of no demon. I'm afraid of what I'm willing to do to stop him."

"I think I can pull Ivy down!" Another voice boomed from behind them. Aurora.

Energy poured off of her, cascading down over Mark.

"No!" Mark protested. "It won't work. I've seen it."

"What happened to your eyes?" Aurora asked.

Soft, long fingers cupped his face, hands that Mark had once felt on his chin, on his body, in his hair. Aurora. It was no longer love between them. But nothing would take away what they'd had, what they'd been through. They'd matured so much together and been there for each other whenever life got weird. That couldn't be cut away. Not by a Fate, not by the end of the world.

He felt soft fabric drape over his face as Aurora tied something to cover his eyes.

"We're almost high enough," Beth said with certainty. "I can reach Puka from here."

"Beth," Mark pleaded, "you can't give up like this."

"Silly, boy," she said. "Dying ain't giving up. It's just the biggest fight ever."

Mark released the sword completely to her grip.

"I may be able to hit them with wind and rain, knock them off balance," Aurora said.

"No," Mark refused, "that won't work either."

"Well, we have to do something!" panic rose in Aurora's voice.

"Another ten feet..." Beth said, voice rising with her preparation.

"Look at the connections. The way the Fates do. They're like ropes connected to everyone's chest."

"Okay," Aurora said before her voice dropped lower with recognition, "Oh, wow."

"Tell me what you see."

"I've seen it before, but this is more. So many threads and paths going everywhere. Heavy ropes between the Fates. One from me to Ivy, but it's frayed. Fibers have been trimmed away."

"Fibers?" Mark asked.

"Five feet..." Beth readied herself.

"They cut away fibers," Aurora explained, "part of the connection that makes us act because of each other. Ivy won't stop for me. Her connection to them is now stronger."

"I'm about to jump..." Beth said.

"Then repair it," Mark said. "And that's what they have to cut off from Iowa."

"What's Iowa?"

"Mark, I love you," Beth interrupted. "I know you don't love me back, and that's fine. I just...never loved anyone before, and I had to tell you."

Mark stuttered, reaching for words that weren't there, unable or unwilling to reject someone who meant so much to him at such a crucial moment.

He didn't have to say anything, though. "Here goes nothiiii-ing!" Beth's voice faded as she jumped away.

For a moment, there was only the sound of the storm.

"Mark, What's Iowa?"

"God," Mark said numbly, falling back to sit. Stupefied into not acting.

Beth

She flew.

Rain rushed by as the ground below rushed up. She reared back the sword, clasping it with both hands. She tried to remember how Mark taught kids to hold the bat. Hands choked up. Loose grip. Swing from the hips.

The tangle of wings flew up toward her, or rather, her toward them. She could barely make out where one of the biblical beings began and the other ended. Long spiked black fingers, animal claws, and bloody sickles ripped into flesh in a mass.

Lightning flashed.

In an instant, she saw Anthony flying high above. She hadn't seen him with such energy in weeks. High-kneed trot from his strong, lithe body. The energy of a younger horse.

"I love you, friend. I'm so sorry," she whispered.

And before the light faded, she saw him. Puka. The tormenter who had haunted her life for years. Her disgusting little secret she'd carried with her, ashamed to show anyone but unable to shake. A body of muscle and fat, tar-black skin shiny and wet. That disgustingly handsome face with long ears that turned her stomach.

She rotated her hips. She dragged her arms across her body. She swung the sword with all her might, the blade in a shining arc, slicing through the rainy air, coming straight into Puka's body.

The blade chopped into his side. He roared, disengaging from his fight, turning and grabbing her by the throat. He easily removed the sword with his free hand and held it. His eyes bored into her soul.

"Gratitude for the weapon, Elizabeth," he said in his Irish lilt as he swung it down onto her head, killing her.

The Creature

The blood sang in his veins as his heart drummed a rhythm.

The animal demon had fallen away. The women controlling the Reaper could not keep up. Even the Reaper himself was no match, for he feared pain and his own death. The Creature coveted them. Pain proved he still had time left to fight, and death meant victory. There was only fighting, no other meaning on this mortal plane.

The Reaper's blood was delicious. Rust, red, and salt. Sinking fingers into flesh gave a satisfying squish. But receiving the violence was even more satiating. His nerves burned, flushing cold as air discovered interior parts of his body. The sickles were especially sharp, opening the meat of his muscle with biting chops.

It wouldn't last much longer; the Creature had to savor each moment. His hands caught each sickle, sharpness traveling through his palms. He lunged forward, snapping for a bite of the Reaper's face.

This Reaper was tiring, as were the women controlling him. He was not meant for such glorious violence. Maybe originally, his form had such a purpose, but he had no passion for it. Passion for blood was the Creature's greatest possession. He pushed further, blades sliding deeper into his palms. The Reaper's face was closer to the Creature's long, dark teeth.

The Creature would enjoy devouring his body.

A tear across his back screamed. The animalistic demon had returned, now armed with a sword. The Creature twisted and yanked, pulling his mangled hands free from the Reaper's blades. Surrounded now, his opponents chopped at him with powerful swings, weakening his body and nullifying his limbs. One blow caught his wing, then another, and another. The Creature toppled. Good. The ground flew up to him. He soared downward, ready for the triumphant end to his campaign of suffering. The end. Good.

He stayed awake long enough to hear his bones crack on impact.

Mark

It was Hell sitting there. Mark could hear Aurora's struggle, tying up the parts of her connection to Skelton. Every few moments, she would check in with him.

"See anything yet?"

Maybe she was seeking his guidance. Maybe she was trying to make him feel involved.

It shouldn't have been so hard to do nothing, to let those more powerful than him act. But Mark had always acted. He always found a way to swing at a pitch. He never stopped working to quiet the visions, whether it was drinking, smoking, or drugs.

When he was inactive, he'd been held completely helpless, stolen and overpowered, tied and nearly drowned, left to die. After that, he worked even harder to fight, to constantly push.

Despite the world ending, everything was so peaceful. The

constant rain gave a gently shushing noise, blanketing him in constant warmth. The ground roared beneath, vibrating a calming buzz. Even thunder rumbled without booming or cracking.

The rain poured onto his head around the makeshift mask Aurora had given him, dripping down his cheeks into his mouth. The coppery taste was all that separated this moment from the memory of water forced down his throat, tied up, held captive in a trunk.

But this was not then. He was not being held against his will. And since then, he had grown. He'd gained friends.

He hoped Beth had succeeded.

He'd let go of his grip on Aurora. And she'd flourished without him, growing into some goddess.

And he'd found Baz, who was going his own path at the moment but would come back to him. He just had to.

"Help me!" Aurora called out, but Mark knew it wasn't for him. It was for the woman she loved now. She no longer needed Mark's help. And that was okay. He'd helped enough.

He could barely hear as Aurora explained to the Fates the plan: to take humanity's connection with Iowa, separate those fibers that made humankind act in fear or malice, and spin it into its own thread.

The series of directions was interrupted by an impact. A wet thud a few feet from Mark. It wasn't the Fates; they were still working out the threads connected to the god. Beth had sailed off the mountain to fight her demon a few moments ago.

So it must have been either Morrigan or Baz. Either way, he had to check.

Sitting had stiffened his joints, and he groaned his body back into motion. The injury in his hand throbbed with his heartbeat as he crawled on all threes toward the sound of the landing.

Then he felt it, a body. Wings and muscles, skin growing cold. He felt around the face, searching for the flowing hair that set Morrigan apart.

This was Baz.

Mark scrambled to feel for a pulse. But did angels even have a pulse in this body?

"Baz! Baz!" But Mark heard no answer. He poked and nudged, feeling for a reaction. There was none.

Baz was dead. Mark cradled his head in his good arm, tears singing the cuts in his eyes as he sobbed.

This was an angel and honest-to-God fallen angel who dropped right into Mark's lap. He drove him mad sometimes and filled him with feelings that confused his body. And Mark had been stupid enough to destroy his own eyes in some bizarre ritual of loyalty. It had been a swing and a miss.

Baz hadn't needed Mark to sacrifice his sight. He definitely didn't need a pledge of allegiance. Baz had needed companion-ship. And Mark had never given it fully. When Baz opened up with the truth, like a vulnerable wound, Mark had withdrawn his companionship completely. And now he was dead.

"You'll never know..." Mark sobbed, "I never said..."

He leaned down to press his forehead against his angel's and whispered, "I love you." And kissed Bazrael's dead lips.

Bazrael

The Creature whimpered a final breath, and Bazrael was resurrected. He gasped a wet, ragged inhale and looked up into Mark's face. A thin white cloth had been tied over the

All-Star's bleeding eyes, a look of shock across his face.

Bazrael was laid out on the slope of the growing earth mound, his head in Mark's lap. It took a moment to understand the situation, to piece together what had happened.

"True love's kiss," Mark admitted sheepishly.

Bazrael rose to kneel and embrace Mark, who flinched and squealed in pain.

"Sorry."

Bazrael's human was so delicate. *His* human. Mark had confessed his love. Mark loved him. And Bazrael loved Mark back. They were each other's. They kissed again, dripping wet from rain and blood, but they were alive, damnit.

The night was not over.

"What are they doing?" Bazrael asked, seeing Aurora had joined the Fates as they were cutting into some invisible item below.

"Hopefully saving everyone."

Above, the Reaper and the animalistic demon continued their battle, weapons now clanging against one another. Without steel of his own, there was no use fighting them. But that was exactly what Bazrael had to do. He stood.

"Where are you going?" Mark asked.

"To battle."

"But, you're unarmed, and Morrigan's out of his mind."

"And the demon has procured my sword."

Mark was silent for a second, the news sitting heavy on him, before stating simply, "You can't take them both on."

"I must."

"Why?"

"Because I am a weapon."

"No, you're not! You don't have to be. You can just be...mine.

Be my boyfriend. Even if the world ends, we can just...watch it end together."

Bazrael considered this for a moment. It did sound nice. What a wonderful means to die, a perfect perspective of the end of days, witnessing with the one he loved. But of course it couldn't be.

The combatants saw him, each falling into a dive, sailing down straight for Bazrael as they tussled, pushing and slashing at one another.

"Mark, I can't." Bazrael's throat went dry, and words betrayed him.

There was a moment of peace, the two of them touching, sitting on the hillside. For that instant, nothing else mattered. Nothing else occurred. Just two humans in love. It warmed Bazrael from the inside until his heart burned searing hot and his skin flushed. He could even see his own halo brightening.

"Mark, it's not working!" Aurora Marie Seitsinger, the summoner, called out from the air below them, where she and the Fates worked. "The scissors can't cut it."

None of it was working. None of Mark's grand plans would stop the inevitable. But it was good for humans to try the impossible. It was their way.

Mark cursed to himself, then shouted. "Break off his destiny! Bazrael's path! Snap it free from him so he can wield it!"

The eyes of the Fates glowed as they each threw a hand in Bazrael's direction. Their waves of magic flooded him, a directed tsunami.

The winged assailants were almost on top of them when the blue glow caught his eye. From his chest, as wide as his hips, a flat blue crystal, nearly as tall as Mark. It caught all light and bounced it back a thousandfold.

Bazrael's destiny. A wide but short path headed to one inevitability. It cracked, pieces of crystal crumbling away until the entire slab of it fell. Bazrael caught it from one jagged end and realized what his destiny had formed: a sword. Wide, flat, and blue crystalline.

The animalistic demon and dark Angel of Death fell upon him, swinging their weapons downward. Bazrael's wings unfurled as he stepped to keep Mark safely behind him. With the glowing sword of his own destiny, Bazrael batted away the attack easily. He kicked the demon, then jabbed at the Reaper, disarming one sickle. He blocked another offensive just in time to swing the destiny blade around and parry the demon's attack.

They were no match for him armed.

Even with the Fates failing, Bazrael could die fighting, protecting Mark.

Or...

If the Fates were failing because they were unable to cut something, could Bazrael help? Could the destiny of a fallen angel help penetrate their impossible obstacle? He had to act fast and get some distance between him and his attackers. And of course, he couldn't leave Mark here in harm's way.

"Climb on," he said.

"What?"

"Get on my back." With a grunt, Mark's weight fell onto Bazrael, an arm reaching around to hold his chest.

Bazrael swung his sword at the two combatants, backing them off, before leaping into the air. Wings beat, leaving behind the moving ground of Earth. He dove for the cluster of flying women, his feathers catching just enough air to sail directly at them.

The Fates hovered around Aurora Marie Seitsinger, who held

out both fists as if she pulled a rope taut. The Fates worked their scissors at the space between.

Descending toward Aurora, Bazrael held the enormous sword overhead and swung it down right where the scissors were biting into the air.

The invisible material, whatever it was, was unbelievably strong. It gave a little but didn't cleave. Bazrael felt it push his arms back as he realized he had no more strength or momentum to give. He'd failed. It was unbreakable.

Then, Mark's warm hand fell over his. Letting go of his grip on the angel's chest, Mark gripped the sword handle alongside Bazrael and added his own strength.

The invisible rope began to fray.

War cries broke out behind him as the demon and Reaper raced to catch up.

High above, the circle of horses screeched as the mountain reached up to meet them.

Rain poured. Earth bubbled.

Lightning flashed blinding white.

But not from the sky.

Aurora's gripping fists fell away from each other. The invisible material gave, and as it broke open, electrical energy burst.

Something collided with Bazrael's wings, knocking him down. He and Mark tumbled. The Reaper had fallen into him, but his eyes now held human recognition. This wasn't the dark Angel of Death possessed, but Cain Morrigan. On his face was a very human expression that hadn't been present for the fight. They both twisted in the air to face the charging demon. Sickle and sword tore the evil figure apart.

Bazrael dropped his crystalline sword, his angel's destiny,

to scoop Mark up, hugging him tight as they plummeted to the ground.

Dirt, mud, and grass cascaded down alongside them, collapsing from a rising mountain back into a patchy field.

Fissures in the Earth creaked shut as the orange glow from beneath faded out.

In the sky, lightning in the shape of a horse dissipated, reaching out across the clouds and chasing away into nothing. A pile of bones that had made up another horse tumbled down and clattered onto the grass. Next to it, a colorful eraser from a child's school supply box bounced away. And with a soft plop, a dingy, well-loved stuffed animal of a brown horse with expressive eyes and a big smile landed on its hindquarters, looking up at Mark and Bazrael.

Bazrael didn't let go of Mark as the rain died out and the sirens grew louder. They were soon encircled by fire trucks and ambulances. The Reaper, the conjurer, and the Fates never landed, escaping into the night. Surrounded by humans in uniform shouting attempts to help, Bazrael and Mark stood alone, holding each other tight.

And finally, in a moment of surreal peace, they shared in a white-hot kiss.

Two Months later

MaKayla

Officially, it was a deadly seismic event, the worst to hit New York State since 1944. One canal side building collapsed. The waterway itself had millions of dollars in damages. The baseball fields were devastated, including the field house, bleachers, fencing, and scoreboard. Mark Cecilia, named in the news as a local athletic phenom, was permanently injured, blinded by falling debris. And local hero, high school student Beth Sweet, who just weeks before had braved an unseasonal blizzard to rush an elderly citizen to the hospital via horseback, lost her life.

With national media attention, the rebuild was fast. Of course, the canals were fixed immediately. Then the baseball fields were stripped and graded, still a giant patch of gravel and piping for drainage. A new scoreboard went up fast, mounted on the new fieldhouse. And underneath, the city had commissioned a mural in memory of Beth. They were originally going to hire a painter who'd done an installation on Market Street until a local artist volunteered, a high schooler who'd known Bethany Sweet personally.

It was the biggest work MaKayla had ever attempted. Luckily, she had plenty of resources and help. Everyone in town practically tripped over their own feet to support her. She took Beth's own piece, a collage of her pet horse Anthony, as the subject. The result was an enormous blown-up portrait of the animal created from wreckage. Bent beams from the field house, fenceposts which had held chain link, and even rebar from the recently collapsed interstate made up a resilient mane. Painted shards of the old scoreboard fit together for the face, chunks of concrete filled in the animal's forehead star. MaKayla was almost done, awaiting one final element.

Cain had been with her every day she worked. He mostly read, gave opinions when asked, and made sure she ate. She was up in the cherry picker, painting sealant, when everyone started arriving.

Baz and Mark arrived first, Baz moving the caution tape and the set up chairs out of the way of Mark's walking stick. Mark tried to stop the hullabaloo several times. "Baz, it defeats the purpose of me learning how to use this if I can't feel my way around."

"The doctor said to focus on hearing the tapping as you walk. Listen for the sound bouncing. It's like echo-location," he added with a raised eyebrow to Cain, trying to impress.

MaKayla knew Cain hated encouraging the angel, and smiled at him as he ignored the approaching couple.

"I brought lemonade!" Baz announced. "It's sweet *and* tart."

"He insisted on making it from scratch," Mark complained as he settled into a camping chair.

"The children on our street sold me a cup the other day, but it was made from powder! They'd exerted almost no effort but demanded a ridiculous price."

"They're kids with a lemonade stand, leave it alone," Cain grumbled. "And they're your neighbors, now, too. You have to be nice to them."

Baz worked diligently, pouring cups for everyone, checking in with Mark constantly to make sure he was comfortable.

"I've just got a little more to finish, then I'll head down," MaKayla said. She could have easily stopped at any point, but it was good to force Cain to spend a little time with his newly adopted brother. Cain was with her every waking second he could be, so this was their chance to bond, even if Cain hated it.

Finally, Aurora and Ivy arrived with bags of diner food. Ivy was done up with her now-signature goth makeup, complete with dual-tone black and silver lipliner, and Aurora's designer top was on inside out. MaKayla noticed and made a mental note to tease Aurora about it later...if they were still friendly enough to poke fun about each other's sex lives.

Aurora carefully laid out a blanket then doled out food with Baz while Ivy stood off to the side, squinting and looking up at the nearly complete collage. MaKayla lowered the giant mechanical arm down and joined them.

"I wasn't sure if anyone had any dietary restrictions, so I just got a bit of everything," Aurora said.

Baz immediately made a small plate for Mark, putting one of each item down and saying out loud to Mark, "Cheese stick at twelve o'clock. Chicken wing three o'clock. Seven French fries at six o'clock..." And on and on until he identified a dipping sauce. "Ranch?! That's ranch, isn't it?" He bubbled, so proud of himself.

"Will you keep it down?" Cain growled.

"I think it's sweet," MaKayla said to Cain before addressing the fallen angel. "I think it is ranch, Baz, you're right."

But the wind had been taken out of Baz's sails, who apologetically tried to make eye contact with Cain. He wasn't having it. Mark must have sensed it.

"Thanks, Baz," he said in a comforting tone.

"So," MaKayla dragged out the word, letting everyone know she expected answers from all around the picnic blanket. "Has everyone signed up for their electives for senior year?"

"Shop, maybe," said Cain.

"I'm going to take Bible as literature again," said Aurora.

"Latin three," Ivy muttered.

"Jesus!" Mark exclaimed. "I didn't know that class existed!"

"Were we supposed to sign up already?" Baz asked, worried.

"Don't fret," Cain said, dipping a fry in ketchup. "Mom doubled you up on Spanish and Hispanic studies to acclimate you to her ways."

"How's the adjustment been?" Aurora asked Baz as Ivy slung an arm over her shoulder.

"It's *a lot* to get used to," Cain said, refraining from specifying that Bazrael himself was a lot to get used to.

"It's amazing!" Baz answered at the same time. "I love having a brother!"

"He's Mom's little angel," Cain grumbled.

"How about you, Mark?" MaKayla asked. "What's the schedule look like for your last year of high school?"

"Well, I kinda *have* to take braille, but the school doesn't offer it, so they're bussing me over to Canisius College. Which is fine because my new job is over there."

"I didn't know you got a new job," Aurora said.

"Paid internship at a physical therapist," Mark said with his mouth full of chicken wing. "Sports rehab. Maybe I'll major in it?"

"*You* are going to be a doctor?" Ivy asked incredulously.

"God, no," Mark said. "Just a guy who wraps ankles and tells high school All-Stars to take it easy."

"I hear they don't listen," Baz laughed.

"So what about your parents?" Aurora asked Cain. "How are they with the full house?"

Cain shrugged. "Mom's in heaven with a son who wants to spend time together. And Dad..."

Cain and Baz finished the thought together: "Dad works."

Ivy pried further, "How are they taking the news you aren't... going into the family business?"

"I think we kind of are," MaKayla answered, taking Cain's hand in hers. It was warm. Like her. "Just in our own way."

"Like, what, end of life euthanasia?" Ivy asked.

"Wait," Mark said, confused. "You're moving to Asia?"

"No, we're just figuring it out on a case-by-case basis," MaKayla answered.

Cain expanded, "MaKayla and the book have a lot of answers to things I never knew. Like there was this eternal flame in our basement that told Dad and I what souls to harvest. But turns out it was actually a model of destinies for the Fates."

"A model of destinies?" Mark asked.

"It was the ribbons," MaKayla answered, "the paths of human destiny that we see, just conglomerated into a ball. Cain and his father were just seeing the paths that were coming to an end."

Ivy redirected the conversation. "So back to how are you two going to work together, then?"

Aurora elbowed her.

"What?" Ivy asked, "It's not fair that MaKayla gets a

personal Grim Reaper and all I have are books to study."

"What do you think, Mark?" MaKayla asked, "How do you see Cain and I working together in the future?"

"I try not to look," Mark answered. "Just let the visions come to me. But there is one thing pretty obvious. Even I can see Ivy's clown makeup."

Cain busted out laughing. Aurora and MaKayla, too, though they tried to hide it.

"Shut up, Mark," Aurora said.

"You can't even see," Ivy whined.

"I can literally smell the makeup from here."

Everyone had a good laugh, then calmed down.

Ivy broke the lull. "There is something we do need to discuss."

"Yeah," Mark said, "you were supposed to tell us more about Beth."

MaKayla's breath hitched. Even with all the work that went into the collage, she hadn't really talked about Beth's passing with any of her friends. The thought had plagued her with every element she added to the mural. Was MaKayla responsible? Had she taken away all of Beth's options? Was this just the beginning of an eternity surrounded in death?

"I meant..." Ivy said. "About Gods' End. Because like it or not, there is a powerful infrastructure out there. Notes and rituals they left. And obviously, from what Beth and Mark endured, this occult legacy can really harm a lot of people if left unchecked."

A mission was exactly what MaKayla needed. The art piece would be done soon, then what? Working at the store for the rest of the summer? Going back to school and pretending to be a normal overachieving student? She'd changed as much as the baseball fields. As much as the city. There was no going back. "So what," she asked, "are we going to find Lachesis and hunt down any notes and artifacts from Gods' End?"

Baz clapped his hands. "Are we going to be treasure hunters?"

Mark calmed him by settling a hand on Baz's shoulder. "Easy, boy."

"I think," Aurora said slowly, taking the time to look at everyone as she spoke, "it would make sense for *us* to take up the cause of Gods' End. This group has a direct connection to the original through MaKayla's and Ivy's grandparents. And we have the powers to actually help people."

"Aurora's right," Ivy said. "We can use the knowledge of the old Gods' End, but not selfishly."

"But I thought Baz said God was dead." Cain sounded confused. "How do we end Him?"

"Maybe the purpose isn't to end gods," Baz explained, "but to stop the unfair control that the supernatural exert over mortals."

MaKayla nodded to herself and spoke, her voice cracking, "Absolutely. We could help people in danger. Like Beth."

Her name hung in the air for a second. Heads bowed solemnly, eyes teared up. Mark raised his glass of water. "To Beth."

Everyone joined in. "To Beth." They drank and patted each other's hands and hugged. Aurora, MaKayla, and Mark sniffed away tears.

"So," Cain asked with resignation, "we're demon hunters, then? Baz and I will be fighting more of them?"

"That's actually what I was going to say about Beth," Ivy said. "When she was little, She had made a deal with a Puka, a shapeshifting Irish water cryptid. Probably more closely related to fae than demon.”

“Then that’s who we’ll fight,” Mark said. “Cryptic Irish water fairies. And anyone else controlling mortals.”

Everyone agreed.

“Ivy and I could find them,” MaKayla volunteered. “We could use the eternal flame in Cain’s library. If it’s just a collection of human destinies, there has to be a way to read them, I’m positive.”

They made brief eye contact, Ivy giving a curt nod and the slightest hint of a smile. It was the most affection she’d shown since they discovered they were cousins, but it was a start.

The rest of the meal went by like any group of normal teens talking: jokes, laughs, innuendos. MaKayla may never go back to being who she once was, but at least she had this group. They’d be different together. And even though she tried not to read the futures of people, she could see the connections, the destinies intertwining. She even saw how on-again-off-again Ivy and Aurora’s relationship would be. But they’d stay together. They all would. The convocation of Gods’ End.

Lunch was winding down, everyone explaining their plans for the evening. Baz taking Mark on some sort of adventure as an excuse to practice using his walking stick. Ivy and Aurora staying in for the evening and avoiding family as best they could. Of course Cain would hang out, doing whatever MaKayla wanted. But there was only one thing pressing.

“We have to get a group photo before we leave,” she demanded.

“Awesome!” Baz exclaimed.

“I’m not even wearing anything cute,” Aurora complained.

“Yes you are,” Ivy argued. Adorable.

"Did you bring the thing?" Cain asked.

It had completely slipped MaKayla's mind. It was the initial reason for the group meeting, the final piece of the mural. They'd used it as an excuse for everyone to share a meal before school started up again.

"Oh!" Aurora said, "I forgot to bring him!"

"Him who?" Baz asked.

Instead of answering, Ivy arched an eyebrow to her girlfriend and said, "Unless...?"

Aurora dug into her huge purse and pulled out a floppy brown stuffed horse. Anthony. "I hope it's okay, it darkened when we sprayed it with water-proofing."

MaKayla's throat dried out at the sight of the little toy. "It's perfect."

"The city is going to seal up the whole thing when MaKayla's done anyway," Cain said, adding to MaKayla, "Are you ready for the final touch?"

Aurora handed the stuffie to MaKayla. The soft fluff of the floppy little toy filled her with emotion. This had been Beth's. It was a part of her. The only part they had left.

"*I'm sorry, Beth.*" MaKayal thought, sending the sentiment out.

"It's okay," Cain said matter-of-factly.

"What?" MaKayla asked, surprised he answered.

"What?"

"Why'd you just say that?"

"I don't know." He smiled and shrugged in that adorable way Cain did. "I just...Felt it."

Baz gave his brother a big hug, "That's so sweet!"

Cain made a production out of pushing Baz away while everyone had a laugh. But MaKayla couldn't shake the feeling that Cain had just carried a message from beyond.

It's okay.

"I'll do it," MaKayla finally said, wiping away tears. "But we need a picture of everybody together."

"What?" Ivy said, looking up at the two-story mural. "Up there?"

"I don't think we'll all fit in the basket," Aurora said.

"That's fine," Baz added. "Most of us can fly."

Everyone hushed him, even though none of the construction workers were within earshot.

"Ivy," Mark asked, "Think you can hide us from sight?"

Instead of answering, Ivy turned some rings on her fingers, pulled an amulet from inside her shirts, and whispered words to herself. Her hands flew quickly through motions and a lightness, a swirl of magic surrounded the group.

Stuffy in hand, MaKayla felt the scissors holstered under her coveralls, pressed against her thigh. Her Fate powers poured over her, and she floated up to the mural. Beside her flew Cain, not flapping wings, but hovering. Ivy took Aurora's hand, and they delicately rose beside them. Baz shifted into an enormous blond angel, took up Mark in a hug, and beat his wings to stay above the others.

Aurora held out her phone as if to take a selfie, then released her grip. It floated out a few feet, bobbing midair. The flash went off as they took a few photos, then MaKayal went to finish her work. In a small glass cube in the center of the giant mural's horse eye, she placed Anthony the stuffed animal.

The phone clicked a few more shots, and the second gathering of the young people of Gods' End had their group photo.

The End...for now

253

How did Cain learn he was a Grim Reaper?

If you're wondering how Cain not only discovered his lineage and immortality, but came to despise humanity and human feelings, then read the free prequel novella, Angel of Brimstone!

Cain Morrigan was a normal freshman, but instead of getting onto the basketball team, he got dragged through supernatural realms of existence with a Greek immortal. Now they must awaken the power within Cain before a godlike entity known as the Beyond uses him to reach our plane of existence and enslave all life. A high school romantic comedy. Plus, you know, death and despair.

Go to Jeffriesbooks.com now and read the prequel novella, Angel of Brimstone for free!

Special Thanks

I am so thankful that this project was entirely funded via Kickstarter campaign. Huge gratitude to my backers:

Ben Dawson
Tanya Hagel
Alexandra Corrsin
Dead Fish Books
Angela
Joseph Harkreader
Jeremy Morang
Samantha Newberry
Morgan
Fleur DeVillainy
Rich Madison
Seth Remington
Jenny Allen
Ophelia Wells Langley
Scottie Armstrong
Helen J. Roberts
Shayla Morgansen
Ruth Dillon
Lea Thompson
Gee Rothvoss
AingealWroth